Alexander McCall Smith is the author of over eighty books on a wide array of subjects, including the award-winning The No.1 Ladies' Detective Agency series. He is also the author of the Isabel Dalhousie novels and the world's longest-running serial novel, 44 Scotland Street. His books have been translated into forty-six languages. Alexander McCall Smith is Professor Emeritus of Medical Law at the University of Edinburgh and holds honorary doctorates from thirteen universities.

PRAISE FOR THE DETECTIVE VARG NOVELS

'Heaven is in the detail with this sort of escapist writing. It's like AA Milne meets Karl Ove Knausgaard. McCall Smith knows how to create a world full of sweet things and emotionally true moments and in this new series of "Scandi blanc" delivers exactly what his fans will be hoping for'
Financial Times

'Wonderfully soothing and relaxing; the books do not make you sit on the edge of your seat but sink deeper into your chair'
Telegraph

'Alexander McCall Smith's continuing warm-heartedness makes Ulf such unfailingly good company'
Reader's Digest

By Alexander McCall Smith

THE
DEPARTMENT
OF
SENSITIVE
CRIMES

ÄLEXANDER
McCALL SMITH

ABACUS

First published in Great Britain in 2019 by Little, Brown
This paperback edition published in 2020 by Abacus

1 3 5 7 9 10 8 6 4 2

ISBN 978-0-349-14333-0

Typeset in Galliard by M Rules
Printed and bound in Great Britain by
Clays Ltd, Elcograf S.p.A.

Papers used by Abacus are from well-managed forests
and other responsible sources.

FSC
www.fsc.org

MIX
Paper from
responsible sources
FSC® C104740

Abacus
An imprint of
Little, Brown Book Group
Carmelite House
50 Victoria Embankment
London EC4Y 0DZ

An Hachette UK Company
www.hachette.co.uk

www.littlebrown.co.uk

This book is for Bob McCreadie

CHAPTER ONE

Free Association, Charged at Normal Rates

'Søren,' said Dr Svensson, gravely, but with a smile behind his horn-rimmed glasses; and then waited for the response. There would be an answer to this one-word sentence, but he would have to wait to see what it was.

Ulf Varg, born in Malmö, Sweden, the son of Ture and Liv Varg, only too briefly married, now single again; thirty-eight, and therefore fast approaching what he thought of as a watershed – 'After forty, Ulf,' said his friend, Lars, 'where does one go?' – that same Ulf Varg raised his eyes to the ceiling when his therapist said, 'Søren.' And then Ulf himself, almost without thinking, replied: 'Søren?'

The therapist, *kind* Dr Svensson, as so many of his patients described him, shook his head. He knew that a therapist should not

1

shake his head, and he had tried to stop himself from doing it too often, but it happened automatically, in the same way as we make so many gestures without really thinking about them – twitches, sniffs, movements of the eyebrow, the folding and unfolding of legs. Although many of these acts are meaningless, mere concomitants of being alive, shaking one's head implies disapprobation. And kind Dr Svensson did not disapprove. He understood, which is quite different from disapproving.

But now he disapproved, and he shook his head before he reminded himself not to disapprove, and not to shake his head. 'Are you asking me or telling me?' he said. 'Because you shouldn't be asking, you know. The whole point of free association, Mr Varg, is to bring to the surface – to outward expression – the things that are below the surface.'

To bring to the surface the things that are below the surface … Ulf liked that. That, he thought, is what I do every time I go into the office. I get out of bed in the morning to bring to the surface the things that are below the surface. If I had a mission statement, then I suppose that is more or less what it would be. It would be far better than the one foisted on his department by Headquarters: *We serve the public.* How bland, how anodyne that was – like all the communications they received from Headquarters. Those grey men and women with their talk of targets and sensitivity and more or less everything except the one thing that mattered: finding those who broke the law.

'Mr Varg?'

Ulf let his gaze fall from the ceiling. Now he was staring at the carpet, and at Dr Svensson's brown suede shoes. They were brogues, with that curious holed pattern that somebody had once explained to him was all to do with letting the shoes breathe, and was not just a matter of English aesthetics. They were expensive, he imagined. When he first saw them, he had decided that they were English shoes, because they had that look about them, and that was precisely the sort of thing that a good detective noticed. Italian shoes were thinner, and more elegant, presumably because the Italians had thinner, more elegant feet than the English. The Dutch, of course, had even bigger feet than the English; Dutchmen, Ulf reflected, were tall, big-boned people. They were large – which was odd, in a way, because Holland was such a small country ... and so prone to flooding, as that story he had been read as a child made so clear – the little Dutch boy with his finger in the dyke ...

'Mr Varg?' There was a slight note of impatience in Dr Svensson's tone. It was all very well for patients to go off into some reverie of their own, but the whole point of these sessions was to disclose, not conceal, and they should articulate what they were thinking, rather than just think it.

'I'm sorry, Dr Svensson. I was thinking.'

'Ah!' said the therapist. 'That's precisely what you're meant to do, you know. Thinking precedes verbalisation, and verbalisation precedes resolution. And much as I approve of that, what we're trying to do here is to find out what you think *without thinking*. In other words, we want to find out what's going on in your mind. Because that's what—'

Ulf nodded. 'Yes, I know. I understand. I just said *Søren* because I wasn't quite sure what you meant. I wanted to be sure.'

'I meant *Søren*. The name. Søren.'

Ulf thought. Søren triggered nothing. Had Dr Svensson said *Harald*, or *Per*, he would have been able to respond *bully* or *teeth* because that was what he thought of. They had been boys in his class, so had Dr Svensson said *Harald*, he might have replied *bully*,

3

because that was what Harald was. And if he had said *Per* he would have replied *teeth* because Per had a gap in his front teeth that his parents were too poor to have attended to by an orthodontist.

Then it came to him, quite suddenly, and he replied, 'Kierkegaard.'

This seemed to please Dr Svensson. 'Kierkegaard?' the therapist repeated.

'Yes, Søren Kierkegaard.'

Dr Svensson smiled. It was almost time to bring the session to a close, and he liked to end on a thoughtful note. 'Would you mind my asking, why Kierkegaard? Have you read him?'

Ulf replied that he had.

'I'm impressed,' said Dr Svensson. 'One doesn't imagine that a . . . ' He stopped.

Ulf looked at him expectantly.

Dr Svensson tried to cover his embarrassment, but failed. 'I didn't mean, well, I didn't mean it to sound like that.'

'Your unconscious?' said Ulf mildly. 'Your unconscious mind speaking.'

The therapist smiled. 'What I was going to say – but stopped myself just in time – was that I didn't expect a policeman to have read Kierkegaard. I know that there's no earthly reason why a policeman should not read Kierkegaard, but it is unusual, would you not agree?'

'I'm actually a detective.'

Dr Svensson was again embarrassed. 'Of course you are.'

'Although detectives are policemen in essence.'

Dr Svensson nodded. 'As are judges and public health officials and politicians too, I suppose. Anybody who tells us how to behave is a policeman in a sense.'

4

'But not therapists?'

Dr Svensson laughed. 'A therapist shouldn't tell you how to behave. A therapist should help you to see *why* you do what you do, and should help you to stop doing it – if that's what you want. So, no, a therapist is certainly not a policeman.' He paused. 'But why Kierkegaard? What appeals to you about Kierkegaard?'

'I didn't say he appealed. I said I had read him. That's not the same thing as saying he appealed.'

Dr Svensson glanced at his watch again. 'I think perhaps we should leave it at that,' he said. 'We've covered a fair amount of ground today.'

Ulf rose to his feet.

'Now what?' asked Dr Svensson.

'Now what, what?'

'I was wondering what you were going to do next. You see, my patients come into this room, they talk – or, rather, we talk – and then they go out into the world and continue with their lives. And I remain here and think – not always, but sometimes – I think: *What are they going outside to do?* Do they go back to their houses and sit in a chair? Do they go into some office somewhere and move pieces of paper from one side of the desk to another? Or stare at a screen again until it's time to go home to a house where the children are all staring at screens? Is that what they do? Is that why they *bother*?'

Ulf hesitated. 'Those are very profound questions. Very. But since you ask, I can tell you that I'm going back to my office. I shall sit at my desk and write a report on a case that we have just closed.'

'You close cases,' muttered Dr Svensson. 'Mine remain open. They are unresolved, for the most part.'

'Yes, we close cases. We're under great pressure to close cases.'

Dr Svensson sighed. 'How fortunate.' He moved to the window.

5

I look out of the window, he thought. The patients go off to do significant things, such as closing cases, and I look out of my window. Then he said, 'I don't suppose you could tell me what this case involved.'

'I can't give you names, or other details,' replied Ulf. 'But I can tell you it involved the infliction of a very unusual injury.'

Dr Svensson turned round to face his patient.

'To the back of somebody's knee,' said Ulf.

'How strange. To the back of the knee?'

'Yes,' said Ulf. 'But I can't really say much more than that.'

'Odd.'

Ulf frowned. 'That I should not explain further? Is that odd?'

'No, that somebody should injure another person in the back of the knee. Of course, the choice of a target is hardly random. We injure what we love, what we desire, every bit as much as that which we hate. But it is odd, isn't it? The back of a knee . . . '

Ulf began to walk towards the door. 'You'd be very surprised, Dr Svensson, at how odd people can be. Yes, even in your profession – where you hear all sorts of dark secrets from your patients, day in, day out. Even then. You'd be surprised.'

'Would I?'

'Yes,' said Ulf. 'If you stood in my shoes for a few days, your jaw would hit the table in astonishment. Regularly.'

Dr Svensson smiled. 'Well, well.' His smile faded. The jaw. Freud, he remembered, died of a disease that affected his jaw. Alone in London, with enemies circling, that illuminating intelligence, liberating in its perspicacity, flickered and died, leaving us to face the darkness and the creatures that inhabited it.

6

CHAPTER TWO

A Very Low Crime

Ulf's office was in a high-gabled building in the old town of Malmö, the Gamla Staden. The visitors who flocked to the area had no idea that behind the unmarked doorway, halfway down the winding lane that led to the Malmö Konstmuseum, was the home of the Sensitive Crimes Department of the Malmö Criminal Investigation Authority. Those visitors who sat for any length of time in the café directly opposite this entrance would, if observant, notice that this was an unusually busy office, judging by the number of people who went in and out of the otherwise unexceptional doorway. Had they lingered for any length of time, such visitors would also have noticed that many of these people walked directly across the street and into the café itself, where they conversed, either at the bar or at a table, in hushed tones, as people do who are discussing, in a public place, those matters that are not to be talked about openly.

Ulf's desk was in Room 5 of this office. He shared the room with three others: two colleagues, Anna Bengtsdotter and Carl Holgersson, and a clerical assistant, Erik Nykvist. Anna and Carl were rough contemporaries of Ulf's, although Carl was a few years older. Erik, though, was in his late fifties, and was talking about retirement. His career had hardly been stellar: after thirty-eight years in the department he had progressed from postal clerk to clerical assistant – a progression of three steps on a ladder with seventeen well-defined rungs. He did not particularly care: his passion was fishing, and the need to earn a living was nothing more than a minor distraction in the battle between man and fish that dominated his waking thoughts. Retirement would be bliss, he believed, as his wife had inherited a modest cabin on an island in the Stockholm archipelago, a stone's throw from the sea. His pension was generous enough and they would have few expenses in such a place. The cabin had a small patch of land attached to it – enough to grow sufficient vegetables for their needs – and they would eat fish five days a week, just as they currently did. 'What could be a better prospect than that?' he once remarked to Ulf. And Ulf replied that he found it difficult to imagine a more ideal existence than the one that Erik would almost certainly be leading once his retirement began.

Anna Bengtsdotter, whose desk faced Ulf's, was from Stockholm, where her father was the proprietor of a small travelling circus. This circus had been in the family for three generations, and Anna had been under pressure to join several cousins who fielded a highly popular musical ride. She refused, and insisted instead on taking a college course in human resource management. This had led to a job in the police, in the personnel department, from which she had transferred, by dint of persistent and determined application, to the Criminal Investigation Authority. Anna was married to an anaesthetist, Jo Dahlman, a quiet person whose abiding passion was philately. She had twin daughters who were keen swimmers, and already making their mark in Malmö swimming circles.

Although both Anna and Ulf were conscientious in their approach to their work, they freely admitted that Carl was the hard worker of the team. He was always first in each morning and last out in the evening, in spite of having a young family. It was Carl who willingly – and remarkably cheerfully – took on the extra shifts when the exigencies of the department's under-manning required somebody to stand in for a sick colleague. It was Carl who volunteered for assignments that were either extremely tedious or exceptionally distressing. 'If I don't do these things,' he said, 'then somebody else has to. He or she won't like it any more than I will, and so I might as well do it, don't you think?'

This was a distributive logic that Ulf felt was somehow flawed, unless altruism was the central value that underpinned one's universe. And for most people, Ulf thought, this was not the case. 'You have to look after yourself, Carl,' was his reply.

To which Carl responded, 'Not if you're Immanuel Kant, Ulf.' And quickly added – for Carl was always somewhat diffident, 'Not that I am, of course.'

Erik, who had overheard this exchange from the other side of the room, interjected, 'Which section is he in?'

Carl might have laughed, but did not, and nor did Ulf. 'He retired a long time ago,' Carl said. There was no point, he thought, in explaining Kant to somebody like Erik, whose universe seemed restricted to fish, and ferry timetables, and island weather.

Ulf had wondered where Carl's sense of duty came from, and

had concluded that it was probably attributable to his father, a Lutheran theologian who made regular appearances on a television programme, *What You Should Think*. This dealt with practical moral issues of the day, such as vegetarianism, the reception of refugees, environmental protection – all the dilemmas and headaches that could make life a moral minefield. Professor Holgersson spoke in a slow, grave way that made for compulsive television. People could not take their eyes off him as he made his contribution to the debates, nor could they stop listening to his sonorous, measured tones. He had become well known – even to people who would otherwise have no interest in such issues – and there was now a radio advertisement in which an actor, imitating the professor's voice with that mimetic genius that some actors seem to possess, exhorted the listener to buy a particular brand of pre-packed, home-assembly furniture.

It was no surprise to Ulf, then, that Carl should be so hard-working, methodical, and utterly reliable. Nor that he should be bookish – professors' sons, surely, could be expected to be bookish. This meant that at odd moments, perhaps during a coffee break in the café over the road, or travelling in a car to the scene of some crime, Carl would regale Ulf and Anna with unexpected facts about some issue he had encountered in a book or article that his father happened to have mentioned to him. On occasion these had to do with philosophy, or even theology, but it seemed that the professor's reading was much broader than that, and included books and magazines dealing with subjects as diverse as primatology, civil engineering and medicine. An auto-didact in any of these fields might not be the ideal work companion, but Carl was never boring, and there had been many occasions on which one of his passing remarks had sent Ulf off to the library to read up on some abstruse subject or other.

'Carl is very clever,' observed Erik one day. 'Why isn't he a professor somewhere – like that dad of his – rather than a detective?'

'He's here because he believes in justice,' said Ulf. 'And because he thinks it's the right thing to help others.'

Erik looked thoughtful. 'What does he do in his spare time?'

Ulf replied that he thought that Carl had very little spare time, what with the demands of his young family and the long hours he worked in the department. Yet he clearly found time to read, and so that must be what he did.

'Just read?' said Erik. 'Just read books and so on?'

'Yes. I think so.'

Erik shook his head in wonderment. 'I should ask him whether he wants to come fishing some day.'

'You could,' said Ulf. 'But I doubt if he could find the time.'

Erik shrugged. 'If you can't find the time to go fishing, then . . . well, what's the point?'

Ulf did not feel that further discussion would be profitable. So he simply said, 'True, Erik,' and left it at that.

The case that Ulf had mentioned to Dr Svensson at the end of his last therapy session had started, as many of the department's cases did, with a simple report from the local police. Their resources were strained, and if anything happened that looked as if it might require complicated investigation, they referred it to the Department of Sensitive Crimes. These cases could go to the normal Criminal Investigation Authority, but the local police enjoyed a close relationship with the authority and tried to avoid burdening them excessively. The fact that these referrals were often made rather hastily inevitably meant that some of the issues with which Ulf's department was landed were not all that sensitive, but by and large the system worked. Only occasionally did they have to protest that the routine disappearance of a teenager, or the theft of a laptop computer, was not really the sort of issue for which they had been set up.

The report that came in one morning stated simply: 'Market stabbing. No severe injury, but unusual *locus*. No witnesses, and the victim himself saw nothing. Please investigate.'

Ulf read the report out to Anna. 'Unusual *locus*? What does that mean?'

'Strange place, I imagine.'

'But the *locus* could be the *locus* of the crime or the *locus* of the injury.'

Anna laughed. 'Hardly the latter, surely. No, I think it's probably a stabbing that took place in the back of a puppet theatre, or under a table laden with peace movement literature – the anti-war people have a stall down there most days. Something of that sort.'

Ulf sighed. 'I suppose we'd better go and ask around. The local police say somebody will be there to fill us in with such information as they have. I don't think that'll be much – no witnesses, they say.'

Anna closed her laptop and reached for her handbag. 'I was hoping to do some shopping anyway,' she said. 'Count me in on this one. I need to buy broccoli. And free range eggs.'

They travelled to the market in Ulf's ancient light grey Saab. It had once been silver in colour, the pride of Ulf's uncle from Gothenburg, but it had faded with age. 'It's the Kattegatt air,' the uncle explained. 'Salinity is bad for certain paints, and I think silver is especially vulnerable. But inside, Ulf, the car is perfect. Real leather. Everything works. Everything.'

The uncle's eyesight had deteriorated and he had reluctantly given up driving. 'It'll give me great pleasure to know you're

12

looking after it, Ulf. And I hope it gives you as much pleasure as it's given me.'

It did. Ulf loved the car, and on occasion, when feeling low for whatever reason, he would take it for a drive – not to anywhere in particular, but simply to be out on the road, comforted by the smell of the old leather upholstery and surrounded by the sounds of a perfectly functioning mechanical creation: the tick of the clock on the dashboard, the smooth hum of the engine, the well-lubricated munching sound that accompanied the changing of gear. Inevitably, he returned from such outings feeling vastly better, making him wonder whether the money he spent on his sessions with Dr Svensson would not be better expended on fuel for more aimless, but clearly therapeutic, journeys in the Saab.

ABSOLUTELY CERTAIN!

Anna, too, enjoyed travelling in Ulf's car, and as they drove the short distance to the old market she sat back, closed her eyes, and caressed the cracked leather of the seat. 'The best part of any investigation with you, Ulf,' she said dreamily, 'is being in your car.'

Ulf smiled. 'I'm sorry my company rates so lowly, Anna.'

She opened her eyes. 'Oh, I didn't mean that, Ulf.' She paused. 'You know what I mean? Being in your car is like being in the old Sweden.'

'You mean it's a social democratic experience?'

Anna grinned. 'Something like that. A return to a time of innocence. Everybody wants that, don't they?'

Ulf said that he thought some did. They could be misunderstood, though: nostalgia and reactionary sentiment could come perilously close.

The conversation drifted. Anna told Ulf about a row at her daughters' school. A strident parent had accused one of the teachers

13

of making her child feel undervalued. 'The truth of the matter, though, is that the child in question is actually a bit of a dead loss. I don't mean to be unkind, but it would be hard to undervalue that kid.'

'We have to pretend,' said Ulf. 'We have to pretend about so much these days. We have to pretend to like things we don't like. We have to try so very hard to be non-judgemental.'

'I suppose so,' said Anna. 'I suppose teachers have to pretend that every child is some sort of genius.'

'Yes.'

'Especially when talking to the parent.'

'Yes,' agreed Ulf. 'Especially then.'

'Perhaps it's for the best,' mused Anna. 'Perhaps if we pretend hard enough about these things, we'll end up believing the things they want us to believe, and everybody will be happy.'

'Nirvana,' said Ulf. 'We could change Sweden's name to Nirvana – officially.'

The conversation switched again – this time to an internal office memo that had everybody up in arms – and then they were there, arriving at the edge of the sprawling market. Anna got out to guide Ulf into a tight parking spot, and then the two of them made their way towards the place where they had arranged to meet the local policeman who had first investigated the stabbing.

He was called Blomquist, and Ulf and Anna had worked with him once before, on an investigation into fake whisky that had briefly appeared in the market a year or two earlier. Blomquist remembered them, and greeted them warmly at the top of one of the lanes along which the market stalls were pitched.

'I remember that whisky business,' he said. 'That was strange, but this one!' He whistled. 'This is a real puzzler.'

14

Ulf shrugged. 'That's why we're here, I suppose.'

Blomquist nodded. 'Oh, I know that you people have a reputation for sorting these things out, but I think this one is going to test you.'

Anna glanced at Ulf. 'We'll see,' she said, assuming a business-like manner. 'Tell us what you know.'

Blomquist pointed to a stall further down the lane. 'You see that stall over there? The one where that man is showing that woman a scarf?'

Ulf looked in the direction Blomquist was pointing. A stout man in a leather jacket was concluding the sale of a scarf to a young woman in jeans and a vivid red top.

'That'll be cashmere,' said Anna. 'I know those people.'

'That's the brother of the victim,' said Blomquist. 'He's looking after the business while his brother is in hospital. We can go and talk to him, if you like. You'll see where it happened.'

'How long will this man be in hospital?' asked Anna.

Blomquist made a dismissive gesture. 'Only a day or two, I think. It's not a serious injury, but it's in a difficult place apparently. The back of the knee. Apparently there are all sorts of cables that run down there . . . '

Anna interrupted him. 'Cables?'

'I think you mean tendons,' said Ulf. 'We have tendons at the back of our knees.' He paused. 'And I think in the front as well. Or certainly the sides.'

'I play tennis,' said Blomquist. 'I know all about that. If you twist your knee, you know all about it.' He looked at Ulf. 'Do you play, Mr Varg?'

'I used to,' said Ulf. 'I was never much good, but I enjoyed it.'

'Sport is for enjoyment,' said Blomquist. 'And the wonderful thing about tennis is that you can enjoy it even if you aren't very good.'

'As long as your opponent is roughly the same standard,' Ulf cautioned. 'If you're up against a power serve and you aren't much good, the game gets pretty one-sided.'

'That's true,' said Anna. 'But should we go and speak to this man? What's his name, by the way?'

'Oscar Gustafsson,' replied Blomquist. 'And his brother, the victim, is Malte. Malte Gustafsson.'

'I was here at the time,' said Oscar. 'I didn't see it happen, but I was here, helping my brother out. He owns the stall, you see – I work on the railways but I'm on shifts and in my time off I come here and help Malte.'

Ulf looked about him. The market was quiet, and it did not look as if there were many people who would be interested in the display of scarves and sweaters that fronted the Gustafsson stall. He reached out and fingered one of the scarves. Oscar was a stocky, thickset man with short-cropped hair; he was not someone with whom one would readily associate cashmere.

'Cashmere?' Ulf asked.

For a moment Oscar hesitated. Then he said, 'Close enough. It depends on what you mean by cashmere.'

Anna stared at him. 'I know this is just a personal view, but when I say cashmere, I tend to mean cashmere.'

Ulf made a placatory gesture. 'That's not why we're here,' he said. 'Tell me about your brother, Mr Gustafsson.'

Oscar looked relieved. 'He's been a market trader for about ten years. He was a mechanic before that, you know – quite a good one. He looked after motorcycles mostly. Harley-Davidsons. Then he had enough of that because he developed eczema and his skin reacted to soap. Working can be a problem if your hands get greasy every day and you can't tolerate soap.'

Blomquist nodded his assent. 'Definitely,' he said. 'Eczema is a difficult condition. And some of those creams they give you thin the skin, you know. You have to be careful about using them.'

'Only the stronger ones,' said Anna. 'If you use the less powerful steroids, it's better.'

'Malte's had trouble with all that,' said Oscar. 'Even after he stopped fixing motorcycles. He uses a soap substitute now, but he still gets patches of dry skin.'

'Hydration,' said Anna. 'You have to watch hydration, particularly in cold weather. I suppose being a market trader means that you're out in the open a lot.'

'He should be careful,' said Blomquist. 'Cold weather and wind are a really bad idea if you have dry skin.'

Ulf tapped the toe of a shoe on the pavement. 'But Malte – tell me more about him.'

'Malte,' began Oscar, 'is a very mild guy.'

Victims, thought Ulf, so often are.

'He's a few years older than I am,' Oscar continued. 'I always looked up to him. You know how it is with brothers: you think your older brother can do anything. You want to *be* him, I suppose. And with Malte, it was very much like that because he was so good with machinery. I tried to be, but never really made much progress. I joined the railways, hoping to get a mechanical apprenticeship, but I never made it. I went into line maintenance, which is what I do today. It has its compensations.'

Ulf nodded. 'Many of us have to settle for something,' he said.

17

'And then we find the thing we've settled for is as good as the thing we wanted to do in the first place.'

'True,' said Oscar. 'And that was the case for Malte as well, I think. He had to settle for market trading after his problems with his skin, and then he discovered that he liked it very much. He never looked back.'

Ulf thought for a moment. 'You said that Malte fixed Harley-Davidsons. Does he still ride?'

Oscar replied that his brother still had two Harleys, one a 1965 model, the other a mishmash he had put together from various spare parts. 'He calls the one he made from various bits and pieces a Davidson-Harley – because it's the wrong way round.'

Anna laughed. 'Very funny.'

Oscar looked pleased that his brother's joke had been well received. 'Some people don't get it,' he said. 'At least, some of the bikers don't.'

'Ah, well,' said Ulf. 'Humour's an odd thing. But tell me: does he belong to a bikers' group? A Harley-Davidson club, or something like that?'

'You mean a gang?' asked Oscar. And then, smiling, he explained that although Malte did belong to a bikers' group, the membership was very atypical of a bikers' gang. 'There are about twelve of them,' he said. 'Ten of them are retired – only Malte, who's the youngest, and one of the others are under fifty. Malte's forty-eight, you see.'

'So these bikers are pretty tame?' asked Anna.

'Yes,' Oscar replied. 'Their rides are very sedate. Those big Harleys can be like armchairs, you know. You sit back and take the corners carefully. They don't go far, those guys – they like to get back home early.'

'Back to the *old ladies*,' quipped Anna. 'That's what they call them, don't they?'

'These guys call them their wives,' said Oscar. 'I told you – they're very respectable.'

'So you don't think that this could have anything to do with biker issues,' said Ulf. He knew that one did not normally discuss theories with witnesses, but the question slipped out.

Oscar's lip curled. 'Them? No chance. They're a bunch of kitty-cats.'

'Appearances can be deceptive,' said Anna.

Oscar shook his head vehemently. 'It's nothing like that,' he said. 'Oscar was on very good terms with all of them. He helped them with their bikes – as long as it was something he could do wearing gloves. Gloves protected his skin. They all liked him.'

'So,' said Ulf, 'if it wasn't a biker feud, what do you think it could be? You don't get stabbed for nothing. Was there anybody who had a grudge against him?'

Once again Oscar was adamant. 'Listen,' he said, 'nobody – and I mean nobody – dislikes Malte. He's the sweetest guy imaginable. He'd never—'

'A dissatisfied customer?' interjected Anna, gesturing to the stock. 'An argument over rejected goods?'

Oscar gave her a contemptuous look. 'Malte's honest,' he said. 'He never cheats. And his prices are fair, too.'

Ulf asked about Malte's home life. Was he married? Was the marriage a happy one?

'Malte got married at twenty-eight,' Oscar replied. 'He and Mona recently celebrated their twentieth anniversary. She's a kindergarten teacher. She trained late – just ten years ago – after their own kids got a bit bigger. She comes from a dairy farm about forty kilometres outside town. They make their own cheese – it's quite a successful business.'

'Is Mona involved in it?' asked Anna.

Oscar sighed. 'She should be. There were two of them – her and her brother. The old man still runs the place and Mona's brother, Edvin, helps him, and does more and more these days. Mona would like to be more hands-on herself, or at least have a proper say – after all, it's a family business – but Edvin doesn't seem to want her. He's got round the old man, and so Mona is never consulted. They recently built a whole new milking parlour – state-of-the-art stuff – and they didn't even tell her about it. Not a word. Yet she's technically an equal partner with her brother in the business – along with the old man, of course.'

'What does Malte think about that?' asked Ulf.

'He was furious. He told Mona she should stand up to her brother.'

Ulf and Anna exchanged glances. 'So there's bad blood between Malte and his brother-in-law,' he said.

'Yes, there is. Not that it's Malte's fault. He took it up with the family lawyer. He complained that if the business is a company – which it is – they should run it like a proper company, with shareholder meetings and properly minuted decisions – all of that stuff. Edvin did not like that, I can tell you. He threatened Malte . . .' Oscar stopped himself. 'I mean, he told him that he was the one who did the work on the farm and he would run it as he pleased.'

'You said he threatened him,' Anna pointed out. 'What exactly did he threaten to do?'

Oscar's expression was sulky. 'Edvin didn't stab Malte. I can tell you that for nothing. Edvin wasn't anywhere near this place when it happened.'

'How do you know that?' said Ulf. 'The market can get pretty crowded.'

Blomquist had been silent throughout these exchanges. Now he spoke. 'It was certainly busy at the time of the incident. I arrived ten minutes afterwards, and there were big crowds.'

'Remember I was here too,' retorted Oscar. 'If Edvin had been hanging around, I would have seen him. He wasn't. And anyway, there's a reason why he wasn't here. A good reason.'

They waited for him to explain. And when he did, he did so with a certain air of triumph. 'Because he was in Canada. Some cousin was getting married in Winnipeg, and both Mona and Edvin had been invited. Mona didn't want to go, but Edvin and his wife did. They left at the beginning of last week and don't return until next Tuesday. Malte told me about it. He wouldn't have minded going, but Mona said she couldn't stand Edvin's company for a whole wedding. She's the one who decides what they do, generally.'

Accompanied by Blomquist, they were taken by Oscar to the scene of the incident. This was behind the stall, in a small canvas enclosure, a sort of lean-to tent that seemed to serve as an office. There was a desk, a folding chair of the sort used by campers, and a pile of cardboard boxes.

'I came in here when I heard Malte shout,' said Oscar. 'I was dealing with a customer when I heard him yell. I thought he was just calling me to tell me something, but I soon realised that something was wrong. Malte was standing over there, bent over, holding his knee. He was in considerable pain.'

'And was there anybody else in here with him?' asked Ulf.

Oscar shook his head. 'Not a soul. And Malte said he didn't see anyone.'

Ulf frowned. 'Could somebody have been in and then left in a hurry?'

Oscar looked perplexed. 'I just don't see how anybody could have done that.'

Ulf asked if there was any way in and out, other than the gap in the canvas through which they had walked. There was not, said Oscar, apart from a small split in the canvas at the back. 'A small child could get through that,' he said, pointing to the split. 'But not an adult.'

Ulf bent down to examine the split. Parting the canvas, he saw that behind it there was an alleyway of sorts stretching down the back of the stalls. It would have been possible for somebody to walk along that, he thought, although there were many obstructions: a petrol can, an abandoned spare wheel, a few wooden crates upended and rotting.

He turned back to face Oscar. 'Which way was Malte looking when you came in?' he asked.

'Towards me,' said Oscar.

'Away from the split in the canvas?'

'Yes, I think so.'

Ulf bent down again to examine the canvas where it split. 'There is blood on the canvas here,' he said quietly. 'Look.'

Blomquist peered over his shoulder; Anna bent down and looked from the side.

'This is where it happened,' said Ulf. 'Somebody reached in from outside – with a knife – and plunged it into the first thing that came to hand. That was the back of your brother's knee.'

'So that's why he never saw him,' muttered Oscar.

'I assume so,' said Ulf. 'Anna, what do you think?'

'It's a credible hypothesis,' said Anna. 'But it's a hypothesis that answers no questions. Any hypothesis that uses the word *somebody* takes us no nearer a solution.'

Ulf disagreed. 'It answers the *how* question, though. It leaves open the *why* question, and the *who* question, but to have answered one of three questions is better, surely, than to have answered none at all.'

'Marginally,' said Anna.

She left to buy her broccoli and eggs while Ulf and Blomquist, who seemed to have attached himself to their investigation, searched the narrow space behind the tent for any piece of evidence that might shed light on the case. They found nothing, of course, but the detritus of urban existence: the cellophane wrappings of instant food; an abandoned, exhausted ballpoint pen; a crumpled shopping list, dropped by some passer-by, a memo-to-self that listed purchases: potatoes, vitamin pills, kitchen towels, French chalk; a ticket for a rock concert that had taken place months earlier – a Danish group that everybody had heard of, even Ulf, who did not like rock music.

'Nothing significant,' said Blomquist, at the end of their search, and added, 'People are such litterbugs, aren't they?'

'They are,' agreed Ulf. He pushed at a collapsed cardboard box, left by some trader to disintegrate in the rain. A beetle, disturbed in its sodden home, scurried off in search of shelter.

CHAPTER THREE

The Singing Tree

There had not been much to do at the office when Ulf and Anna returned from the market. In their absence, Carl had been hard at work: a routine report, one that they were all due to have contributed to, had been completed, Carl having sacrificed his lunch hour to get it finished. All the report required now was signatures, after which Ulf had at his disposal what he called *thinking time*, an opportunity to let the mind mull over the details of the investigation so far. Something missed? Something suggested by the circumstances that had yet to dawn on him? The obvious, Ulf once observed, is rarely the obvious until the passage of time has proved it so. This was the wisdom of hindsight, which claims that anyone could have foreseen what eventually happened, and was not something that Ulf had ever supported. 'We are usually in the dark,' he once said to Anna. 'All of us – you, me, Carl – three people in the dark, fumbling around, trying to find our way out of the woods.'

'And yet we have a reasonable rate of success,' she countered. 'Which shows that light can sometimes penetrate this darkness.'

'I think that may just be coincidence,' Ulf said. 'Sometimes we stumble over the truth. We think we find it, but it finds us.'

Anna asked, 'Does that matter? What counts is the result, not the route by which one reaches the result. It's often all a matter of luck.'

Ulf pondered this. The role of luck in human affairs had always intrigued him. So much of what we did was influenced by factors that were beyond our control – the vagaries of others, sequences of events that we initiated in ignorance of where they would lead, chance meetings that led to the making of a decision that would change our life. Ulf had met his wife, Letta, that way: he had bumped into an old friend who had invited him to a party. He met the old friend because he returned to a shop to retrieve a purchase he had left on the counter. Had he not forgotten to pick up the item, he would not have gone back into the shop and would not have met the friend and received the invitation. And then he would not have gone to the party where he met his wife. Their marriage had been a contented, uneventful one, and then she had met a hypnotist, and his world had come tumbling down. Had he not forgotten that item, he would not have known the happiness he knew, nor the sadness. It would all have been different.

But this was no time to think about that. Dr Svensson had once counselled him to think of the things you're doing rather than the things you *did*. It was useful advice – he knew that – even if the therapist liked to claim he was not dispensing advice, but helping him to work out what was the best thing to do. That was the trouble with Dr Svensson, thought Ulf: he often denied that he was there – an odd thing to do, especially when you charged so much for being present.

So Ulf sat at his desk during this thinking time, and thought about the strange assault on Malte Gustafsson. He felt that there was a missing factor that he should be seeing, but he was uncertain whether that factor was to do with the victim, or with the *modus*. He had yet to meet Malte, but he felt that he had a reasonable idea of who he was. A man's description of a brother should normally be treated with caution – we never recover from the jealousies, and loves, of childhood, and this may influence the way we see people. Ulf knew of feuds that had started in the nursery and ended in the retirement home. And yet he thought that Oscar's insistence on Malte's good nature and popularity was probably justified; it certainly felt that way to Ulf.

He was in no doubt about what Oscar had said about Malte's motorcycling colleagues. In Ulf's experience, any assault on a biker was almost certainly the act of another biker, and could usually be pinned on a member of a rival gang. Identifying as a biker was an act of machismo, and machismo always provoked animosity. But it was different when bikers reached a certain age: the plumage may say one thing, but the spirit says another. Middle-aged bikers might want to travel at two hundred kilometres an hour, but they usually settled for one hundred. They might have pictures of skulls on the backs of their leather jackets, but in their case these were really pictures of their last X-ray rather than threats. It was probably the case that at least some middle-aged bikers would have started to have prostate problems and as a result liked short trips. And no biker – of whatever age – would ever consider picking a fight with a motorcycle mechanic, even one who could not tolerate soap and had to be careful about exposure to grease.

No, there was no point in pursuing anything in that direction. And nor, it seemed, was there anything to explore on the family front. Malte's wife, Mona, might be alienated from her brother, and that might seem a good line of inquiry, but the brother had been in Winnipeg at the time of the attack and so that removed him from suspicion. Unless, of course, he had arranged for somebody else to do the stabbing. That was a thought: if one wanted a cast-iron alibi, go to a wedding in Winnipeg, but get somebody to do the deed on your behalf.

Ulf realised he had perhaps been too quick to exclude Edvin from suspicion. Farmers – particularly dairy farmers – might be phlegmatic, but when it came to an argument over land – and milking parlours, presumably – they could become intensely passionate. Rural feuds about who used which field or whose cows had broken out and eaten whose turnips were famous for their intensity. Wasn't *Cavalleria Rusticana* all about rural passions and their dramatic consequences? You did not have to be Italian to experience such things, although no Swedish composer could have written *Cav* and been taken seriously.

But no, it just did not seem right, and Ulf had learned to trust his instincts. No dairy farmer would get somebody to go off and stab his brother-in-law in the back of the knee. It just would not happen.

And that left him with no surmise and nothing to think about, let alone work upon. So Ulf looked at his watch and decided it was time to go home and take Martin, his dog, for his evening walk before giving him his dinner. He could still think about the case while he did this: he might have reached a dead end when it came to the *who* question, but there was still the *why* question. Why would anybody stab Malte in the back of the knee? Had that really been sheer chance, as he initially thought, or was there a reason why the assault had been carried out at a low level? At a low level . . .

Ulf decided that in that particular feature lay the key to the whole matter. There was something critical about it that he had yet to figure out. He was now sure of this, and it boosted his confidence about finding a solution. Now he knew where to look: not up there, but down there, down at knee level.

Martin gave him an ecstatic welcome – as he always did. Ulf had read that dogs believed when their owners left them behind in the house they would never see them again. Dog memory, however long it might be when it involved smells, and the remembrance of smells, was not all that strong on events, and a dog might well forget that his owner usually returned after going out. So the poor dog would go through the agony of abandonment – seemingly permanent – every single day, sometimes more than once a day. And when the owner returned, the dog's joy would be immense, as great, in its way, as the joy of Penelope on the return of Odysseus. Or, for that matter, of the hero's dog when his master turned up once again in Ithaca, although poor Argos, lying on his dungheap, was too old to do much more than raise his ears and wag his tail, much as he would have liked to turn somersaults, bark with delight, and confer slobbering canine kisses.

It was not easy, keeping a dog in a flat, especially an active one like Martin, who had poodle and Labrador blood in him – both being sociable breeds fond of exercise and human company. It would have been impossible, in fact, were it not for Ulf's neighbour, Mrs Högfors, a retired schoolteacher, who was only too happy to take Martin out for walks along the street several times a day and look after him while Ulf was working. Martin loved Mrs Högfors, and she adored him in return, allowing him to sleep on her sofa, feeding him a constant diet of fattening treats, and refusing to countenance any talk of faults on his part. So when Martin ate a set of stereo headphones belonging to Ulf, and gnawed a hole in Mrs Högfors' own hall carpet, these *peccadillos*, as she called them, were put down to his desire to be helpful.

'And we have to remember,' she said, 'Martin suffers from a handicap. We have to make allowances.'

The handicap to which Mrs Högfors referred was deafness. Martin was hearing-impaired, and had been so since puppyhood. Ulf had first discovered this when taking Martin, as a young dog, for a walk in the park near his flat. Two troublesome youths, who had been setting off firecrackers, tossed one so that it landed immediately behind Martin. The resulting explosion had no effect on Martin, who sauntered on unperturbed. Ulf had been surprised by this, given the sensitivity of most dogs to fireworks, and had arranged for Martin to be examined by the local vet. Ulf's suspicions were confirmed: Martin was unable to hear anything, even with the temporary assistance of a special canine hearing aid that the vet inserted in his ear.

'There's not much we can do,' said the vet. 'You're going to have to watch him on the roads. He won't hear cars, you know.'

That was a danger, of course, but Ulf found it possible to avoid the more serious consequences of Martin's deafness by remembering that for a dog, smell is more than capable of compensating for lack of hearing. So, rather than call Martin for his dinner – as most dog owners would do – he would open a can of dog food and then blow across the open top, wafting the smell off to Martin's attentive nose. Similarly, when it was time for Martin to be taken for a walk, Ulf would wave his leash about in the air, allowing Martin to catch a whiff of the leather and to come bounding up for the outing.

These techniques had worked well enough, but then a chance

remark by the vet had led Ulf to adopt a whole new approach to Martin's handicap. 'It's a pity,' said the vet, 'that nobody's ever thought of teaching dogs to lip-read.'

Ulf had quizzed the vet. 'Nobody's done that?'

The vet shook his head. 'Not as far as I know. But I can't see why they shouldn't. Dogs can read signals – look at sheepdogs – they understand hand movements for left and right. Dogs are no fools, you know.' He paused. 'Well, some are. Some dogs are truly stupid, Ulf. But Martin certainly isn't; his poodle genes prevent that. I've never met a stupid poodle in all my twenty years of practice. Not one. Stupid spaniels – plenty of those; stupid terriers – now and then; but stupid poodles – never. They just don't exist.'

Ulf had said nothing, but the vet's comment, a casual, throwaway observation, started him thinking. Why shouldn't dogs lip-read? Dogs understood language – to a limited extent. Dogs knew single words – *walkies*, *biscuits*, *bad*, *sit* and so on – although their grasp of grammar was solipsistic. All verbs, in a dog's mind, are governed by a pronoun, and that pronoun refers to themselves. So the verb *sit* must always be read as *me sit*. Adjectives and nouns, too, are similarly qualified: *bad* is *me bad*, and *biscuits* is *me biscuits*. And if they understood words, even imperfectly, and even in this remarkably self-centred way, then surely they could understand the equivalent sign – a gesture or lip position that accompanied the word?

Ulf decided to put the matter to the test. Starting with a simple command – one that most dogs were capable of understanding and acting upon, *sit* – he stood in front of Martin, said *sit* in such a way that the position of his lips was exaggerated, and then pressed firmly on Martin's hindquarters, forcing them down.

Martin looked up at his owner in mute incomprehension. Many

dogs spend a large part of their lives in such a state of unknowing: they try to understand the human world, to which they feel – and are, by ancient compact – attached, but can simply make no sense of it. Such were Martin's feelings now: why did Ulf, whom he worshipped, whom he regarded as God incarnate, want him to lower his hindquarters when there was clearly no need to do so? But that was a question too advanced in its implications for a dog, and Martin did not even try to understand it, and so he sat. And in the course of time he established a connection between the position of his owner's lips and the need to sit, thus becoming the first dog in Swedish history to lip-read a command successfully.

Ulf took Martin outside briefly when he arrived home that evening, and then fed him. After that, with Martin asleep in his basket under the kitchen table, Ulf sat down and opened the latest copy of a magazine to which he subscribed, the reading of which he eked out, as one might prolong the pleasure of a box of chocolates. This magazine arrived in the post every third Thursday of the month, and, through the exercise of willpower, could be made to last ten days, with roughly eight pages – or one article – being read each day. Then the magazine would be placed, along with earlier issues, on a living-room shelf specially set aside for it, filed in correct sequence and therefore readily available for further reference.

The magazine was *Nordic Art*, a popular art history publication specialising in Scandinavian art but occasionally including articles on the art of other northern countries – Canada, Russia, Iceland and Scotland. Ulf read these other articles, of course, but not with the interest he reserved for those dealing with Scandinavian art of the twentieth century. That was what interested him, and that was his principal intellectual passion, along with philosophy, which he read less frequently, and with rather less engagement.

31

That evening there was an article in *Nordic Art* that he had been looking forward to reading. This was a prolonged reflection by a prominent art critic of a painting that Ulf had seen on a visit the previous year to Norrköping. The Vargs, his family on his paternal side, originally came from Östergötland, and there were still family occasions – weddings, baptisms, funerals – amongst a large tribe of cousins, to which Ulf would occasionally have to travel. On his last visit, made for the seventy-fifth birthday of a senior Varg aunt, Ulf had been able to pay a quick visit to the Norrköpings Konstmuseum, the local art museum, and had found himself standing in front of *Det sjungande trädet*, *The Singing Tree*, a large painting by Isaac Grünewald. This painting, which a small informative label told him was painted in 1915, was Chagall-like in its colours and dreamy, flowing quality. An autumnally leafed tree, predominantly red, curled its trunk up the central section of the painting. Behind it, in public gardens, a carousel was filled with children, watched, to judge by their clothing, by two sailors. Further in the background, but still in the gardens, a striped tent-roof sheltered a throng of people, talking, or dining, or simply thronging. Now this picture was being subjected to the gaze of an art historian, and was featured, in full and vibrant colour, above the article in *Nordic Art*.

The painting had made an impression on Ulf, and he was pleased to see it again. He started reading: this picture, wrote the critic, is all about the incorporation of nature, represented here by the tree, within our growing urban environment. The tree still celebrates its essential *treeness* through song, as nature will do whatever we impose on her. Birds still sing their ancient songs in the middle of a bustling city, with all its cacophony of man-made sounds. Dry leaves still rustle like dice even when growing against concrete or hewn stone. Out of a tiny crack in a pavement will crawl a perfectly formed insect, a creature of curves and protrusions amidst a linear world of man's engineering.

Ulf's eye wandered from the text to the reproduction of the painting. In the foreground, more important than any of the other figures on the canvas, was a woman holding the hand of a small child. The child, a boy in a striped shirt, was about half the size of the woman. He tugged at her arm as if wanting to go off to the right-hand corner of the painting; she, sheltering under a blue parasol, seemed to be intent on staying where she was. She was co-operating with the painter, standing still, while the child had more pressing business elsewhere. It was a small detail, but it interested Ulf because he had not seen it before. He had viewed the figures as just being there coincidentally, rather than being there to say something about the tree. And now it occurred to him that the child complemented the tree. The tree had its own song – so did the child. The adult represented the world that had entrapped the tree – taken it out of the forest, so to speak, out of nature, and placed it in an urban environment. The child would be taken out of the world of childhood – a world in which trees might well be expected to sing – and put in the serious, non-singing world of adulthood.

Then the thought occurred to him: what if the child were not a child, but a small man? What if these figures represented a woman who lived with a midget, a husband or lover who was much shorter than she – half her height? It was perfectly possible. Tall people took up with small people, and sometimes the disparity in height could be considerable. He looked at the painting again, and told himself that this interpretation was clearly fanciful: the small figure was definitely a boy. But then he stopped. He stood up, dropping *Nordic Art* to the floor. Under the kitchen table, Martin opened an eye, not because he had heard the sound of the magazine hitting the floor – he could not – but because he had been observing Ulf from under not-quite-shut eyelids, watching his mouth for any sign of the lip position for *walkies* or *biscuits.*

Ulf reached for his telephone and dialled Anna's number. She was making dinner at home, steaming the organic broccoli she had bought in the market; she would serve this with cod and potatoes to her husband, the girls having eaten earlier, to allow them to attend practice at the swimming club. She was used to getting office calls at all hours, and so was not surprised when she received Ulf's request for Blomquist's mobile number. She had made a note of this at the beginning of their visit to the market, and gave it to him now.

'He'll be pleased to hear from you,' she said, holding the phone with one hand and with the other lifting the lid of the vegetable steamer. 'He's very keen to be involved in this investigation.'

'He might be able to help us,' said Ulf. 'I won't take any more of your time just now, but I might have something to talk about tomorrow.'

Anna was curious. 'A suspect?'

'Maybe. It depends. At the moment it's just a supposition.'

Anna said that she had also been thinking about the case. 'It's nothing to do with the dairy farm,' she said. 'It's not them.'

'No,' agreed Ulf. 'I think they're in the clear.'

'So that leaves the bikers. I think this has all the hallmarks of a crime of passion. You only stab somebody in the back of the knee if you're feeling very sore about something. You don't want to kill your victim, you want him to feel pain. You're effectively saying *You've caused me pain, and now I'm doing the same thing to you.*'

Ulf hesitated. The silence between them was being transmitted

34

through the air, from communication tower to communication tower. Silence. Then he said, 'Possibly.'

They rang off, and he dialled Blomquist's number. 'Blomquist,' he said. 'Did you see any really small people in the market that day? Not just short, but really short?'

Blomquist coughed. 'Sorry,' he said. 'My chest. I've had this cough that's been with me for two weeks now. Stubborn. I have this codeine syrup stuff that makes me feel vaguely drowsy. I don't like taking it – and I don't think it works all that well.'

'I hate having a tickle in my throat,' said Ulf.

'A dry cough,' said Blomquist. 'Yes, those are the worst. I like the expression a *productive cough*. You bring up the phlegm. Much better that way, I think. Lots of phlegm.'

'That helps,' said Ulf. He waited a few moments to see if Blomquist had finished. A productive telephone call, he thought. Brings up the facts. Lots of facts.

'Yes,' said Blomquist at last. 'There was somebody.'

'Known to you?'

Ulf waited. On this answer, he thought, hangs the fate of this investigation.

'Yes,' said Blomquist.

Anna looked at Ulf in astonishment. 'A dance studio?' she asked. 'Did I hear you correctly? Dance?'

They had met, quite by chance, in the café opposite the office. Ulf rarely went in there before mid-morning, but Anna was a regular on what she called the 'early caffeine shift'. She liked to buy a large cup of coffee that she would nurse for a few minutes, scanning the morning's newspaper headlines, before making her way into the office. On this particular morning, she was surprised to see Ulf, and even more surprised by his mention of a visit he proposed they should make later that day.

'I spoke to Blomquist last night,' he said. 'He went on and on about a cough he's been suffering from. You know what he's like.'

'I barely know him,' she said. 'I remember him from that whisky case, but you had more to do with him than I did.' She paused, and took a sip of her steaming coffee. 'You say he has a cough?'

'Yes,' said Ulf. 'He told me he'd had it for two weeks.'

'That's hardly persistent.'

'No. I would have thought a two-week cough was hardly worth mentioning.'

Anna took another sip of her coffee. 'I spoke to somebody who's been coughing for four months. She told me that the doctor has given her one of those steroid inhalers. It's meant to calm the airways.'

Ulf nodded. 'But you don't want to use too many steroids.'

'No,' said Anna. 'But if you carry on coughing, what can you do?'

Ulf raised the issue of athletes. 'If you're a cyclist, for instance, and you have to have one of those inhalers, surely you could get into trouble with the anti-doping people? Like that American? What was his name? The man who had his Tour de France win taken away from him.'

Anna had only a vague recollection of the affair. 'I suppose I'll have to talk to the girls about doping one of these days. If they start getting into these big competitions with their swimming, I imagine they'll have to be careful about what they take – for coughs, and things like that, of course.' She paused. 'Two weeks is nothing. Some of these infections last for ages.'

Ulf nodded. 'I cut a finger on an oyster shell once,' he said. 'I was shucking some oysters . . . '

'I love oysters,' said Anna.

'Do you eat them raw?'

She did not mind: either raw or cooked.

'Anyway, I cut my finger on the shell. You know how difficult it is to get them out of their shells? Well, I was being careful and I still managed it. The cut wasn't very big at all, but it wouldn't heal. It became infected and they had to try several antibiotics before it got better. They were quite worried, I think.'

'The doctors?'

'Yes. They were worried. They told me they had only a limited number of antibiotics at their disposal – what with resistance – and when they didn't work it was always an anxious moment.'

Anna sighed. 'We depend on antibiotics, don't we? We take them for granted, but they're a very hard-pressed defence line. Jo worries about that, you know.' Jo was her anaesthetist husband, a mild, rather oppressed-looking man – just the sort to worry about antibiotics, thought Ulf.

Then Anna asked, 'So Blomquist had some information?'

Ulf told her of his conversation with Blomquist and the response he had received to his question about small people at the market. 'I had an idea, you see, that the person who stabbed Malte was very small.'

'Because of that small split in the canvas?'

'Yes, but also because of the site of the injury.' Ulf waited. He was not sure how his supposition would be received.

'Down low?'

'Precisely. If you are small – very small – and you reach out to stab somebody, then the injury will be on a lower part of the body, won't it?'

Ulf watched Anna as she considered this. He valued intelligence, and Anna was a highly intelligent woman. But as well as valuing her opinion, he was worried about her pouring cold water on his ideas. What if she were to laugh? What if she were to say that this was absurd, and that linking the site of injury to the height of the assailant was just too unsophisticated?

She did not laugh. Instead she nodded gravely. 'It's possible,' she said. 'Just possible, I suppose.'

Ulf's relief showed. 'Blomquist replied almost immediately,' he said. 'He said: "Oh, there was Hampus, of course. I saw him there. He works nearby and you often see him."'

Anna put down her cardboard cup. 'These things get too hot,' she said. 'They make them too thin these days.'

'Or the coffee's made too hot,' said Ulf.

'That too. But who's this Hampus?'

Ulf smiled. 'Well, this is the interesting bit. Apparently Hampus runs a dance studio – one of these places where you go to learn the waltz.'

'And the cha-cha? And the quickstep?'

'Yes, all of that stuff.' Ulf did not like dancing.

'I used to go to one of those places,' said Anna. 'When I was seventeen. I thought I might become one of those professional dancers. You know the type – they wear all those sequins and they whirl around.'

'We all have our dreams,' said Ulf. 'And you ended up as a detective.'

'A better career. Much better. I don't think those dancers have much of a life. Constant practice. Forever watching your weight so that your bottom doesn't look too big.'

Ulf lowered his eyes.

Anna was looking at him. 'That made you think of Saga,' she said accusingly. 'Go on, admit it.'

He looked up, and smiled. 'I suppose so.'

Saga was a colleague who specialised in financial crime. She had a problem with weight distribution.

'I don't know how she fits in her chair,' said Anna. 'But I don't suppose I should think about that sort of thing. We're not meant to, are we? We're meant to ignore people's bottoms.'

Ulf shrugged. How could one ignore something so fundamental? 'This Hampus,' he said. 'He's very small, Blomquist said. He's a midget.'

Anna raised an eyebrow. 'A midget? Do we use that word?'

Ulf said that he was not sure. 'Perhaps it's safer to call him a very small person. I wouldn't want to use a derogatory term.'

'Probably safer,' said Anna. 'If you use the wrong word in a report, you get your knuckles rapped. So he's not a dwarf, then?'

'Not as far as I know,' said Ulf. 'I asked Blomquist, who said that he thought a dwarf didn't have normal bodily proportions. Midgets – I mean, small people – do. They have small bodies, but otherwise they look normal.'

Anna frowned. 'I'm not sure that you can say *normal*, you know. Perhaps say *average*. Nobody gets offended if you say that they're not average.'

They were both silent for a while. Anna took another sip of her coffee; Ulf looked out of the window. A man was walking past with his hat pulled down over his eyes and the collar of his coat turned up. As he drew level with the café, he glanced in and made eye contact with Ulf. They both looked away.

'I have to say,' Ulf continued, 'that I found the thought a little strange. Here's this very small person running a dance studio. Blomquist says that he dances with his customers. That's what he said.'

'Not surprising,' said Anna. 'The owners of these places are usually dance instructors.'

'Yes, but can you picture it? What if the customer is ... is normal – I mean is average height? Wouldn't it be a bit difficult for Hampus to dance with a person who's much taller? How could he put his hands round her shoulders?'

Anna shook her head. 'It can't be easy.'

'No,' said Ulf. 'But that's not for us to speculate about. The real question is this: could Hampus be the very short person who stabbed Malte in the back of the knee? That's the question, I'd say.'

'I'd say that too,' agreed Anna. She looked at her watch. 'We'd better get over to the office; Carl will have been there for hours already.'

Ulf prepared to leave. 'I saw Carl's father on television last night.'

Anna thought of Ulf, alone in his flat, watching a television programme about moral dilemmas.

'He was talking about the ethics of criticising other people's lifestyle decisions.'

Anna picked up her half-finished cup of coffee. 'Such as?'

'Oh, vegans telling schools they shouldn't keep animals in the classroom. You know, guinea pigs, hamsters and so on. Schools sometimes have them in the classroom.'

'Yes,' said Anna. 'The girls did, when they were smaller. Mind you, the kids aren't going to *eat* these creatures. So what's the vegans' beef?'

Ulf smiled. 'Apparently they argue that this inculcates ideas of animal husbandry in the children's minds.'

'Oh, really!' Anna exploded. 'Where's their sense of proportion?'

Ulf did not answer. He was wondering whether there was anybody who would object to his keeping Martin? And if so, what would they say he should do with the dog? Let him go free?

But Anna had more to say about classroom pets. 'The girls' school had a guinea pig called Walter. The kids took turns to take it home at weekends. Until somebody's dog ate it one weekend.'

Ulf whistled. 'Disaster.'

'Yes. But what was Carl's father's view?'

'He said it depends,' said Ulf. 'But he said it in that fantastic voice of his. And everybody in the studio audience started to nod. He only has to open his mouth, and people start to nod. It's amazing.'

They left the café and crossed the road to the front door of the office. Erik was arriving for work just ahead of them, and he nodded a greeting. Ulf noticed a magazine rolled up under his arm: it would be one of Erik's angling magazines, with its pictures of reels and floats and all the paraphernalia of fishing; the things that made life bearable for him, his props. He thought about Professor Holgersson, and what he might say about such a life. Or what Kierkegaard might say, for that matter. They would approve, he suspected, because it was an honest, authentic life, lived with integrity and without pretence, which was more than could be said of so many more sophisticated lives.

'Poor Erik,' muttered Anna.

'No,' said Ulf. 'No. Not poor Erik – fortunate Erik.'

Anna gave Ulf a dubious look. 'But all he thinks of ... '

' ... is fishing. Yes, but does that make him unhappy? Quite the contrary: Erik is utterly happy. Erik is completely resolved.'

Anna looked thoughtful. 'What do you think Erik thinks of us?'

'I have no idea,' said Ulf.

41

'He admires you,' said Anna. 'He's told me so on more than one occasion. He says you're kind.'

'That's generous of him. Of course, he's the kind one.' Ulf paused. 'I know he likes you.'

Anna remembered that she had had an invitation from Erik to join him and his wife for ice fishing one winter. She'd had to think quickly to come up with an excuse.

'Ice fishing is extremely dull,' said Ulf. 'You sit there round a hole in the ice and wait for fish to bite.'

'I know,' said Anna. 'Poor Erik.'

Ulf smiled. 'Don't condescend,' he said playfully.

She took his reproach seriously, and was apologetic. 'I'm sorry. You're right. Erik doesn't need our sympathy.'

Ulf assured her that he didn't mean to sound critical. 'I'm not trying to tell you how to think about your colleagues. I'd never do that.'

It was a curious moment, and he felt as if an unspoken boundary of intimacy had been crossed. He thought that she felt the same, as he saw her blush and turn away just as they reached the outer door of the office. He wanted to reach out and touch her arm, and he began to do so, but stopped himself, converting the movement into nothing significant – just a raising and dropping of the hand.

The morning was taken up with a seemingly interminable section meeting during which their immediate superior, an enthusiast for bureaucratic procedures, spent more than two hours detailing the latest procedural guidelines. Somewhere in the organisation, high in its upper reaches, were minds that churned out page after page of guidance notes, instructions and policy statements. Most of these were filed and forgotten; seldom did they make any difference to the way in which people carried out their duties. But the procedure for procedures had to be gone through, in accordance with further procedural guidelines. Ulf sat in his chair, staring at the ceiling, while Carl, ever conscientious, feverishly scribbled notes on what their superior officer said. This pleased the speaker, who paused considerately from time to time, in order to allow Carl to catch up with the flow of his lecture, and occasionally said, 'Please stop me, Mr Holgersson, if I speak too quickly or if anything I say is not quite clear.'

At the end of the meeting, as Ulf and Anna, and the dozen or so other officers who had sat through the ordeal, rose to their feet, the superior officer approached Carl.

'Please forgive me,' he said. 'I'm sure that people are always asking you to do this sort of thing.' He slipped a book out of his briefcase and placed it in front of Carl. 'Your father's latest book. The one on Kierkegaard. Would you mind getting it signed for my wife? She's a huge fan.'

For a moment Ulf pictured the huge fan – an immense woman, flowing out of her clothing – so huge as to find it difficult to walk. But that was not what huge meant here, he thought; language is not a literal business, he reminded himself. And then he thought: Kierkegaard. And that led to an image of Dr Svensson, with his horn-rimmed spectacles, and his layman's view that the life of a member of the Department of Sensitive Crimes was somehow more exciting than that of a psychoanalytically inclined psychotherapist.

'Kierkegaard,' said Anna under her breath.

Carl was gracious, as he always was, for the moment the son of the hypnotically urbane professor. 'But of course. It's no trouble. I shall be seeing him on Sunday and I'll ask him to dedicate it to her then.'

'She'll be very appreciative,' said the superior officer. 'She watches him whenever he's on television. She really is a huge fan.'

Ulf closed his eyes. He saw the professor being pursued by a group of his fans, the huge ones struggling to keep up with the thinner, more lithe fans, dropping exhausted and disappointed. He opened his eyes. Anna was looking at him, and smiling discreetly. He thought that perhaps she had been thinking the same thing, which was unlikely, but a nice thought anyway – that two people who liked one another should think the same thought at the same time.

The Johansson School of Dance was on the ground floor of a building not far from the market. The building was slightly shabby, the stucco on its front in need of attention, the door, although once fine, now drab in appearance. The impression it gave was of faded grandeur, which Ulf thought rather suited a ballroom dancing business: lights and glitter, but underneath an inevitable tawdriness. Dance was illusion, a triumph over gravity and awkwardness, but only a temporary one. The lights would always have to be switched off, the music stopped, the movement of the dancers lapse back into stasis.

They found a parking place for the Saab, and then Ulf and Anna rang the school's front-door bell. *Please ring, and then wait* said a small sign beside the bell.

A woman in a leotard appeared, and opened the door.

Ulf said, 'Is Mr Johansson in?'

As he spoke, he showed her his identity card. Anna did the same. The woman glanced at the cards and frowned. Gesturing for them to enter, she led them wordlessly along a corridor framed with pictures of ballroom dancers.

'Your graduates?' asked Ulf.

44

The woman nodded, but did not say anything. Then, at the end of the corridor, she pointed to a door in which there was a large glass panel. 'This studio,' she said curtly, and then disappeared through another, unmarked door.

They approached the door and looked through the glass. Music drifted from inside: somebody was playing the piano.

Neither was prepared for the sight, and for a moment Ulf felt an urge to burst out laughing. Anna gave a slight gasp of astonishment. In the centre of the studio dance floor, a very small instructor was dancing with a remarkably tall woman, his hands held up into hers, as if she were pulling him up towards her. They were doing what appeared to be a waltz, and the music confirmed this. 'The Blue Danube'.

Ulf pushed at the door, and the pianist, a man, stopped playing. The instructor turned to stare at the intruders. He detached himself from his dance partner and crossed the floor to face Ulf and Anna.

'Hampus Johansson?' said Ulf.

Hampus looked up at Ulf. Then he looked at Anna, before shifting his gaze back to Ulf.

'You don't have to tell me who you are.' The voice was high-pitched, and sing-song in its tone.

'We're—' began Anna, only to be interrupted by Hampus.

'I know who you are. And I know why you're here.'

Ulf studied the man standing before them, just over waist height. He saw the sweat stains on the tight T-shirt he was wearing. He noticed the rings on both hands – four altogether. He saw the piercing in the left ear – small, discreet, golden.

'Malte Gustafsson,' said Ulf.

Hampus looked down. 'I didn't mean to hurt him,' said Hampus.

Ulf and Anna waited.

'He laughed at me, you see.'

Ulf frowned. 'Laughed at you?'

Hampus looked up again. Ulf saw that tears had appeared in his eyes. He wanted to reach forward and wipe them away, but that was not for a detective to do.

'He's seeing Ingrid,' said Hampus. 'She works here. She must have let you in. She and Malte ... They're close friends.' He hesitated, his voice cracking with emotion. 'They're lovers. He came here and he watched me dancing with Violet and I saw him laughing. He was laughing at me. I hated him then.'

'You don't have to say anything more,' said Ulf. 'Not here. You can make a statement at the station.'

Hampus shook his head. The tears were more evident now; Anna winced.

'You people will never understand,' Hampus continued. 'You don't know what it's like to be stared at. Every day. Every single day. All the time. People stare at anybody who doesn't fit in, who's too short or too ugly or a different colour or whatever it is. They stare. But the difference with me is that you sometimes hear them laughing, as if I'm some sort of joke. You hear them. They laugh.'

Anna shook her head. 'I'm sorry,' she said.

'And it was hard,' Hampus went on. 'Because Ingrid is my friend and I've always hoped she might love me, and she doesn't. She doesn't. She loves that man whose cashmere is all fake. She loves him instead.'

'You don't have to say anything more,' said Ulf. 'You'll need to speak to a lawyer.'

Hampus shook his head. 'A lawyer can't save me. I've done a terrible thing. I'm finished now.'

He moved his foot and Ulf saw how his dancing shoe, a tiny patent-leather pump, like the shoe of a child, made a mark in the French chalk that covered the floor. *French chalk* . . . He had seen a reference to French chalk recently, but where?

'You know, it may not be as serious as you think,' Ulf found himself saying.

Anna looked at him in surprise, but he could tell that she welcomed this. What was the point of being an agent of the state's vengeance if one could not show mercy?

'We can charge you with minor assault,' Ulf continued. 'We can cite special factors – provocation, for instance. You were undoubtedly provoked. There need not be a prison sentence, you know. I can make special recommendations to the prosecutor. He is my friend.' That was Lars, who, unknown to Ulf, lived for him.

Hampus muttered something.

'What did you say?' asked Anna.

'I said: I'll never do anything like that again.'

She looked at him, and believed him. 'I'm so sorry,' she said. 'You think we don't understand, but we do, you know.'

'She's right,' said Ulf.

Hampus wiped at his cheek. 'I suppose I have to come with you.'

Ulf nodded. 'For a while. But I'm sure you'll be able to go home before too long.'

'Though maybe not tonight,' said Anna.

CHAPTER FOUR

Bim

Bim lived with her mother, Elvinia Sundström, a tapestry restorer. Bim was twenty and a student at the University of Malmö, where she studied human geography. She and her mother occupied a small flat with a balcony, on which in the summer they cultivated flowers and herbs: rosemary, basil, sweet william. Elvinia's husband, Fredrik – Bim's father – had left them when Bim was eight. He had been an officer in the Swedish navy at the time but was now believed to be running a hotel in the north of the country, with his second wife, the woman whom Elvinia believed had ruined her life by stealing her husband and depriving Bim of her father.

'He was weak,' she said to a friend. 'All men are. So I don't blame him as much as I blame her. She knew he was married; she knew he had a young child; all she had to say to him was thanks but no thanks. Did she do that? She did not.'

'Perhaps some women are weak too,' said the friend.

Elvinia would have none of this. 'No, they aren't,' she said. 'Women are strong.'

At first Bim missed her father acutely and often talked of his return. 'Daddy will come back soon, won't he?' she said to her mother. 'Daddy's ship will be coming home, won't it?'

It was hard for Elvinia. Although at first Fredrik made an effort to stay in touch with Bim – he sent her letters and parcels – he visited infrequently and then, after a year or so, not at all. Elvinia tried to explain to Bim that her father loved her, but that it was hard for him to see them as much as he would like.

'He's a sailor, you see,' she said. 'Sailors are usually away a lot. They live on their ships. They have cabins, with beds, and all their things in lockers. That's how sailors live, darling. They're always away from home. I think he's in the Faroes now – very far away. That's how it is.'

'But I saw him from the bus,' said Bim. 'Remember? Just a week ago. We were on the bus and we saw him walking along the street in his uniform. Remember? I banged on the window, but he didn't hear, and the bus was going too fast anyway.'

'That might not have been him,' said Elvinia. 'Many men look the same, darling. That was probably somebody else.'

It was a small lie; of course it had been Fredrik, and that woman, that husband-stealer from the north, that seductress, had been with him. Of course she had. It had been a small lie intended to protect a child from the brutal truths of adult selfishness. But, like many small lies, it had consequences. Telling a child that what her eyes tell her is not what's really there, is an invitation for subsequent psychological complication. But what could Elvinia do? It was all very well for people to insist that one always told children the truth – that by doing so one allowed them to come to terms with the hard face of the world – but, she wondered, did that make children any happier? Or did it simply destroy the hope, the innocence, that should be the background music of childhood? Did she want Bim to grow up thinking that her father did not love her, that he had wilfully deserted her, or should she be encouraged to believe that only the demands of being a naval officer kept him from showing the love and affection he undoubtedly felt for his family? To Elvinia, the answer was obvious: Bim should be encouraged to respect her absent father, because having a father, even one who was not there, was better than having no father at all. That was what she thought, and she believed – or persuaded herself to believe – that she had read somewhere, in a magazine perhaps, that this was the right thing to do in such circumstances. There were risks of course, and these might have consequences later on. But everyone knew that, just as everyone knew that all our behaviour has roots in what people have done to us: the lies they have told as much as the truths.

At least Fredrik never defaulted on Bim's maintenance payments; Elvinia had to give him credit, albeit reluctantly, for that. She realised, though, that when Bim reached the age of eighteen the agreement sanctioned by the divorce court would come to an end. For her own security, as much as for Bim's, she decided that she would need a career, her early marriage to Fredrik having put paid to her ambition to train as a physiotherapist. Enrolling on a university course was not an option: she had Bim to look after and she simply could not afford to pay for several years of childcare. So, looking around for an apprenticeship, preferably in a craft that would allow her to indulge her artistic interests, she eventually stumbled upon a small fabric conservation studio run by a weaver called Hanna Holm. Hanna was single-handed, both as a mother and a conservator, and she understood the juggling of times and commitments required of a woman in Elvinia's position. She listened sympathetically to Elvinia's story, shaking her head at more egregious instances of Fredrik's perfidy.

'I thought naval officers were meant to be gentlemen,' she said.

'Oh, that's all changed,' said Elvinia. 'The only gentleman left in this country is the King.'

Hanna nodded, although she did not entirely agree, at least in respect of the paucity of gentlemen. The man who sold her fish was a gentleman – she was sure of that – and so was her recently retired postman, even if he was a somewhat unconventional one. She thought of the King. 'Poor man,' she said. 'It can't be easy.'

Elvinia looked thoughtful. She remembered that Carl XVI Gustaf had been nine months old when his father's aircraft crashed near Copenhagen and had not been told about his father's death until he was seven. If she had been keeping the truth about Fredrik from Bim, then here was an even more extreme example, although the King's sister had not approved of this, saying publicly that a child's questions should not be met with silence. Elvinia felt ashamed; she would have to tell Bim the truth: that her father was not out at sea, but was still there in Malmö – this was before he went to live in the north to run that so-called hotel – with his *soi-disant* wife. Although she was really just his lover, she thought bitterly; and he could have come to see them if he were minded to do so.

'Well,' said Hanna, 'if you want to do this, why not give it a try for a couple of months, and then you can decide? I'll be very flexible with the hours I expect you to work.'

They agreed, and shortly afterwards Elvinia embarked on her training. She proved good at the work, and Hanna was relieved when she said that she would like to undertake the entire apprenticeship.

'I've found the thing I really want to do,' Elvinia said to Hanna. 'Working with thread and wool, with fabrics . . . '

'And with love,' interjected Hanna. 'Love is the most important ingredient in any artistic work. You have to love the work.'

'I do,' said Elvinia.

'I can see that,' said Hanna.

Elvinia could not have found a better-qualified teacher. Hanna had trained at the Swedish History Museum in Stockholm, where she had learned the skills required of a general conservator. It was fabrics, though, that particularly interested her, and she had eventually specialised in that area. As a newly qualified conservator and restorer, she had been allowed to work on the Skog Tapestry, a late medieval tapestry that featured three enigmatic crowned figures. There had been much discussion as to who these figures were, with the possibility being raised that they were the old Norse gods, Odin, Thor and Freyr. The identification of Odin rested on the fact that he appeared in the tapestry to have only one eye, a disability borne by Odin since he exchanged an eye for the gift of wisdom. This theory, however, was spoiled by the discovery that the reason why the figure in question only had one eye was that the stitches depicting the other one had simply fallen out. With that theory dispatched, the three figures became the Magi, although once again it was difficult to reconcile that with the fact that two of them appeared to be armed, one with an axe, and another with a sword. Unless the sword was a cross . . .

Hanna was ready to retire, and was happy to pass on her workshop and her clients to Elvinia. There was more than enough work, with the result that over the next few years Elvinia enjoyed a life of relative comfort and security. She and Bim got on well, and the teenage years, for so many parents a period of bickering and disagreement, were for Elvinia a time of company and harmony. By the time Bim was ready to go to university, rather than move out into a student flat she chose to stay with her mother. Elvinia was happy to have her at home, although she secretly hoped that Bim would cultivate friends of her own, and possibly even find a boyfriend. She was worried that with her own suspicion towards males, she might have put Bim off men. She did not want that: she hoped that Bim would find a boy who, unlike her father, would stick with her and make her happy.

Female friends proved easier to find. By the end of her first year, Bim was a member of a group of young women who did just about everything together. There were three others in this group: Linnea Ek, Signe Magnusson and Matilda Forsberg. These three were students of English, Swedish literature, and Earth Sciences respectively. All three had boyfriends of varying degrees of seriousness: Signe had, in fact, two boyfriends, not out of any inherent lack of fidelity, but because she could not bring herself to choose between them, and liked them both. She was also concerned about hurting the feelings of the one whom she eventually dismissed, and so she ran these two young men in parallel, avoiding any meeting between them or any slip-up that might reveal that they did not have as exclusive a claim on her affections as they imagined.

'Don't ever, ever tell anybody,' Signe begged Bim. 'The last thing I want – the very last thing – is for people to think I'm, well . . . ' She became silent in an evident search for the right word. Eventually she decided: 'Greedy. I wouldn't want people to think I was greedy.'

'Of course you're not,' said Bim. 'You're just generous-hearted.

Or is it warm-hearted and generous-spirited? Anyway, you're both of those.'

Signe was grateful. 'That's good of you, Bim. And you know something, having two boyfriends is rather fun. You should try it.' She was not serious, but she immediately regretted the remark. Bim did not have even one boyfriend, let alone two.

'I'm sorry,' Signe continued. 'That's tactless of me. I'm sure you'll find a boyfriend at some point.'

Bim sighed. 'I wish I could,' she said. 'I've tried, you know.'

Signe looked at her friend with interest. 'I'm surprised you haven't got somebody,' she said. 'You're very attractive, Bim – you really are. Why do you think boys don't like you?'

Bim's face fell, and immediately Signe felt guilty again. 'I didn't mean to say that. I'm sure that boys *do* like you.' And then she added, 'But maybe not in *that* way.'

Bim looked away. 'Well, if they do, why do I never get asked out? Never.'

'Do they know how to get in touch?' asked Signe.

'I do all the things you're meant to do,' said Bim. 'I go on social media. I've tried internet dating – nobody responded, except some horrible scumbags. One of them was actually in prison, and the other had an electronic tag. There were no nice boys, anyway – or none that I could see.'

'Don't give up,' said Signe, and changed the subject. She now had an inkling as to why her friend had met with no success. Men could tell when a girl was desperate, and if there was one thing that put them off, it was any sign of desperation. She had never been able to work out why this should be, and had ended up with a shaky socio-biological theory that desperation signalled a lack of breeding competitiveness that made males instinctively look elsewhere. Or was it something to do with Bim's essential domesticity – with her herb window boxes and her home cooking? These were most likely not things that young males valued. They wanted a girl who would go clubbing, who would smoke herbs rather than grow them.

The conversation with Signe depressed Bim. She now looked for signs in her friends' attitude that they pitied her, and when the other three stopped talking about their boyfriends, she interpreted this – correctly, as it happened – as their trying to avoid drawing attention to her boyfriend-less state.

This made it all the worse for Bim, and one weekend she decided that she could bear it no longer. She would make up a boyfriend for herself – she would create one. She would tell the others all about him, and that would end her sense of being a social and emotional failure. Obviously, she would not be able to produce this newly acquired boyfriend to show them, and so she would need to explain that Sixten – his name had already come to her – had a job that required him to keep unusual hours. He would be a paramedic, she decided. He would save lives daily. He would be strong. He would be decisive. He would drive an ambulance. He would be the best-looking ambulance driver in Malmö – by far. Such a man would rarely find the time to socialise with others: he would have far more important things to do with his time.

CHAPTER FIVE

He Went to
the North Pole

'A boyfriend!' exclaimed Signe. 'I never thought you'd manage it.'

She immediately apologised. 'Sorry, Bim. I meant: where did you find him?'

Bim waved a hand in the air. 'Oh, we just bumped into one another – started to chat. One thing led to another.'

This did not satisfy Signe. 'But where? Where did you meet this ... what did you call him again?'

'Sixten. He's called Sixten.'

Signe nodded in encouragement. 'And?'

'Well, that's what he's called.'

'No, silly: what I want to know is, what's he like? Is he ... is he *hot*?'

Bim smiled. 'I don't kiss and tell, Signe. I don't ask you if your boyfriend ... boyfriends ... are hot, do I?'

Signe understood. 'All right, not that. But is he good-looking?' She did not give Bim time to respond, but answered the question herself. 'I bet he is.'

'Yes,' said Bim. 'He's good-looking.'

'Have you got a photograph?' asked Signe.

Bim hesitated. 'Not on me,' she said.

'But you will get one, won't you?'

Again Bim hesitated. Then she replied, 'Yes, I'll get one.'

'Tomorrow?'

Bim's silence was interpreted as agreement. She had not thought about that; she had not really thought about any of the implications of Sixten's creation. She had imagined that she would be able to keep him in the background and that the others would understand that he was too busy to get involved in their social circle. But here was Signe asking for a photograph – and here she was promising to get one, and tomorrow at that.

Later, as she sat with her mother on the balcony after dinner – it was a fine, warm evening – she came to a decision on the photograph. It was simple, really: she could take a selfie with a boy – any boy – and then claim that was Sixten. If she went downtown and asked a passing boy if he minded doing a selfie with her, he would probably be bemused and agree. Why should he refuse?

She told her mother that she was going out for an hour or so. 'I just want to get out. Nowhere in particular, but it's such a lovely warm night and ... '

'You don't have to explain, Bim,' said her mother. 'Go off and enjoy yourself.'

She travelled into town by bus, and then made her way on foot to Lilla Torg. The restaurants and bars were busy, and there were crowds of visitors milling about. This was exactly what she wanted, and soon enough she had identified a young man who would make an ideal Sixten. He was roughly her age, tall, and certainly good-looking. In fact, she wondered whether he might not be just a little bit too good-looking for the purpose; she did not want Signe to think that he was simply too good to be true. But he was immediately appealing, in an open-faced, wholesome way, and he was just the sort she would choose anyway. As to his appearance – she wanted them to think that she had landed a film-star-handsome boyfriend; that would teach them to pity her, to think her incapable of finding a man, let alone one who could stop the traffic with his looks.

The young man was with two friends, and they were standing outside a bar, as if they were waiting to meet others. One of the friends had angry-looking skin; the other, who was shorter than his companions, had a cherubic face, fringed with fair curls, making him look like a fourteen-year-old choirboy. Neither of them would do: it had to be the young man she had identified as Sixten.

She approached them, her phone in her hand, as if about to make a telephone call. As she got closer, they noticed her, and she took a deep breath and stepped towards them.

'Hi, do you think you could help me with something?'

She addressed her request to Sixten, and it was he who replied. 'Yes, of course.'

She was pleased that he spoke Swedish; her English was strong, but she felt more comfortable doing this with a Swedish boy. Sixten – the imaginary one – was certainly Swedish.

'I want to test my phone. It was taking things out of focus.'

The young man reached out. 'Give it to me. I don't know much about these models, but let's see.'

She stepped forward and stood beside him. 'Try a selfie,' she said.

Sixten was slightly taken aback, but after a moment's hesitation he smiled. 'All right, a selfie then. You and me. Get in a bit closer.'

She did as he suggested. The flash went off, although she did not think it strictly necessary.

She held out her hand for the phone, and he gave it back to her. 'Perfect,' she said. 'I think it's working now.'

One of the other boys – the one with the angry skin – made some remark out of the side of his mouth. The choirboy muttered something in reply. She did not hear what they said, and it did not bother her anyway. She had what she needed.

She showed the photograph to Signe the next day. Her friend took the camera and peered at the picture of the boy from Lilla Torg. For a few moments she studied the screen, before turning to Bim with a look of unconcealed admiration. And envy.

'I can't wait to meet him,' she said.

Bim had noticed the envious look. Sixten's photograph was having the desired effect: there was no doubt that Signe had received the desired message – Bim, poor, mousy Bim, who lived with her mother and who had never had a boyfriend, now had the sort of boy whose photograph one saw in the magazines, who had to do nothing more than stand there, breathing, to look drop-dead sexy. She, Bim, whom Signe had felt moved to comfort and console in her single state, *she* now had *him*.

At the same time it was surprising that Signe should be envious. She already had *two* boyfriends; did this mean she wanted a third? Or was it that people, for all they wished their friends well, never actually wished them *that* well? Some relationships, of course, depended on the superiority of one party, and a change in the balance of advantage could destabilise them. That, she decided, was happening here. Signe wanted her to feel inferior because that somehow made her – Signe – feel better about herself. She was the big, more successful sister; she was the popular one; she was the one who could dispense advice and crumbs of comfort. She did not want an equal relationship, and she certainly would not want to be eclipsed.

Signe was looking at her. 'When can I meet him?' she asked.

Bim affected nonchalance. 'Sixten is pretty busy,' she said. 'As I told you, he's a paramedic.'

'Yes, but surely he doesn't work all the time. Even paramedics get time off.'

Bim agreed that this was so. 'Yes, he does get some time off, but he's studying at the moment. He's planning to go to medical school.'

Signe bit her lip. Quite unintentionally, Bim had said the one thing that would be guaranteed to cause her friend pain. It would be some years before Signe would want to commit to marriage – after all, marriage would be a problem for somebody with two boyfriends; one cannot marry two men – one would have to decide. But marriage was nonetheless an inevitability in her mind – perhaps one of the boyfriends would die, one never knew – and in so far as it would eventually *happen*, then she had always imagined it would be with a doctor. She would be married to a doctor who would be kind and gentle, but at the same time firm, sympathetic and good-looking. He would be a surgeon, perhaps. Yes, a surgeon would be perfect. And while she was prepared to imagine Bim being involved with somebody on the fringes of medicine – in a strictly subsidiary role, a male nurse, perhaps – she found it difficult to see her with a professional equal to her own, as yet unidentified, surgical boyfriend.

Signe looked away. 'Medical school's pretty competitive,' she said. 'I know lots of people who haven't got in.'

Bim was not ready for this, but with the confidence of her new status, she worked out the rebuttal.

'Sixten already has a place,' she said. 'He's been told that provided he passes this exam he's doing – and a bare pass will be enough – then he's in. They really want him, you see.'

Signe pouted. 'Why?'

'Because of his experience,' said Bim. 'He's seen so much while he's been working on the ambulances. He's saved a lot of lives, you know. There are probably hundreds of people walking around just because of him.'

Signe said nothing. One of her boyfriends worked in a tax consultant's office; the other had a job as a barista in a coffee bar. She shuddered. 'I suppose somebody has to do that sort of work,' she said. 'Not for me, though. All that blood and screaming and so on. Not a chance.'

'It's a good thing,' said Bim firmly, 'that we have people like Sixten, then. If everybody had your attitude, what would people do?' Then she answered her own question. 'I suppose they could get jobs as baristas.'

Signe looked sour. She tried to smile. 'I'm really pleased for you, Bim,' she said. 'A boyfriend at long last.'

Bim had not intended to tell her mother about Sixten, but then she lent her her telephone. She had not been thinking at the time, and when Elvinia left her own phone at a friend's house, Bim did not hesitate to offer her mother the use of her own. Elvinia needed a telephone for business calls – she was expecting the confirmation of an important restoration contract to repair the Persian carpets of a luxury hotel in Copenhagen, and the Danish agent who secured the business for her said she would be calling that day. Since she was going to be in and out of the office, Elvinia would need to give her a mobile number: 'I know you need your phone, Bim, but could I use it just for one day? You'll get it back this evening when I can get out to Katerine's place and get my own phone back – I promise, promise.'

'Of course,' said Bim, handing the phone over to her mother. 'Keep it charged – the battery doesn't last very long.'

Bim thought nothing more about it at the time, and it was only in the middle of the day, when she was sitting through a lecture on the psychology of the interview, that she remembered the photograph. Lending a phone to somebody is not lending her your life, she thought, even if the borrower is your mother. You don't expect your mother to read your emails or look at your photographs – unless she should press the wrong button, of course, and that was exactly the sort of thing that a mother might do. *What's this button, darling? Oh, photographs . . .*

Bim knew the moment she saw her mother that evening that she had found the photograph. As she handed the phone back to her daughter, Elvinia gave her a look that Bim understood perfectly. It was the look that she had always given her when there was cause for reproach – and often that reproach was associated with an implicit accusation of exclusion. 'We should have no secrets from one another,' the look said, 'and yet . . . '

But the reproach was short-lived, and was almost immediately replaced with a conspiratorial look – such a look of understanding and delight as might cross a parental face when the parent discovers her child has done something immensely distinguished and has been too modest to boast about it. So might a parent look on finding out that her daughter has been chosen for a university ski team, when she thought all along that she was only a moderately competent skier; or if she discovered that her daughter was in the running for a 'Young Woman of the Year' award and had said nothing about it; or when, as in this case, she found out that her daughter had at last managed to find a nice-looking boyfriend with no visible tattoos or facial piercings.

'Tell me,' said Elvinia coyly, 'what's his name – this new friend of yours?'

Bim looked away. She was by nature truthful and she would never lie to her mother. Yet she could not bring herself to tell her the full story of what she had done – it would sound so odd, so childish. She told herself that she should never have done it in the first place, and that it would inevitably become complicated and, with equal inevitability, lead to embarrassment. But it was too late for that now – she had done it – and whatever she said, short of a confession, would be a lie. So if she said that it was just a boy she had met by chance and that there was nothing more to it, then that would be in a superficial sense correct but, at the very least, completely misleading.

'Sixten,' she said. 'He's called Sixten.'

She had not really intended to say this, but it followed as inexorably as a railway carriage, if pushed by an engine, will follow the rails set out before it.

Her mother smiled. She was about to say, 'Now, that's a coincidence,' but she stopped herself. She wanted to play this carefully. So she asked, instead, 'And what does Sixten do? Did you meet him at the university?'

'He's a medical student,' muttered Bim. And then she added, 'It's nothing serious, Mother. We're just good friends.'

Elvinia nodded. 'Of course, of course. Early days. But I must say

I'm so pleased you've found ... a friend. Will you bring him here some evening? For dinner perhaps?'

'He works very hard. Medical students have to.'

Elvinia was quick to agree. 'I know that. I went out with a medical student once – a hundred years ago, of course; well before I met your father. He was always working. When we went out on a date he sometimes took his books along with him.'

Bim, being keen to change the subject, welcomed the direction in which the conversation was going. 'What happened to him?' she asked.

'He became a cardiologist, I believe. I saw him at a gallery opening – one of the textile shows. He had his wife with him. She teaches art, I think. She's a nice woman.'

'Had he changed a lot?'

'Not really. Some people look the same all the way through, don't they? They get a few more lines here and there, but the face remains the same. Others find their face sags as the years go past. It seems to sink somehow. Gravity, I suppose.'

Bim laughed. 'Not yours, Mother.'

'You're very sweet.'

The danger had passed. Two small lies had been told, but they would be reversed. Bim had made up her mind. She was going to end her relationship with Sixten.

A week later, when they were sitting together in a university coffee bar, Linnea Ek told Bim that she was planning a party in her flat – nothing big, just a few friends – and she would like her to come. 'Bring Sixten,' she said. 'We're all itching to meet him.'

Bim hesitated before replying. 'What day are you thinking of?' It would be easy to come up with an excuse – they knew that Sixten worked odd hours.

But Linnea's reply precluded such an easy way out. 'You decide,' she said. 'I've spoken to Signe and Matilda, and they say virtually any day will suit them. So, you – you and Sixten, that is – can choose the date. That'll work fine for us.'

Bim thought quickly. This was exactly the sort of difficulty she should have foreseen, she told herself; she should have broken up with Sixten days before this.

She said the first thing that came into her mind. 'Sixten's gone to the North Pole,' she said. 'He went last week.'

Linnea looked at her friend in frank astonishment. 'The North Pole? The *actual* North Pole?'

'Well, it isn't a pole – not a real one. It's the Arctic.'

'Yes, I know that,' snapped Linnea. 'I'm not stupid. But what's he doing in the Arctic?'

Bim explained once more that Sixten was a paramedic. 'There's a Swedish research station up there. They need a paramedic in case somebody . . . falls through the ice, or gets frostbite, or cuts himself. All sorts of things can happen up at the North Pole.'

Linnea took this in. 'Yes, I can see that. But how long is he going to be up there?'

'A year.'

'A year!' exclaimed Linnea. 'A whole year!' She stared at Bim, as if trying to make sense of an impossible situation. 'What are you going to do?'

Bim did not reply.

'Bim? Is it over?'

Bim nodded silently.

'I'm so sorry,' said Linnea. 'That's really bad luck, isn't it? You meet this guy – who sounded fabulous, by the way – and then he goes off to the North Pole. That's really tough luck.'

'I know,' said Bim. 'I know. I was hoping that . . . ' She paused. And then she began to cry. It was not contrived; the tears were real, such was her relief at the ease with which one could bring subterfuge to an end; at the ease with which one could stop lying to friends and return to one's truthful self; at the ease with which a boyfriend might be dispatched.

Linnea was effusive in her sympathy, as, a few minutes later, were Signe and Matilda, when they came into the coffee bar. Signe had arranged to meet one of her boyfriends in town, but could not remember which one. She would need to make a phone call to sort that out, and wanted to borrow Bim's phone. Bim gave it to her, and then went to the counter to buy herself a Danish pastry. When she returned, Linnea had obviously told the other two what had happened, as she was greeted with looks of concern and sympathy. Handing back the phone, Signe put an arm around Bim's shoulder. 'Don't be upset, Bim,' she whispered. 'Don't let it get to you too much. There'll be somebody else in good time. There really will be. And if there isn't – which I suppose is possible – then you'll still be happy single. Single people can have a perfectly good life, you know. A bit lonely, perhaps, but not too bad, all things considered.'

And Matilda, who agreed with this, said, 'If you've got happy memories – and I'm sure you have – hold on to them. Don't let them go sour.'

'It's not as if he left you for somebody else,' Linnea pointed out. 'He . . . well, he went to the North Pole, didn't he? That's different.'

'Still,' said Matilda. 'It's a bit selfish, isn't it? Presumably he didn't *have* to go.'

'I suppose not,' said Bim.

'Did the two of you discuss it?' asked Signe. 'Did he say some-thing like, "Would you mind if I went to the North Pole?"'

They waited for her answer. She looked at them. Should she just tell them? Should she confess that Sixten never existed? No, she could not do this. The whole ridiculous episode was almost at an end; all she needed to do was to pretend for just a few minutes more. Then Sixten need never be mentioned again. She would say it was just too painful, and they would respect that.

'We talked about it,' Bim said. 'We talked for hours, in fact. He said that it was a really good opportunity for him to get more experience in polar medicine. Apparently, it's different from ordinary medicine.'

Signe nodded. 'Yes, I suppose it is.' But then she thought of something. 'But what about medical school? You said that he'd been offered a place.'

'Yes, he was.'

'So, he's not taking it up?' asked Linnea.

'When he comes back,' said Bim.

Linnea looked puzzled. 'But that's going to be in a year's time, you said?'

'Something like that.'

'Oh, well,' said Signe. 'That's men for you.'

Then Matilda said, 'My uncle's a climatologist. He goes to that research station place from time to time. He's sometimes away for weeks. Not a year, of course. He'll probably meet Sixten up there.'

Nobody paid much attention to this remark – except for Bim. She heard it, and looked away. She felt the back of her neck getting warm.

CHAPTER SIX

The Smell of Envy

It was a quiet time in the office. The report on the Malte Gustafsson affair had been written, proofread, and then sent off to a higher authority two floors above. Once that had been done, there was little with which Ulf could occupy himself until the next inquiry began. That might be later that day, or the next, or even not until the following week: the Department of Sensitive Crimes depended on referrals, and these tended to be irregular. Sometimes as long as ten days could elapse between cases, meaning that there were periods when all three members of the Room 5 team found time hanging heavily on their hands.

'It's an odd feeling,' Ulf observed during one such fallow period, 'sitting here hoping that somebody out there does something outré.'

Anna agreed. She had knitting in her drawer, and could have kept herself occupied with that, but Ulf had warned her that were the Superintendent to drop in on the office – and he sometimes did that unannounced – then it would not look good if one member of the team were doing her knitting and another, Erik, were tying fishing flies at his desk.

'We have to look busy,' he said, 'even if we aren't. Otherwise we'll suddenly hear that we're losing a post.'

'Me,' said Erik, raising a hand. 'I'd be very happy to be made redundant.'

'Yes, you might,' said Carl. 'But I wouldn't. I wouldn't know what to do if I didn't have a job to come in to.'

Ulf followed his own advice. He put an old issue of *Nordic Art* into one of the folders used for inquiry files. That meant that he could sit at his desk reading about Scandinavian art without giving any visitor the impression that his mind was elsewhere.

He paged through the magazine. There were two articles on the art of Greenland, several review articles dealing with the latest books on Swedish and Danish painting, and an analysis of the use of artistic themes by Finnish nation-builders in the late nineteenth and early twentieth centuries. Ulf perused the index; he had read most of the contents – the edition was three years old – but found that he had forgotten most of what he had read. This was the fascination of *Nordic Art*: he could go back to past editions time and time again and refresh his memory of facts and opinions he no longer remembered. When I retire, he thought – not that retirement was anything but the most remote prospect – I shall spend my time reading *Nordic Art*, with every bit as much enjoyment as Erik will get from spending his own more imminent retirement catching fish.

Ulf glanced across the room towards Erik, who was concentrating on winding a small piece of thread around the shaft of a hook. A tiny feather, only barely visible to Ulf, was being attached to the hook by this thread, making at the end of the process a miniature trick, a minuscule act of fraud. Why, thought Ulf, should a grown man seek to defraud a gullible fish? *Here is a tasty morsel – no! A concealed hook! Foolish, foolish fish . . .*

Erik looked up and saw Ulf watching him.

'We call this the Red Dipper,' he said, holding up the now completed fly. 'Fish can't resist it. They take this almost every time.'

Ulf nodded. 'Fish are very stupid, aren't they?'

Erik put down the fly and looked angrily at Ulf. 'Fish, stupid? Oh no, far from it. Fish are very intelligent.'

Ulf shook his head. 'No, they aren't. Fish are stupid. Their brains are . . . well, almost invisible, I imagine.'

Erik drew in his breath. 'With the greatest respect, Ulf, I don't think you know what you're talking about. Fish are *not* stupid. I know a lot about fish, and one of the things I know is that they are *not* stupid.' He paused. 'Let me tell you: if you want to catch a trout in a stream, you have to stalk it.' Erik stared at Ulf with the triumphant air of one disclosing a clinching argument. 'Did you know that? You don't just stroll up to the riverbank and cast the fly. You have to try to merge in with the vegetation. Fish are watching, you see.'

Carl looked up from his desk. He, at least, had found some work to do; the perusal of cold case files – cases the department had not solved and probably never would. But there was always the chance that something would occur to somebody reading the papers again. 'How do you know that fish are watching, Erik? I'm not trying to catch you out, but how do you know what fish are doing? You can't really see them down in the water. So how do you know they're watching?'

Erik shrugged. 'How does anybody know anything?' he challenged.

Ulf replied. 'By observation,' he said. 'That's how we know.'

Erik did not reply at first. Then he said, 'I'm telling you – fish watch us.'

'They watch *you*, perhaps, Erik,' muttered Ulf. 'They watch you because they know you're out to get them. You've made it personal.'

Carl tried to mask his grin, but failed to do so. Noticing this, Erik looked away in disgust. 'I find it odd,' he said, 'that people who know nothing about fishing should talk about it with such apparent authority. Strange, but I suppose we live in an age of strong opinions.'

Ulf caught Carl's eye. 'Do you think fish have opinions, Carl? I'm not sure about it myself, but I thought I might just ask.'

Anna sighed. 'I think Erik has a point, you know. I don't think it's appropriate for us to spend our time talking about fish. I really don't.'

'You're right,' said Ulf, struggling to contain himself. 'Politics, religion and fish: three no-go areas for civilised conversation.'

'And sex,' added Carl. 'Don't forget sex.'

Ulf nodded. 'Of course. Mind you, do fish have sex?' He addressed himself to Erik. 'What do fish do about sex, Erik?'

Before Erik could answer, Anna's telephone rang. Picking up the receiver, she listened to a brief message from the front desk.

'Back to business, everybody,' she announced as she rang off.

All three went along the corridor to Room 2, the interview room. As the most senior – marginally – of the detectives, it was for Ulf to decide who should lead the interview.

'You're in the chair, Anna,' he said. 'Whoever this young woman is, she'll probably appreciate a female presence.'

Anna nodded. 'They said she's a Miss Magnusson. Signe Magnusson.'

71

'There was an actress called Signe Magnusson,' said Carl. 'My father used to talk about her.'

Anna remembered her. 'I saw one of her films once. A long time ago.'

'My father said she was one of the most beautiful women of her generation,' continued Carl. 'He said she had great big eyes – wide eyes.'

'Like the eyes of a fish?' asked Ulf.

Anna threw him a warning glance.

They went into the room. Signe, seated at a small table, her hands folded on her lap, looked up.

Anna introduced herself, and then the others. 'A few formalities,' she said. 'Could we have your full name, your address, and your occupation? And your age, too, please.'

Signe gave them the details.

Anna's voice was warm and, she hoped, comforting. 'Now then, Signe,' she began. 'What can we do for you? The police have referred you to us, you see. We're a unit that deals with more sensitive issues.'

Signe listened intently. Then, when Anna had finished, she said, 'Is this all kept confidential?'

'Of course,' said Ulf.

'Completely,' added Anna. 'You don't have to worry about that.'

But Signe required further reassurance. 'Does that mean you'd never tell anybody outside – anybody you spoke to, for instance – you'd never tell them who came to you in the first place?'

Anna nodded. 'As we told you, this is a special unit for sensitive issues. We're very well aware of people's concerns in that regard.'

Signe sat back in her chair. 'I feel really awkward about this,' she said.

Anna looked at her enquiringly. 'Would you prefer to speak only to a woman?' She gestured to Ulf and Carl. 'I can easily ask my colleagues to withdraw, if you'd prefer it that way.'

'No,' said Signe. 'It's nothing like that.' She paused. 'You see, this concerns a friend of mine – somebody I know well.'

There was silence. Anna waited. Then, gently, she pressed Signe to continue.

'It started about a month ago,' Signe said. 'Or five weeks, actually. Anyway, something like that. This friend of mine, Bim, told us – that's me and my friends, Linnea and Matilda – that she had met a boy. A boyfriend. We were pleased for her because she hadn't had a boyfriend, you see, and she lived with her mother and everything. So it was good news as far as we were concerned.'

Anna nodded encouragingly. Carl made a note on a pad of paper. Ulf listened.

'She told us quite a bit about him,' Signe went on. 'She said that he was called Sixten and that he was a paramedic. She said that he was planning to go to medical school. She showed us a photograph; he was very good-looking. She was standing next to him – I think it was a selfie. I've got a copy of it here, if you like.'

Anna frowned. 'How did you manage to get that? Did she give it to you?'

Signe replied that Bim had left her phone on the table in the café while she went to the counter. While her friend was away from the table, she found the photograph and emailed it to herself. 'Maybe I shouldn't have,' she said, 'but I did.'

'We won't go into that,' said Anna. 'Please continue.'

'Then,' said Signe, 'just a couple of weeks after she had met Sixten, she told us that he had left Malmö. Just like that. So we asked her what happened and she said that he'd gone to the North

Pole. There's a research station up there. She said that they needed a paramedic and that he was going up there for a year.

'I was really surprised. I wondered why somebody who was planning to go to medical school would go and spend a year in the Arctic. It seemed a bit odd, to me – really odd – but I thought that maybe Sixten was a bit strange. Anyway, I felt sorry for Bim. She seemed quite upset – she cried, in fact.

'I didn't think much more about it for a few weeks, until one of the others – Matilda, it was – told me something that made me think. She has an uncle who's a climatologist. He goes up north quite a bit, she said, and he had just come back from a week up there – letting off balloons or whatever it is he does. I think they use balloons to test temperatures.'

'They do,' said Carl. 'They take the temperature at higher levels that way. Meteorological balloons.'

'Yes,' said Signe. 'I know.'

'Please continue,' said Anna.

'This uncle of Matilda's went for dinner at Matilda's parents' place. It was her mum's fiftieth birthday and so Matilda went along too.'

'The uncle who's the climatologist?' asked Carl. 'The one from the Arctic?'

'Yes, him. He's not from the Arctic permanently, of course – just occasionally.'

'Nobody lives up there permanently,' said Anna.

'It depends what you mean by Arctic,' Ulf said. 'The Sami live up in the Arctic, but not as far north as where you're talking about.'

'Are we talking about the actual North Pole?' asked Anna.

'No, not quite,' said Ulf. 'But I think this research station place is close enough.'

74

'Does it matter?' asked Carl.

Anna returned to Signe. 'Just carry on, Signe.'

'Well, Matilda mentioned to this uncle, the climatologist one, that she knew of somebody who had just gone up to the research station. She told him about Sixten and about how he was a paramedic. Then the uncle shook his head and said there was nobody of that name up there. Nor was there anybody going – he knew that because he was on some planning committee that runs the station. He said they had no paramedic; rather, they had a rota of doctors who liked to spend time up there for research purposes. If you have a doctor, then you don't need a paramedic.'

'So Bim was making it up?'

'That's what I thought initially,' said Signe. 'I thought that maybe he had dumped her and she came up with this story as a sort of face-saving excuse. But then I noticed that if I mentioned him – which I did from time to time – she became really jumpy. It was as if she was hiding something. I became suspicious. And then something happened that made me really worried.'

They waited. Somewhere in a neighbouring street, an ambulance siren wailed.

'Bim's mother has a car that she lends to Bim from time to time. Bim even calls it her car, but it's really her mother's. Linnea and I were going somewhere with Bim in her car – to a party that somebody was holding out of town. Anyway, when we were at the party I discovered that I had left a sweater in the car and so I borrowed the keys from Bim, and said I'd go and fetch it.

'When I got to the car I remembered that Bim had put some stuff in the boot of the car, and I thought my sweater might be there. So I unlocked the boot and found it. But I also found something else. There was a small shovel, with some dirt on it. And something else besides.'

The room was now in complete silence.

'It was a cloth – an ordinary white cloth about so big – and there was dried blood on it. Not much, but definitely blood. It was tucked in behind the shovel. And that was when I started to put two and two together. I wondered whether Bim had . . . well, you know, got rid of Sixten.'

Anna cleared her throat. 'I'm not sure whether such a conclusion would be entirely justified,' she said.

'Maybe not. But then there was something else – something Bim had said that made me think. I only remembered it later, but it really stuck in my mind.'

'And that was . . . ?' asked Anna.

'Something Bim had said to me a few weeks back, before she and Sixten broke up. We had been talking about boys who two-timed, and I said that I could understand why a boy might on occasion have two girlfriends. Not that I was justifying it, of course, but I said that we had to be tolerant. And then she said, quite strongly as it happened, "If I discovered a boy was cheating on me, I'd be tempted to kill him – I really would." Those were her actual words.'

'Did you say anything to her about all this?' asked Ulf.

Signe shook her head. 'No. I was confused, and I suppose I was also a bit frightened. If she had actually killed Sixten, then she could kill me too. You never know.'

Anna reassured her that she thought that extremely unlikely. 'You mustn't jump to conclusions,' she counselled. 'People disappear for all sorts of reasons. They go away. Then they come back. It happens all the time.'

Signe was not convinced. 'But why would she lie about his going to the North Pole?' she asked. 'And why was there blood on that bit of cloth?'

Ulf intervened. 'Those are things that we can look into,' he said. 'You've done the right thing by bringing this to our attention.'

Signe said that she felt bad about it. 'She's a friend. And here I am accusing her of getting rid of somebody . . .'

'You haven't accused anybody of anything,' said Anna soothingly. 'You had some perfectly legitimate doubts, and you have done the right thing by bringing them to the attention of the police. If everybody were as conscientious about that as you've been, the crime rate would go right down.'

'Exactly,' said Carl. 'You have no reason to reproach yourself. No reason at all.'

Signe relaxed. 'I feel so stupid,' she said. 'Imagining things.'

'You're not stupid,' said Anna. 'And now, could you show us that photograph of Sixten?'

Signe slipped a piece of paper across the table. 'I've printed it on ordinary paper. I can send you a file, if you like. You might be able to sharpen it – you know, increase the definition.'

'Erik can do that,' said Carl.

They looked at the photograph.

'A nice-looking young man,' said Anna.

'Who are the others in the background?' asked Ulf.

Signe had no idea. 'His friends, perhaps. Passers-by.'

'And that's Bim with him?' asked Carl.

Signe nodded. 'That's her.'

Anna slipped the piece of paper into the folder she was carrying. 'Could you give us Bim's address, please? And her phone number.'

Signe looked worried. 'You're going to talk to her?'

Anna explained that they would have to do this. 'It will be our starting point,' she said. 'There may be a perfectly good explanation. We need to see if she can throw light on it.'

'But you won't mention me, will you?' Signe pleaded. 'Not by name.' She looked anxious; her eyes were searching out Anna's, for reassurance.

'We shall not mention you,' said Anna calmly. 'You have my word.'

When Ulf returned to his flat that evening, Martin was with Mrs Högfors. He gave silent thanks, as he often did, for this arrangement, made possible because Mrs Högfors was always in. Ulf had never known her to go anywhere, although she did reveal that four years ago she had, in fact, gone to Copenhagen, but had returned the same day as she said that it had not agreed with her. There had also been a trip to Stockholm to visit a cousin, but that, she said, had not been a success either.

'I take the view,' she once said to Ulf, 'that if you live in Malmö, then that is the place you are intended to be. Högfors' – she always referred to her late husband by his surname – 'said the same thing too.'

'So Mr Högfors never went anywhere either?' said Ulf.

The widow shook her head. 'He was a man of the very broadest outlook, but he never believed in going anywhere. He had a very sensitive stomach, you know, and that is always a disincentive to travel. If you have a sensitive stomach, it is undoubtedly best to remain at home.'

Ulf had glanced at the picture of Högfors on the table in Mrs Högfors' living room. A cheerful-looking, well-built man, not visibly suffering from the consequences of a sensitive stomach, stared out of the framed photograph. He was wearing, Ulf noticed, a nautical cap.

'He sailed?' asked Ulf, gesturing towards the photograph.

'No,' said Mrs Högfors. 'But he was a great supporter of the navy. Högfors was very distrustful of the Russians – he always was, even as a small boy, I believe. He said that Sweden needed her navy to constrain the Russians. And he was right, in my view. The Russians are everywhere, Mr Varg – everywhere. Not just in Russia, where you might expect to find Russians, but all over the place in their submarines and what-not.'

In spite of her disinclination to travel, Mrs Högfors was an eager reader, and was perfectly happy to read about exotic places that she would never visit. Rather to Ulf's surprise, she also read books on popular science, although she was undiscriminating as to their date of publication. This meant that she would sometimes talk about what she described as exciting new possibilities well after those possibilities had been translated into reality. Thus she had excitedly told Ulf that she had read a book predicting that one day man would undoubtedly set foot on the moon.

'It's hard to believe,' she said, 'but apparently there's a good chance of it happening. I was just reading about it.'

Ulf had replied that he thought it was just possible that this had already occurred.

'Oh, I don't think so, Mr Varg,' she said. 'I was reading that it's still at the planning stage.'

The book had been produced to show him – a tattered-looking volume, discharged after long service in the local library, that she had picked up from a church bazaar. From the biographical note on the back cover, Ulf ascertained that the author had been born in 1897.

That evening, Ulf found Mrs Högfors looking concerned.

'Martin is not quite himself today,' she said. 'Normally he's so excited to see you, but look at him now.'

Martin lay on a rug under Mrs Högfors' dining table. She was right – it was unlike him to be indifferent to the presence of his owner.

Ulf bent down to pat the dog. Martin opened an eye, half-heartedly wagged his tail several times, then closed his eye again.

'Did he eat, Mrs Högfors?'

'Yes,' she replied. 'I gave him some of those dog biscuits he likes so much. He polished them off. And his nose is wet, you'll see.'

'That's a good sign?'

'Oh, yes. If an animal's nose is wet, then there's nothing too seriously amiss. It's when their noses are dry that you have to start worrying.'

'He could be tired,' suggested Ulf.

That, she agreed, was a possibility, but she thought it was more in his mind. 'I think he might be depressed.'

'Do dogs get depressed?'

Mrs Högfors nodded. 'Yes, I understand they do, Mr Varg. Högfors once told me about a dog that apparently committed suicide.'

Ulf smiled. 'Surely not, Mrs Högfors.'

She assured him it was true. The dog had belonged to a Lutheran bishop who was largely indifferent to it. 'He was a very unhappy man, that bishop,' she said. 'Rather like that bishop in *Fanny och Alexander* – you know that film they've just made. Mr Bergman, I think.'

'I think it was made some time ago, Mrs Högfors.'

'Was it? Oh well, I must get to the cinema more often. Anyway, that bishop was a very buttoned-up man, was he not? I can imagine that his dog can't have had much fun. Anyway, this dog – the dog that belonged to the other bishop – was very much down in the dumps. Apparently, he swallowed a considerable overdose of some pills he sniffed out in the bathroom, and that was that. The vet couldn't do much for him, I'm afraid.'

Ulf raised an eyebrow. 'Somewhat unlikely, surely, Mrs Högfors. Couldn't it have been an accident? Dogs eat all sorts of things.'

'No,' she said, shaking her head. 'It was deliberate.'

'Well, I'm sure Martin won't be that bad. Shall we see how he is over the next day or so, and if he doesn't perk up I'll take him to the vet.'

Martin returned with Varg to his flat, where the dog had a small meal, which was not eaten with any great enthusiasm, but was nonetheless finished. Then he slept, while Ulf made his own dinner and went over in his mind the rather odd interview with that young woman, Signe Magnusson. Something was worrying Ulf, gnawing away at him, as troublesome details so often do. There was something that did not quite add up in the story that Signe had told them. It was hard, if not impossible, to put one's finger on it; perhaps it was more a case of intuition. As a detective one became used to the promptings of the nose, and this, he thought, might be a case where such promptings should be heeded. But what was it? He thought about what Signe had said, but also, more importantly perhaps, about how she had looked when she said it. Did she dislike her friend Bim? Was there envy in the background? Envy had a particular smell, Ulf thought. It was very subtle, but you could always identify it when it was present. The smell of envy.

CHAPTER SEVEN

A Dead Dog Floats

There were two tasks written into Ulf's diary for the following day. The first of these was to attend the trial of Hampus Johansson on charges of assault. The second was to interview Bim in Interview Room 2. Anna had the same commitments entered in her diary. She, like Ulf, was not looking forward to the first of these, while she awaited the second with curiosity mixed with anticipation. That sort of inquiry – the investigation of a crime that might or might not have taken place – was exactly the sort of case that had drawn her to volunteer for the Department of Sensitive Crimes in the first place. And she liked working with Ulf, of course – everyone did. They enjoyed his sense of humour and his occasional unpredictability. That unpredictability, of course, was itself unpredictable, which added to his colleagues' enjoyment of it.

It was not mandatory for investigating officers to attend the trials of those whom they had arrested, and many did not. In cases, though, when they had met the victims personally, they were encouraged to attend as a show of solidarity. From the victim's point of view, seeing the agent of the perpetrator's fall present in court marked a conclusion to the whole drama. It was also reassuring that the police were there at the time of the dispensing of justice. This sent a signal to the accused that any attempt at intimidation or recrimination would be resisted and punished. The trial of Hampus Johansson was different, though, as both officers felt considerable sympathy for the accused, even to the extent of wishing that it had been possible to let him off with a summary penalty order. Ulf had raised that possibility with his friend, Lars, the prosecutor, but had been told that this was impossible where a weapon was used or where the injury inflicted had been a serious one.

'The back of the knee is potentially very vulnerable,' said Lars. 'You can't ignore that sort of thing.'

'I wasn't proposing to ignore it,' said Ulf. 'I was merely suggesting that—'

Lars did not let him finish. 'The decision's been taken, Ulf. Sorry. Johansson is going to court. I'll speed it up, if you like, so that we can get it over with, but it's going to happen.'

Ulf realised that Anna shared his feelings about the trial as they travelled together in his ancient Saab to the new District Court building in Flundran.

'I'm not looking forward to this,' she said. 'That poor man ... '

'Victim or perpetrator?' asked Ulf. 'Who's poor? Hampus or Malte?'

'I was thinking of Hampus,' said Anna.

Ulf laughed. 'So was I,' he said. 'But do you know something? I think it's odd that here we are – agents of the state's vengeance – sympathising with the lawbreaker. Isn't there some-thing strange about that?'

'Everybody loses when a crime takes place. The perpetrator is diminished as much as anybody else.'

Ulf thought about this. He could see the direction of Anna's argument, but it made him feel uncomfortable. 'But don't we need righteous indignation?' he asked. 'Don't we need legitimate anger?'

'Perhaps. But the wrongdoer is still human. He's still in a mess – one of his own creation, sure, but he's still wrecked his own life.'

Ulf agreed. 'Yes, he has. But I suppose we should try to keep the moral contours clear. We need to remember that there's right and there's wrong and that some people are on one side and others are on the other.'

'I know that,' said Anna. 'All I'm saying is that when you see somebody like Hampus standing in the dock, and you think about how he got there, then you surely feel some sympathy.'

Ulf sighed. 'I know, I know. And to tell you the truth, I tried to get this case diverted out of the system. I spoke to the prosecutor about dealing with it as a summary penalty matter. He said no.'

'Your friend? Your friend . . . whatshisname?'

'Lars. Lars Patriksson.'

Anna thought for a moment. 'You and he go back a bit, don't you?'

Ulf had known Lars since they were both seven. 'We were *Spårarscouts* together. And we ended up as *Roverscouts*. All the way through. And at university.'

Anna found it hard to imagine Ulf as a scout. 'I can't quite see it,' she said. 'Young detective with young prosecuting lawyer in your cute little green uniforms. Sweet, but hard to imagine.'

'You didn't serve?' asked Ulf in mock indignation.

Anna shook her head. 'I was a member of a cookery circle. Can you believe it? My mother thought it was appropriate for girls to join something called the Swedish Girls' Cookery Union. Ridiculous.'

'Parents can be so old-fashioned,' said Ulf.

'Mind you,' said Anna, 'we had terrific fun. We went to cookery camp where we cooked all day.'

'Was that all?'

'Yes. There was nothing else to do. It was in the country, in a sort of large farmhouse. There was a lake nearby, and we were allowed to swim, but nobody did because on the first day somebody found a dead dog floating on the surface and nobody wanted to go there afterwards. So we just cooked.' She paused. 'Did you go to camp?'

'Of course. Regularly. We did things in the forests.'

Anna looked out of the window. 'You know, when I was a girl I always suspected that boys were having more fun. I had an idea that they went off into the forests and did things that we didn't do. And that idea never went away, to tell you the truth.'

'You still think it?'

Anna turned back to look at Ulf. 'Sometimes. Men can be evasive, you know. They like to give women the impression that there are things they do which are . . . well, men's business.'

'And women don't do that? There isn't any women's business?'

Anna said that there was, but it was transacted quite discreetly. 'Women are less showy than men,' she said. 'They do their women's things more discreetly.'

'I'd love to know what these women's things are,' said Ulf.

'Wouldn't you just,' said Anna, with a smile. 'But you'll never find out.'

*

Ulf and Anna were seated in Court No. 2 when Hampus came in, accompanied by Blomquist. The policeman spotted them first and waved; then Hampus did too, and exchanged a few words with Blomquist. Then the two of them walked over to speak to the detectives. The judge had yet to enter, and the court was empty, apart from one or two officials and a bored-looking court reporter from the evening paper.

'I thought I'd come with Hampus,' said Blomquist. 'Just to see him through the whole process. After all, it happened on my patch.'

Ulf looked at Hampus. The dance instructor's face was pale and drawn. Ulf saw that his hands were shaking, and that he had clasped them together to still them.

Ulf asked Blomquist if Malte was expected. Before Blomquist could answer, Hampus spoke. 'I didn't mean to harm him,' he said. 'I wasn't thinking straight.'

Blomquist reached down and put a hand on his shoulder. 'Calm down, Hampus,' he said. 'You tell that to the court, not us. When the prosecutor asks you what you did, you can tell him that. Explain it.'

'He hates me,' said Hampus.

Ulf shook his head. 'He doesn't. He's just doing his job.'

'Which is to put me in prison,' muttered Hampus.

Ulf glanced at Anna.

'You shouldn't think like that,' she said. 'Nobody hates you, Mr Johansson. Not even Malte Gustafsson. He told us that he's forgiven you. He feels bad too.'

'Yes,' agreed Ulf. 'He said that he feels really bad about laughing at you because of your height.'

Hampus glowered. 'There are plenty of people,' he said, 'who are shorter than I am.'

'Of course there are,' said Anna quickly. 'What Mr Varg meant was that Mr Gustafsson laughed because he thought you looked funny.' She paused. That was not what she had intended to say, and she could see that it was not going down well.

'He doesn't look all that funny,' said Blomquist. 'There are people who look much funnier than you do, aren't there, Hampus?'

Hampus did not answer. But in the silence that followed, they saw that he had begun to cry. Blomquist reacted immediately. Crouching down, he put his arms around the small man. 'Don't cry, Hampus, don't cry. Nobody's going to prison.'

'I think we should get ready for the judge,' said Ulf. 'And anyway, here's the prosecutor.'

Lars had entered the court from a side door. Wearing his black gown, a couple of files tucked under his arm, he looked every bit the well-organised, dispassionate official. But then he saw Hampus, in tears, being comforted by Blomquist, and for a moment he faltered. Ulf waved to him, and he waved back, but only half-heartedly. Then he sat down, abruptly and too suddenly, as people do when they suddenly feel dispirited – or guilty.

Blomquist led Hampus to a court official, who was standing nearby. The official indicated the defendant's place and gave him a glass of water. Hampus drank it immediately, holding the glass with both hands to prevent spillage. His lawyer came in – a small man, too, although not as small as his client. Blomquist, who seemed to know the lawyer, shook his hand firmly and whispered something into his ear. The lawyer nodded, and then placed a reassuring hand on Hampus's shoulder. Then Hampus was sick, suddenly and uncontrollably. A court official rushed forward, taking a white handkerchief out of his pocket. The judge came in, followed by two lay assessors. They stopped and stood still as they took in the scene before them. Then the judge nodded and indicated they take their places on the dais.

In the back of the court, Ulf whispered to Anna, 'Oh God, oh God, oh God!'

'He'll be all right,' she whispered back. 'Look at your friend Lars – he's almost in tears himself.'

Ulf glanced at Lars, who returned his gaze. Ulf thought: which forest was it? Which one? The exact spot?

The trial did not take long. Under the Swedish non-adversarial procedure, it was not necessary for the lawyer representing Hampus to say very much – the task of mitigation was taken on by the prosecutor himself and the judge, who asked every question he could possibly think of that would put Hampus in a better light. And so, when Hampus was invited to explain himself to the court, the ground was more than prepared.

Hampus took a piece of paper from his jacket pocket and began to read it. Apart from the sound of his voice, the court was completely silent. Nobody moved, or whispered, or shuffled paper. All eyes were fixed on the small figure, dressed in a sombre grey suit, the size of a child's outfit and yet bunched at the ankles, for the trouser legs were still too long.

'I understand what I have done,' began Hampus. 'I lost my temper because everything had become too much for me. I very much regret it. I picked on Mr Gustafsson because he had laughed at me and because there was a person who paid attention to him when I had hoped she would pay attention to me. Nobody has ever loved me. Nobody has ever been anything but embarrassed to be in my company. Nobody has ever called me and asked me to meet them for a drink or for coffee. Laughter – and ridicule – rubs off on others. People don't realise that, but that is what it does. Those who laugh at me will laugh at those who are with me. That is what they do.

'I do not say all this to get your pity. I do not want your pity. I say this only because I am so ashamed of what I did and I want to explain that I am not one to go around using a knife on people. That is not who I feel I really am. That is why I must explain.

'I am now ready to be punished. I deserve punishment. I have not come here to argue about that.

'I ask Mr Gustafsson to forgive me for what I did. I do not know whether he can do that, but if he can find it in his heart to do so, I shall be very pleased. I am sorry. I am truly sorry.'

He sat down.

The judge looked at the assessors on either side of him – they were mute. One adjusted the necklace she was wearing; the other stared fixedly at the ceiling. Down on the floor of the court-room, Lars fiddled with the cuffs of his shirt. He half turned and glanced at Ulf.

Which forest? thought Ulf.

Then the judge cleared his throat. 'Community service,' he announced. 'Two hundred hours of community service. That is all I intend to say.'

The judge arose. His two assessors were momentarily con-fused, but soon stood up, as did everybody else in the courtroom. Hampus looked at his lawyer for guidance; the lawyer shook his hand and said something to him that nobody else could hear. Hampus nodded.

The brevity of the trial meant that Ulf and Anna had an hour to kill back at the office before the interview with Bim. Both had correspondence to catch up with; both found it hard to concentrate on the task in hand. Eventually Ulf rose from his desk, stretched, and said, 'Café.'

'A very good idea,' said Anna, closing the lid of her laptop with more than necessary firmness.

From his desk on the other side of the room, Carl looked pointedly at his watch. 'Late lunch hour?' he enquired.

Ulf was unapologetic. 'No, coffee break.'

Erik glanced at Carl. It was not for a clerical assistant (grade 3) to question a detective (grade 7) but since Carl, who was of equal rank to Ulf and Anna, had made the initial comment, he felt that he could join in. 'Nice to be able to take a coffee break whenever one wants. Very nice.'

Ulf smiled at Erik. 'You can take one too, Erik.'

'You know I can't,' Erik snapped back. 'You know that I'm grade 3 and that the clerical division has strict rules about that sort of thing.'

Anna brought the discussion to an end. 'Ulf and I have been in court,' she said. 'We skipped our lunch hour, as there's always a lot of sitting about to do in court. You know that, Carl. So we're entitled to a break now.' She turned to Ulf. 'Come on, Ulf. Our young friend will be arriving in less than an hour.'

They sat in the window seats of the café – the most sought-after seating, as it allowed people to look out onto the street and observe the comings and goings. At first, neither said anything, as if by tacit agreement they were allowing themselves time to reflect on what had happened in court.

When Ulf eventually spoke, it was despondently. 'It was like crushing a beetle, you know. Just like that.'

Anna looked thoughtful. 'I suppose I see what you mean.

Something large and powerful stepping on something small and powerless.'

'Except ... Well, you could say that about any criminal trial, couldn't you? The defendant is always small and powerless when up against the state. Of course he is. But this was different – this seemed cruel.'

Anna remembered something. 'Did you see his suit? Did you see the legs?'

'Yes. They were too long for him. They were crumpled around the ankles.'

Anna looked at Ulf. They noticed the same things – they always had. Was that because they had worked together for so long, and had learned to do the job in the same way? Or was it something to do with a shared fundamental outlook on the world, what the Germans called *Weltanschauung*? The Germans had a word for everything – a word that could be very focused, very specific, because it could be constructed for a precise set of circumstances. They even had a word, it was said, for the feeling of envy experienced when one sees the tasty dishes ordered by others in a restaurant and it is too late to change one's own order. *Mahlneid*, meal envy, she believed that was the word – if it existed at all. People invented German composite nouns as a sort of parlour game, and most of them would never catch on – though some must, sometimes. For every word there was a first user, an ur-speaker; that was how language developed: somebody considered a particular word right for a particular moment, and began to use it. *Mahlneid* could well catch on because many are bound to have felt that sort of envy as the waiter carries the dishes of others, gorgeously tantalising, past their own table; many might be expected to welcome that particular word.

She reflected on how she and Ulf saw things in the same way.

Whatever the cause of that, she enjoyed it. Unfortunately, she and her husband saw the world quite differently. Of course they agreed on the big things – they both voted the same way and had roughly the same taste in aesthetic matters – but, when it came to what they actually took note of, there was a yawning gulf between them. Jo failed to notice the body language of others. He failed to notice what they were wearing, and what that said about them. There was so much, she felt, that simply passed him by. By contrast, she and Ulf dwelt on the minutiae. Ulf could see a frayed shoelace in somebody's shoe and spin from that an entire theory as to who that person was, what motivated him, what he did for a living, and even more. She found that she could do much the same, and as a result they could sit together in one another's company, saying very little but observing the world about them in all its fascinating detail. Then they would turn to one another and laugh, because they both would have noticed some absurdity and each knew that the other would have seen it too and found it amusing.

Anna did not like to compare Jo and Ulf, mainly because the comparison always seemed to favour Ulf. Jo was a modest man – she thought most anaesthetists were, simply because they are attracted by the thought of quietly sitting in the operating theatre and not having to talk to their patients. Anaesthetists did not feel the need to talk very much, being happy with their gases and their valves and the bleeping of their machinery; they were diffident people by and large, unlike the loud and boastful surgeons whom they served. And yet, perhaps not surprisingly, Anna found the company of anaesthetists tended to put her to sleep, as had happened more than once when Jo had brought his hospital colleagues round for dinner. She had done her best on these occasions but had nonetheless found herself nodding off by the time it came to the cheese course.

Of course there were people who must have an even bigger challenge – Erik's wife, Birghitta Nykvist, came to mind. She and Erik had been married for over thirty years; she had been a bus driver who had met him when they were both on a trip to Stockholm – she in the driver's seat of the bus in which he was a passenger. 'I couldn't take my eyes off her,' Erik said. 'So I made sure that I did the return trip when she was on duty. By the time we got back to Malmö, I had made up my mind.'

This touching story had been narrated at an office party – one to which spouses and partners had been invited. Birghitta had been there, beaming as Erik related the tale of their meeting. 'I had noticed him too,' she said. 'I knew that he wanted to ask me out. You can always tell.'

Anna wondered what they talked about. Did Birghitta like fishing? Erik had once mentioned that she knew a lot about fish, but Anna thought that was probably osmotic knowledge – after thirty years of bombardment with fish lore, some must seep into the mind. Osmotic knowledge does not require an act of conscious acquisition; perhaps she switched off, as long-term spouses tend to do. They have heard everything their husband or wife has to say – they have heard it many times – and so they simply allow it to wash over them. It was a little bit like that with her and Jo, she realised; and blushed at the thought. She had never imagined that she would be in that position – in a marriage where everything that is to be said has already been said, and all that lay ahead would be more of the same, year after year, until the release of dotage or death. The prospect appalled her. It was not what she had signed up for.

Yet surely it would be better, she decided, than the loneliness that must be the lot of somebody like Ulf. She had often thought of that, and pondered whether Ulf would ever do anything about it. It was some years, now, since Letta had left him, and Ulf had had plenty of time to recover from the loss. Losing your spouse when you did not want to lose her – and that had been the case with Letta's departure with that somewhat creepy man (at least she thought he was creepy) – was surely much the same thing as losing your spouse to illness or an accident. What did people say about the grief that came from losing a husband or wife? Did they not say that the deepest grief ran its course within eighteen months and that thereafter one started to recover?

It would have been easy for Ulf to find somebody. Anna was convinced that no matter what progress had been made in bringing about equality of the sexes, there remained areas in which the playing fields had not yet been levelled – and, she feared, never would. One of these was the prospect of marriage, or remarriage, beyond a certain age. In spite of everything that had been done to make life equal for men and women, in this respect it was not: no man – and Anna thought that one really could say *no* man – was unable to find somebody if he set his mind to it, no matter how unprepossessing he was. But women? Could one say the same thing about women? She knew a number of eminently deserving women who would have loved to find a husband but who did not seem able to do so because there were simply not enough men available. Demographic decline – and bad male behaviour – was responsible for that. Men evaded commitment; they were not interested in women; they drank, or fought, or ended up in prison for long periods. And as a final act of irresponsibility, men died, leaving women to fend for themselves and to look, so often in vain, for a man – any man – from the dwindling pool of males. Oh, the sheer waste, the sheer injustice – Anna felt a real sense of resentment over it. And she could not imagine a solution, other than for women to assert that they did not care, that they would be sufficient unto themselves. But the problem with that was that although there were many strong women who were happy without men, there were still many who would have it otherwise, who wanted to find a man and clung to the idea that there would be a man for them one day if only they were patient enough. These were the women who lived their lives under a growing shadow of disappointment.

She had no doubt that Ulf could find a woman friend if he started to look for one. He could go online. That was how people did it these days – they went online and found people who shared their desire to meet somebody. It was simple, and apparently very successful; except, perhaps, in those cases where it was complicated and an utter failure. But whatever the odds, Ulf would have been well placed, as he was a good-looking man with a steady job and a comfortable flat. His dog might not be so much of an asset, but there was no rule that one had to declare a dog on the first date. That could be revealed later, when the relationship was strong enough to allow for disclosure of dogs, or even children. So might somebody reveal only on the fourth date, perhaps, that there were five children at home, the youngest of whom was still an infant. That would test the relationship, of course, but once people have fallen in love, five children is not necessarily grounds for calling the whole thing off.

In spite of his evident eligibility, Ulf had done nothing. Or had he? The possibility occurred to Anna that perhaps she was wrong. Ulf might have a private life that he was keeping, well, private. For her part, she spoke to him freely about Jo and the girls, about the latest school issues and so on, and she assumed that he reciprocated the confidence. But perhaps he did not; perhaps Ulf was seeing somebody but did not care to mention the fact to her. The thought made her feel uncomfortable. It was none of her business, of course, if Ulf chose to have a secret lover, but it hurt her to think that he would not talk about it. And then she realised that what hurt her too was the thought itself of his having somebody else. This was jealousy. It was as simple as that. She did not want Ulf to have somebody else because ... because ... She could not bring herself to admit, even to herself, the reason for her discomfort, and so she put the matter out of her mind. She would not think along those lines; it was disloyal and dangerous. She would not.

As Ulf and Anna finished their coffee and crossed the street back to the office, Ulf turned to Anna and said, 'You know, sometimes, I hate the job I do. This morning was one of those times.'

Anna saw the pain in his expression. 'The fact that you say that,' she answered quietly, 'is proof to my mind that you are exactly the right person to be doing this job.'

CHAPTER EIGHT

He Repaired the King's Bicycle

'Me?' Bim had said to her mother. 'They want to talk to *me*?'

Elvinia gave her an intense look – the sort of look that said *You can speak to me, but you have to tell me the truth.* 'Darling,' she began, 'we all make mistakes from time to time. Sometimes those mistakes are serious ones. But nothing is so serious that it can't be shared with those closest to you.' That was her. There was nobody else. 'You know that, don't you?'

Bim looked confused. 'But what's that got to do with me? Why would the police want to speak to *me*?'

'They didn't say,' Elvinia replied. And then, very tentatively, 'Can you think of anything?'

Bim shook her head. 'Nothing. I really can't. Nothing.'

'Nothing to do with drugs? Not you, of course, but if people around you are using them, maybe even dealing them, then the police might get things wrong and think you—'

Bim interrupted her. 'No, Mother, no! You know that I don't do drugs. I just don't.'

'I know that, darling. I was just exploring possibilities.' She thought for a moment. 'What about witnessing something? Have you witnessed anything recently that they might be interested in?'

Again Bim could think of nothing.

'In that case,' said Elvinia, 'you'll just have to go along and see what they say. No doubt all will become clear.'

And now Bim was at the reception desk in the Department of Sensitive Crimes, asking for a Mr Ulf Varg who had spoken to her mother on the telephone about her coming in for an interview that afternoon. The receptionist consulted a list in front of her and directed her to Interview Room 2. 'There are seats directly outside it. Wait there until they call you in.'

Bim sat outside Interview Room 2. Elvinia had offered to come with her, but she had refused, saying that it was unnecessary. But it was not unnecessary, she had subsequently decided, and now she wished that she had accepted her mother's offer. Being interviewed by the police was exactly the sort of experience that would be easier with some maternal support. All suspects should be given the chance to telephone their lawyers or their mothers, and it would not be surprising if they chose to call their mothers. After all, your mother is far more likely to believe in your innocence than your lawyer.

She did not have to wait long. At exactly the agreed time Anna opened the door, introduced herself, and invited Bim inside.

'This is my colleague, Mr Varg,' she said. 'We work in the same department.'

Bim glanced nervously at Ulf. He smiled back at her warmly, in an obvious effort to put her at ease.

Anna invited her to sit.

'It's good of you to come in,' said Ulf. 'I know that you have lectures and so on at the university. So, thank you for making the effort.'

Bim inclined her head. 'I thought I had to,' she said. 'I thought you said I had to come.'

'No, we didn't,' said Anna. 'We're not arresting you or anything. We just need to ask you some questions.'

Bim bit her lip. It was only dope, and everyone smoked dope now and then. She hardly ever touched it, and the last time had been at least six weeks ago when one of Signe's boyfriends had offered her some. They'd have to arrest the whole university if they started.

Ulf was looking at her appraisingly, and under his gaze she shifted in her seat. If there were two of them, she thought, one will be nice and one will be nasty. That was how these things worked, did they not? Or was that only on film? In reality, were both likely to be nasty?

'What are you studying at the university?' Ulf asked.

The question was posed in a friendly enough tone, but that did not mean, she thought, that he was the nice one.

'Human geography,' she said. 'I'm in my second year.'

'Human geography,' Ulf mused. 'That, I suppose, is different from physical geography. Is that right? You don't study ...' He waved a hand in the air. 'You don't study mountain ranges and rivers and things like that? Maps and so on?'

'All those things may have an effect in the background,' Bim said. 'But the focus of human geography—'

'Where people live is determined by physical factors,' interjected Anna. 'You don't get people living on the top of mountains.'

'Not right at the top,' said Ulf. 'But you do get them living on the sides. What about Nepal?'

Anna frowned. 'They live in valleys there, don't they?'

'And up the slopes too,' said Ulf.

They both looked at Bim, as if to seek support. She said nothing.

'Have you been to Nepal?' asked Ulf.

Bim considered the question. Was this what they wanted to find out? Was this something to do with trafficking drugs from Nepal?

'No,' she replied. 'Never.'

'I'd like to go some time,' said Ulf.

'So would I,' said Anna. 'I'd like to do one of those hikes where they take you right up into the mountains. Somebody in Criminal Records did that. He took his children, but one of them came down with altitude sickness and had to be taken down to a lower level.'

'I hear that you can go to Base Camp on Everest these days,' remarked Ulf. 'They take you in by helicopter and you spend a day or two there before they take you back down again.'

'I'd love that,' said Anna. 'Imagine getting out of your tent in the morning and looking up at Everest.'

Ulf said he would like that, but thought that you might not get a good view of the summit because of cloud. Bim said nothing.

Ulf cleared his throat again. 'You may be wondering why we asked you in,' he said.

Bim nodded. 'Yes, I was.' Surely they had not asked her in to talk about Everest.

'Does the name Sixten mean anything to you?' Ulf asked.

Bim felt a sudden cold within her. That was dread. They were asking about her *lies*. And yet it was not a crime to tell a few lies, was it? You don't have to tell the truth all the time, surely?

Her voice was small as she answered. 'Sixten?'

100

'Yes,' said Anna. 'A young man of about your age. A young man who works as a paramedic.'

Bim transferred her gaze from Ulf to Anna. She had no idea how these people had got to hear of her invention of Sixten. It was bizarre. It was as if they had all stepped out of reality into a work of fiction – which was, of course, what Sixten was. And as she thought this, she was suddenly filled with shame and embarrassment.

'I knew him,' she said. 'I knew a boy called Sixten. And yes, he was a paramedic.'

She had no real idea why she had chosen to perpetuate the lie. Shame, perhaps, lay behind it, but it was also to do with fear. She only wanted to get away, and it would be too complicated to explain what had really happened and why she had chosen to deceive her friends with that ridiculous story. And the original lie, in some strange sense, still had momentum.

'Have you seen him recently?' asked Ulf.

Bim shook her head. 'No. We've split up.'

Ulf waited for a few moments before he asked the next question. 'So, where is he now?'

'He's gone up north. To the North Pole. There's a research station up there. A government place.'

Ulf nodded. 'Yes, so we heard.'

'And you haven't heard from him since then?' asked Anna.

'No. I told you: we split up.'

'Acrimoniously?' asked Ulf.

'A bit. He didn't discuss it with me, you see. He just announced that he was going to the North Pole.' *Why am I telling these lies? This is ridiculous. Stop now.*

'Not very considerate,' Anna remarked. 'I would have felt rather annoyed, if I were in your position.'

'I did. Yes, I did.'

Ulf's next question came quickly. 'You felt angry?'

'Annoyed rather than angry. But anyway, I was getting fed up with him. You get bored with people sometimes. You just do.'

Ulf now asked whether she had any means of getting in touch with him. Did she have a mobile number?

Bim smiled. 'I don't think there's any reception at the North Pole.'

Anna now joined in. '*If* that's where he is. *If.*'

Bim stared at her. This was the way out. 'I thought that too,' she said. 'I thought that he could be making it up.'

'To get rid of you?' asked Anna.

'Yes, it could have been a story. I've been thinking about that – it could all just have been an excuse.'

Ulf tapped the table with his pencil. 'Very possibly. In fact, highly likely. You see, somebody has checked with that research station, and there's no paramedic there. There's a doctor, as it happens, but no paramedic.'

Bim looked away. 'So he wasn't telling the truth.'

'So it would seem,' said Anna.

'You definitely don't know where he is?' Ulf asked.

'No, I don't. I haven't seen him since we split up.'

Ulf tried another tactic. 'Where did he live? Did you ever go to his place?'

Bim shook her head. 'No, never.' She paused. 'He didn't tell me where he lived.'

'So where did the two of you go then?'

It was too late to confess. She had lied inexplicably – and profusely. She would have to continue with the whole farce. She had done nothing wrong, after all – not in the legal sense.

'We met in cafés,' she said. 'We went to clubs at night. Meals out. That sort of thing.'

Ulf made a note. 'But never at his place?'

'No, never. I told you. I didn't know where he lived.'

'Or what sort of place he lived in?' Ulf pressed. 'A shared flat? His parents' house?'

'I just don't know. We never talked about . . . about that sort of thing. And he worked a lot of the time. He was studying, too, and doing his ambulance work.'

Ulf reached into a folder before him and took out the picture given them by Signe. He slid it across the table towards Bim. 'Is this Sixten?' he asked.

Bim could not conceal her shock. 'How did you get that?'

'It was passed on to us,' said Ulf. 'We can't reveal how. It just came into our possession. So, is that him?'

Bim gazed at the photograph. She felt confused. Her mobile was in her pocket – she had had it with her all the time. Nobody could have got the photograph from it. It was impossible.

'Yes. That's him.'

'So let's get this straight,' said Ulf. 'You broke up with Sixten. He said he was going off to the North Pole. It looks as if he didn't. Since then, you haven't seen him. And nor has anybody else. We contacted the ambulance people, you see, and they deny all knowledge of him. Was he lying about that too?'

Bim answered quickly. 'He must have been. Maybe he wasn't a paramedic at all. Maybe he just told me that, for some reason . . . I don't know. Maybe he thought I'd be impressed.'

They sat in silence. Then Ulf, speaking very slowly, asked, 'So you definitely haven't seen him? And you have no mobile number for him?'

'No. And no, I don't have a number.'

Anna smiled. 'Are you telling us that you never called him? That you never texted him?'

Bim looked momentarily flustered. 'We did, of course we did. But . . . but then, when he said he was going off to the North Pole, I deleted him.'

Ulf looked up sharply. 'You deleted him?'

'I deleted his number. His *number*. Not him.'

The silence returned.

'Not him,' said Anna eventually. 'He wasn't deleted?'

'His number,' said Bim.

Afterwards, when Bim had been seen out, Ulf looked at Anna and waited for her to say something.

'That young woman's lying,' she said.

'Yes,' said Ulf. 'It's obvious.'

'Do you think she deleted him?' Anna continued. 'In the final sense, that is?'

Ulf hesitated. 'Possibly,' he said.

'Of course, he was lying as well, wasn't he?'

Ulf agreed. 'That business of the North Pole. That was very evidently a lie.'

'But you think that he really did tell her that?'

Ulf thought for a moment. 'That at least is true,' he said. 'I think he did.'

Anna looked puzzled. 'Where do we go from here? Put out a missing person appeal?'

'We'll probably have to,' said Ulf. 'Unless a body turns up.' He paused. 'She lives at her mother's place, doesn't she?'

'Yes.'

'Then we can get a search warrant for that. And the car as well. We can get a forensic report on the car. Beyond that . . . We'll have to hope that some of his other friends come forward.'

Anna asked whether Ulf thought Sixten was the young man's real name. 'If he lied about being a paramedic, then perhaps he lied about his name.'

'So many lies,' observed Ulf. 'There are so many lies that it's difficult to tell which ones are worth investigating.'

'That's exactly what I feel about this case,' said Anna. 'There's something very odd about it, but I can't put my finger on it.'

Ulf shrugged. 'Do you think she did it?'

'I don't know,' Anna answered. 'Unless it was that other young woman – Signe. What if he'd been leading her on as well? What if young Sixten was playing the field?'

'You mean that he was seeing Signe too, and then dumped her? So she killed him and is trying to get us to think it's Bim?'

Anna developed her theory. 'In other words, Signe is framing Bim for a crime that she committed herself.'

'This is becoming complicated,' said Ulf.

'Life is complicated, Ulf. That's the problem.'

'And we exist to un-complicate it?'

Anna smiled. 'Yes. And isn't it nice to know why you exist?'

Bim seethed.

It was not the interviewers who had made her seethe – the man, she thought, had been kind and sympathetic, and the woman had been polite enough; no, it was not them so much as the fact that they had the photograph of Sixten. As she travelled home on the bus, she reviewed all the possible explanations she could think of as to how the two detectives had obtained the picture. At no point had she printed it, and at no point had she put it on social media. As far as she could remember, the only people to whom she had shown it were Linnea Ek, Signe Magnusson and Matilda Forsberg, her three closest friends. Nobody else had seen it – nobody at all. Except her mother, of course, and the boy himself; he had looked at it after he had taken the selfie, but he had immediately handed the phone back. And his friends, of course – the one with the choirboy haircut and the other one who'd made the snide remarks – she assumed they'd been snide, although she had not heard what he'd said. That was the sum total of those who'd seen the photograph, and yet it had somehow ended up in the hands of the police – of the Department of Sensitive Crimes, or whatever it called itself.

She wondered if her phone had some sort of virus. A computer virus could do extraordinary things, and it was possible, she supposed, that it might instruct a phone to transmit information, or images, without the knowledge of the owner. That was perfectly possible, given the cunning of the people who engineered such things. And so, by some sort of highly irregular process, an innocent selfie taken in the street might end up on the desk of some isolated hacker in Detroit, or some secret agency in Moscow, or even the Department of Sensitive Crimes rather closer to home in Malmö.

Bim quickly discounted this fanciful thought. The only feasible explanation was rather more prosaic: somebody had somehow taken possession of her phone and ... It came to her in a moment of stark insight. Somebody who had borrowed her phone had discreetly emailed the image to himself. And here came the devastating insight: it was not *himself* – it was *herself.* It was Signe. She was the only person, other than Bim and her mother, who had handled the phone: she had asked to borrow it in the university café and it had been in her possession for ten minutes or so. And Bim remembered a further detail: during those ten minutes, she had been at the counter, ordering a Danish pastry. That was it; that was when Signe had sent the photograph to herself. All that was required was a few deft clicks on a few buttons – something that nobody would see unless they were watching very closely. Linnea and Matilda had been there, but they had their own phones to peruse, and they would not have seen Signe's disloyal, cheating fingers tapping out the instructions for the theft.

Cheating fingers ... How apt, thought Bim. Somebody who had two boyfriends, neither of whom realised that he was in a relationship with a consummate two-timer, would, of course, have cheating fingers – and a cheating heart, and a cheating face ... in fact, a cheating everything. Signe was a cheat; she should have spotted that a long time ago and realised that she was no friend.

Then came the even more difficult part. Why would Signe pass the photograph of Sixten to the police? Presumably she imagined that this would in some way cause difficulties for Bim – and it had, because the police obviously thought that she was somehow connected with Sixten's disappearance. But he had never existed, and therefore it was hard to see how he could disappear. Be that as it may, Signe had obviously wanted to hurt her, and that led on to the question as to why she should harbour that desire.

Jealousy, thought Bim. Signe wanted her not to have a boyfriend. She wanted her to envy her with her two boyfriends, neither of whom amounted to very much, in Bim's view at least. One of them had a slight lisp, which made him sound effeminate, and the other had very fair skin, so fair that you could almost see the veins underneath. If she – Bim – had a real boyfriend, then she would at least have the good taste not to have one with visible veins. Bim allowed herself to smile as the thought occurred to her that perhaps the reason why Signe had two boyfriends was that if you put them together, with their obvious defects, you would end up with one, complete boyfriend. She could say that to Signe one day and see what her reaction was.

By the time she reached home, she had decided what to do. Now that she knew that it was Signe who had betrayed her, she could very easily turn the tables on her. She could tell the police that she had seen Signe with Sixten, after his alleged disappearance, and that the report of that disappearance – which could only have come from Signe – was a stupid prank designed to hurt her – Bim. That would amount to wasting police time, which was, she knew, a crime. It was not a terribly serious crime, but Signe would nonetheless be subjected to the same sort of interview that she herself had undergone, and that would teach her to steal other people's selfies. Perhaps they would fine her, which would be good, as a lesson accompanied by a fine was always better learned. Even if Signe could never be punished for having two boyfriends, then at least she could be punished for this. And at the end of it all, Bim decided that she would give Signe a piece of her mind into the bargain. She would say *I always knew you were a false friend*. That sounded rather good. A false friend. Yes.

Walking up the staircase to her mother's flat, Bim no longer seethed. Rather, she reflected with pleasure on the nature of revenge. People said you should never seek revenge. Bim had never subscribed to that view. Revenge was a *smörgåsbord* of delight – to be contemplated with anticipation, and savoured with satisfaction.

She stopped halfway up the stairs. A further thought had occurred to her. What if she were to take a photograph of Signe with one of her boyfriends, and then send it to the other boyfriend? Perhaps she would add a message to it – a simple one. Something like *Who's this then?* Or possibly, *Cheating heart?*

When she eventually reached the flat, Elvinia was waiting anxiously. 'What was that all about?' she asked.

Bim shrugged. 'Nothing, really.'

Elvinia would not let that pass. One did not get invited to the Department of Sensitive Crimes for a discussion about nothing.

'I wasn't born yesterday, darling. Bear that in mind.' Elvinia paused. 'What was it?'

Bim gazed out of the window. 'I should have told you,' she said. 'I was going to, but it slipped my mind.'

'Told me what?'

'Told you that Sixten and I have split up.'

Elvinia was puzzled. 'I'm sorry to hear that. But what's that got to do with the police?'

'Apparently somebody has reported him missing.'

Elvinia frowned. 'Did he tell you he was going away?'

'Yes, he did. He told me he was going to the North Pole.'

Elvinia's jaw dropped. 'The North Pole?'

'Yes. There's a research station up there ... He's a paramedic, you see ...'

Elvinia held up a hand to stop her. 'Darling! Darling! No more, please. Do you really think that Mummy can't tell when you're telling fibs? Do you really think that?'

Bim said nothing. She was six again. That was the problem with living with your mother: it was only too easy to go back to being six again.

When Elvinia spoke, she addressed the light fitting in the centre of the room rather than her daughter. 'I should have realised when you told me this boy's name. I should have realised. Sixten. Of course. It was so obvious.'

Bim continued to look out of the window. She loved her

mother – of course she did – but there were times when she wished she did not live here. There was such a thing as repressive tolerance. There was such a thing as smothering love. 'Realised what?'

'Realised that you were doing what you did when you seven – or thereabouts. You had an imaginary friend. Children often do, you know.'

Bim waited.

'And yours,' Elvinia continued, 'was called Sixten. You said that he was a little boy with fair hair whose father had a small aeroplane that could fly through windows. Sixten worked for the King, you said. He repaired the King's bicycle. You created a whole life for him, you know. It was utterly charming. But then . . . well, apparently children's imaginary friends are written out of the script – suddenly and without warning. And that's what you did. You announced that Sixten had gone to the North Pole. And that was that.'

Elvinia stopped looking at the light fitting and turned to her daughter. 'Darling, you mustn't fabricate,' she said. 'I know how much you want a boyfriend, but you shouldn't make men up.' She paused. 'There are enough men already for us to have to deal with – why add to the troubles of women by making more up?'

CHAPTER NINE

Biscuits, Cats, Basket, Sweden

L ater that afternoon Mrs Högfors called Ulf to tell him that Martin had refused to go for a walk. She was worried, and her anxiety showed in her tone; he had never declined to go outside, she said, and in her view this was final proof, if proof were needed, that something was seriously wrong. 'I am not one to exaggerate, Mr Varg,' she said (she was), 'but dogs can turn their face to the wall, you know. They decide their time has come, and they turn their face to the wall. Just like humans.' Ulf was distracted by this observation. He had never witnessed a turning of a face to the wall, but he assumed it was possible. Perhaps doctors recognised it, when they visited their patients and found them facing the wrong way. Perhaps it happened subtly, by stages, with the patient at first glancing at the wall, then slowly becoming more fixated, and finally succumbing.

His thoughts returned to Martin. He assured Mrs Högfors

that he would make an appointment with the vet that evening. Dr Håkansson conducted an evening clinic for the convenience of those clients who could not make a daytime appointment. It was always crowded, but there had been a cancellation and Martin was fitted in. Ulf had a great deal of faith in Dr Håkansson's diagnostic powers and his ability to find out what was going wrong in his patients. 'Animals can communicate a great deal without saying anything,' the vet declared. 'All you have to do is observe. They'll tell you everything – in their own way.'

Martin had spent the afternoon with Mrs Högfors, and was still there when Ulf returned from work. Ulf had thought that his neighbour might have been over-dramatising the situation, but when he saw Martin he realised that this was not the case. The dog was lying under a table, his head tucked under his forelegs, utterly uninterested in Ulf's arrival. That was unusual enough, but what was even more uncharacteristic was the sigh that he emitted every few minutes. This was a strange, dispirited sound – very close to a human sigh, and redolent, it seemed, of some deep, heartfelt despair. When Ulf first heard it, he looked in alarm at Mrs Högfors, who made an *I told you so* gesture.

'You see?' she said, her voice lowered, as at a sick bed. 'Poor creature. That's the sigh, Mr Varg, of one who is turning his face to the wall.'

Ulf glanced down at Martin. The dog was indeed more or less facing the wall. 'I'll take him immediately,' he said. 'I've arranged an appointment with Dr Håkansson.'

Mrs Högfors nodded. 'Högfors always said that you should never leave things too late. He always said that.'

That was somewhat trite, Ulf thought. If one was always going to say something, then surely it should be something more

112

significant than that. But he did not voice these reservations, saying instead, 'How right your husband was, Mrs Högfors.'

'Of course he didn't always follow his own advice,' she said.

For a brief moment, Ulf wondered whether the late Mr Högfors had turned his face to the wall. 'People don't,' he agreed. 'Advice, in my experience, is often for others, rather than oneself.'

He bent down to pick up Martin, who had shown no signs of being willing to walk. The dog did not resist, but was heavy, and not easily moved. Mrs Högfors fussed about and offered to accompany Ulf to the vet's. He thanked her but said that he would manage. Martin looked at them both with baleful eyes. He sighed again.

Ulf carried him to the Saab, and then, at the other end, he carried him into the vet's clinic. There was a short wait there, as they were early, and then Dr Håkansson appeared at the door and ushered them in.

The physical examination did not take long. Everything, the vet said, appeared to be normal – at least on initial examination. Martin's temperature was exactly as it should be; there appeared to be no abdominal swelling or soreness; and eyes and mouth gave no cause for concern. Standing back, Dr Håkansson looked pensive.

'Do you know that dogs get depressed, Mr Varg?' he asked.

Ulf looked thoughtful. 'Yes, I'd heard of that.' He paused, looking at Martin with new eyes. 'Do you think that's what's wrong?'

Dr Håkansson nodded. 'It's a distinct possibility. We get a lot of dogs in Sweden who suffer from Seasonal Affective Disorder. But that's a winter thing – to do with deprivation of sunlight.'

'And vitamin D?' asked Ulf. 'Isn't it connected with vitamin D?'

'There's some evidence of that,' said Dr Håkansson. 'There's been a Danish study that shows good results with vitamin D supplementation.'

'So his vitamin D levels could be low?'

'Possibly. We could look into that. But remember, this is summer. SAD is a winter condition. I don't think Martin's issue is seasonal.'

The vet reached forward to pat his patient on the head. Martin looked up, but only briefly.

'Have you observed any other symptoms, Mr Varg?'

'My neighbour spotted it,' he said. 'She said that he's been uninterested in things. He didn't want to go out, which is very unusual for him. Normally he loves his walks.'

'And any hyperphagia?'

'I'm not sure ...'

'That's excessive eating,' explained Dr Håkansson. 'People who are depressed may eat too much.'

Ulf pointed out that dogs ate too much anyway. 'Dogs are always hungry, aren't they? They don't turn down food.'

'Possibly,' said the vet. 'What about lethargy? What about decreased libido?'

Ulf raised an eyebrow. 'Decreased libido? But you yourself neutered him, Dr Håkansson. I thought that was the end of his libido.'

Dr Håkansson looked embarrassed. 'Of course. But the reduction of testosterone doesn't mean there can't be a *memory* of testosterone.'

Ulf savoured the phrase. *A memory of testosterone.* It would be a good title for a book, perhaps by a great roué, looking back, from sedentary old age, at the highlights of his roué's career.

'I haven't noticed any change there,' he said. 'Martin was never one to fight or roam, as unneutered male dogs can do, I believe.'

The vet moved to a cupboard and extracted a small box. 'I think we might try him on an anti-depressant,' he said.

'Prozac? Do you give dogs Prozac?'

'Not Prozac itself,' Dr Håkansson replied. 'Prozac isn't intended for animals and there are side effects. No, there's a drug called clomipramine that we use for general behavioural issues. Let's try him on that.'

Ulf was concerned. 'Do we have to medicate him? Isn't there another possibility?'

'Psychotherapy?' asked Dr Håkansson. 'I can refer you, if you like. There's a veterinary psychotherapy clinic that deals with these cases. They work on improving mood.' He paused. 'But frankly, I think we need to do something fairly immediate. Psychotherapy can take a long time.'

Ulf already knew that. His own psychotherapy had been going on for two years now, although he felt that he probably no longer needed any help of that sort. But if Martin started psychotherapy too, then that would mean he would have to pay double what he was currently paying to Dr Svensson. 'Clomipramine,' he said. 'I think we should start with that.'

Dr Håkansson seemed pleased. 'We get good results with it, Mr Varg.'

The vet administered the first dose then and there, Martin accepting the pill with all the resignation of one who does not particularly care what happens. He looked up at Ulf, and then slowly rose to his feet.

'Immediate effect,' said Ulf.

Dr Håkansson laughed. 'We'll see. But at least you won't have to carry him.'

They left the vet's inner office and went out into the waiting room. And it was there, amongst the unhappy canine and feline patients, and their predominantly anxious owners, that Ulf came face to face with Blomquist.

Blomquist was far from anxious. 'Mr Varg!' he exclaimed. 'What brings you here?'

That question, thought Ulf, was the reason why Blomquist would never make it to the Criminal Investigation Authority.

'My dog,' he said, gesturing to Martin standing disconsolate beside him.

'Ah,' said Blomquist. 'What a nice-looking animal.'

'And you?' asked Ulf. 'I take it that's your cat?'

Blomquist gestured towards a small pet-carrier in which a large ginger cat was crouched, staring at Martin with horrified animus. 'It's my daughter's,' he said. 'She always wanted a cat and we gave it to her for her sixth birthday recently. He's here for his regular inoculations. Cat flu, feline AIDS – that sort of thing. There are all sorts of perils in being a cat.'

'There certainly are,' said Ulf. Then he added, 'My dog's suffering from depression, I'm told.'

Blomquist did not seem surprised. 'Dogs don't like cities very much,' he said. 'They pine for the countryside.' He looked thoughtful. 'What do you feed him on?'

'Dog food,' said Ulf.

'Ah,' said Blomquist. 'You might need to think about that. He's probably getting too many carbohydrates.'

One of the other clients, a thin man in a nondescript grey suit, who was nursing a dachshund on his lap, joined in the conversation. 'If you don't mind my saying, that's a very important point. Many people who eat too many carbohydrates get depressed. That's people, of course, but the same undoubtedly applies to animals.'

Blomquist seemed pleased with this support. 'Absolutely,' he said. 'Carbohydrates are all right in moderation . . . '

'Barely,' said the man with the dachshund. 'That advice you get to have three hundred grams of carbs a day is nonsense, in my view. I restrict myself to sixty – at the most.'

Blomquist nodded enthusiastically. 'That's very good. I'm on eighty, but some days I get by with twenty. No pasta. No bread.'

The dachshund owner was in full agreement. 'And no potatoes or sweet things. No chocolate, of course.'

'Chocolate is difficult,' said Blomquist, rolling his eyes heavenwards, as might the weakest of sinners. 'My problem is that I love it. And then there are all those studies that show that if you eat chocolate, your risk of stroke is significantly reduced.'

'I've heard that,' said the man. 'And heart disease, too. Chocolate's now been recognised as a superfood.'

'Except for dogs,' warned Blomquist. 'Chocolate is toxic to dogs.' He turned to Ulf. 'Did you know that, Mr Varg? You haven't been giving your dog chocolate, have you?'

Varg rather resented that question. It was none of Blomquist's business what he gave his dog. And the junior policeman certainly had no right to imply that he was an over-indulgent owner. 'No, I haven't,' he replied firmly.

'Good,' said Blomquist.

'He has a stomach of iron, anyway,' said Varg. 'Chocolate would be no problem for him, I suspect.'

Blomquist looked doubtful. 'No matter how strong his stomach is, you still ...'

He did not finish. 'And he once ate a pair of stereo headphones,' Ulf continued. 'They didn't seem to give him indigestion and we could have left them in – except that Dr Håkansson thought it best to operate.'

'Very wise,' said Blomquist.

The man in the suit now addressed Blomquist. 'Has the low carbohydrate approach worked?' he asked.

'Definitely,' replied Blomquist. 'I've lost four kilos.'

'And you don't feel hungry?'

Blomquist shook his head. 'That's the point about low-carb diets,' he said. 'Because you can have plenty of protein and fat, you don't feel hungry.'

'Exactly,' said the man. 'Fat fills you up. I eat full fat yoghurt – bacon, butter, the works. I never feel hungry.'

Ulf looked at his watch. 'Well, there we are,' he said. He reached into his pocket for his car key and that was when he felt, folded up, the piece of paper on which the photograph of Sixten had been printed. He took this out and unfolded it. He showed it to Blomquist. It was a long shot.

'This has cropped up in an inquiry we're involved in,' he said. 'We were questioning this young woman about this young man.' He pointed to Sixten.

Blomquist stared at the photograph for a few moments and then looked up. 'Yes, I know who that is,' he said. 'The boy, not the girl. I've no idea who she is, but the boy is called Bo. He goes to my gym.'

Ulf drew in his breath. He had not expected this. 'You know him?' he asked, almost incredulously.

'Yes, sure,' said Blomquist. 'Bo ... I can't remember his surname. It'll come back to me, though. You know how it is – things come back to you much later on, when you don't really need them.' He looked up at the ceiling, and it came back to him. 'Pålsson. Bo Pålsson.'

Ulf struggled to contain himself. 'Could you find him?'

'That won't be hard,' replied Blomquist. 'He's in the gym three or four nights a week. I have no idea why he spends so much time there. Always showering. I sometimes meet him in the showers.'

Ulf did not say anything. People showered for different reasons. One could never be sure.

Ulf drew close to Blomquist. 'Listen, Blomquist,' he said, lowering his voice. 'We need to talk to that young man – if he's not dead or at the North Pole.'

Blomquist looked at Ulf in puzzlement. 'The North Pole?'

'There's a Swedish research station there – or somewhere near there. We had information that suggested this young man was up there.'

The man with the dachshund raised a finger. 'Excuse me,' he said. 'I happen to know about that. It's in the Arctic Circle, but it's certainly not at the North Pole, it's in a place called Abisko. And it's not just ice up there – there are trees and marshes and so on.'

Both Ulf and Blomquist stared at him – Blomquist with an expression of some interest. The dachshund stared back suspiciously. Martin stared at the floor. Blomquist's cat stared fixedly at Martin.

The man with the dachshund continued, 'They've been looking at methane emissions recently. It's important work.'

'Methane?' asked Blomquist. 'That's a big problem.'

'Yes,' said the man. 'The permafrost up there has been thawing ...'

'Oh yes, I know that,' said Blomquist.

'And when that happens – when the permafrost thaws – methane is emitted. And that, of course, has consequences for global warming.'

'That's very serious,' said Blomquist. 'Carbon dioxide too. That's an issue.' He paused. 'Cows emit methane, I believe. And dogs too, for that matter. A dog has a large environmental footprint, you know.'

'Yes, they do,' said the man. He smiled. 'Dr Håkansson could tell us all about that, I imagine.'

Ulf turned back to Blomquist. 'I'm sorry, but I need to know something: have you seen this young man recently? And I mean over the last couple of weeks.'

Blomquist answered immediately. 'Yesterday, I think. No, hold on, the day before yesterday. In the shower at the gym, actually.'

For a few moments Ulf was silent. Then he asked, 'Are you absolutely sure?'

Blomquist became the policeman again. 'Yes, I'm quite sure. It was him, beyond all doubt.'

'All right,' said Ulf. 'Could you bring him in? Tomorrow?'

'You mean arrest him?'

'No,' said Ulf. 'Nothing that drastic. Just for questioning.'

'What has he done?' asked Blomquist.

'Nothing. It's not him – it's . . . well, it's complicated, Blomquist.'

Blomquist looked reproachfully at Ulf. *It's complicated.* Well, that said it all! Those people in the Criminal Investigation Authority – especially those in that fancy Sensitive Crimes Division, or whatever they called themselves – thought that ordinary, on-the-street policemen like himself were incapable of handling anything sophisticated. It was so unfair – particularly because he was the source of much of the information they used to solve their sensitive crimes. Me. I give them the facts. I was the one who solved that Gustafsson case. I told them about Hampus. And now I've solved something else for them and he won't even tell me what it is that I've solved. Typical. Absolutely typical of the injustice of the world.

And Ulf thought: we must be kinder to Blomquist. His isn't an easy job these days, what with ... well, what with everything. These are times of everything – the Age of Everything. And it was everything that was straining civil society to breaking point, challenging our world and its certainties. Everything, including methane.

Martin thought ... biscuits, cat, basket, Sweden.

CHAPTER TEN

The Sudden Urge to Cry

At the end of Ulf's next session with Dr Svensson, the psycho-therapist said to Ulf, 'Busy recently?'

'Yes,' replied Ulf. 'Moderately. We had a rather unusual matter to deal with, actually, a ridiculous spat between young women. Twenty-year-olds. Friends disagreeing with one another. Under-the-surface rivalry. That sort of thing.'

'At that age, feelings are very intense,' said Dr Svensson.

'You can say that again,' agreed Ulf. And then, 'Could I ask you something, Dr Svensson?'

'Of course. That's what I'm here for.'

'Imaginary friends.'

'Yes?'

'Are they at all common?'

Dr Svensson shrugged. 'There's literature on the topic, you

know. They crop up in childhood.' He paused. 'Why do you ask?' He grinned. 'Do you have one?'

Ulf shared the joke. 'Not really. Or not one I'd reveal to you, Dr Svensson.'

'Because I'd spoil the friendship?'

'Something like that. No, I'm just interested ... Well, more than just interested – it's something to do with this case we had.'

'The two young women?'

'Yes. One of them, you see, created an imaginary boyfriend. She actually got somebody to pose with her in a photograph – a young man she encountered on the street. Then she "disappeared" him, and so the friend thought she'd done him in. She'd made up some ridiculous story about his going off to the North Pole.'

Dr Svensson's eyes widened. 'The North Pole! That's very significant, you realise. The symbolism.'

Ulf waited for him to explain further.

'The North Pole is a phallic symbol, Mr Varg.'

Ulf frowned. 'But it exists, doesn't it? It's not just a symbol. It has a real, physical existence.'

'No, it doesn't. The North Pole doesn't exist. There is no pole, Mr Varg. It's an idea.'

Ulf did not wish to labour the point. 'All right, there's no actual pole. But if there's no pole, then how can it be a phallic symbol?'

'A word can be a symbol,' replied Dr Svensson. 'Semiotics, Mr Varg!'

'Yes,' said Ulf briskly. 'Anyway, this other young woman – a friend of the first young woman – came to us with the photograph and the story of the mysterious disappearance of the boyfriend, whom at that stage we all thought real.'

'I see.'

'Yes. And we then had a visit from the mother – the mother of the first young woman, that is. She came to tell us that her daughter had told us a pack of lies when we asked her about what happened to her boyfriend. The mother explained that the boyfriend was imaginary and that her daughter had had an imaginary friend as a child – with the same name as the boyfriend she created later on.'

'I see.'

'The mother was very apologetic. She told us that the girl's father, a naval officer, had deserted them and gone to live up north.'

'Ah,' said Dr Svensson. 'North.'

'She asked us to take an understanding view of her daughter's behaviour. She understood that she could be in trouble for giving false information in a criminal investigation.'

'Even into one concerning a non-existent person?'

'Yes, even then. So we did. She was given a warning.'

'And that was the end of the matter?'

Ulf nodded. 'Yes, that was it – as far as we were concerned. But I must say I was curious about this whole business of imaginary friends. Why do children do it?'

Dr Svensson said that he thought it was a form of play. 'They act out the issues that concern them in their real lives. That's what children do. So the imaginary friend will be a projection. The friend will mirror what's going on inside the child.'

'And then they bring the friend to an end?'

'Yes,' Dr Svensson replied. 'It can seem very abrupt to any adult who witnesses it. The parent asks, "Where's Bo?" And the child just says something like, "Bo's gone away." It can seem almost brutal.'

Ulf stared at the psychotherapist. 'Excuse me,' he said. 'Could you say that again?'

'Say what?'

'That last bit. What the parent says, and then what the child answers.'

'The parent says, "Where's Bo?" and then the child replies, "Bo's gone away." I think that's what I said.'

'Why Bo?' asked Ulf. 'Why did you choose that name?'

Dr Svensson did not answer immediately. He turned to look out of the window. 'I suppose that tells you something about me.'

Ulf waited.

'I had an imaginary friend myself, Mr Varg. He was called Bo, as it happens. He was my constant companion until I was about eight. Then, apparently – and I don't remember this part, but my parents told me this is what happened – I got rid of Bo. I just said, "Bo's gone away." That was the end of Bo. And that's why I chose that name. Nothing more significant than that.'

Ulf was silent. He felt sorry for Dr Svensson; for the first time in their acquaintanceship, he felt sorry for him.

'Life is a progression of partings,' said the psychotherapist. 'One by one, people – and things, too – are taken from us. We lose them, they die, they are shown by us to be things of transitory association.'

'I'm sorry,' said Ulf.

'So am I,' said Dr Svensson.

When Ulf returned to the office, there was a message from Anna awaiting him. 'She had to go out,' said Carl. 'She left you a message. It's on your desk.'

He saw the note, placed prominently on his keyboard. 'Have just heard,' wrote Anna, 'that Signe Magnusson has gone missing. Will get in touch.' And then she had put a kiss, an x, before her name. It was the first time she had ever done that, and Ulf felt a sudden thrill. Of course it could be meaningless; many people signed off with an x, and it was probably no more than a mannerism, as meaningless as 'dear' at the beginning of a letter. Or it could mean something more. It could be a little sprig of warmth, of particular affection, put there to make personal the impersonal. Love and kisses, xx. They were such clichéd words and symbols, but there were times they set the heart racing because they meant exactly what they purported to say.

He put the note down. He had assumed they had seen the last of the Sixten affair, but this news from Anna put an end to that assumption. He picked the note up again and examined it afresh. The pleasure he had felt on seeing the casually inscribed kiss was now replaced by anxiety. And that anxiety, insidious and troubling, itself soon gave way to regret. He could not allow himself to embark on this . . . this, what was it? Dalliance? Affair? Hopeless friendship?

He noticed that he was being watched from across the room, and now Carl pointed at the note. 'What does she say?' he asked.

It occurred to Ulf that Carl had read the note. If he had, then he would have seen the kiss. It was very unwise of Anna, he thought; it was reckless.

'Missing girl,' he answered.

'Anything else?'

He folded the note and placed it in his pocket. Carl watched him, and then said, 'Shouldn't you put that in a file?'

At the mention of the word *file*, Erik looked up from his desk. 'Pass it over. If there's no existing file, I'll start one. What's the name of the suspect?'

'There's no suspect,' Ulf said quickly. 'It's just a personal note. There's no suspect and no need for a file.'

Carl sat back in his chair. 'But you just said it's about a missing girl; what's personal about that?'

Ulf turned away, pretending he had not heard.

Carl repeated himself. 'I said: you've just said it was about a missing girl. That's not personal.'

Ulf felt the effect of the blush that he knew must be giving away his feelings. He felt flushed about the face; warm.

'There's some personal stuff in it,' he said. 'Nothing important. Anna has been asking my advice.'

He did not know where that came from. It was a straw grasped at *in extremis*, but he thought it sounded credible.

'About what?' asked Carl.

The direct question gave Ulf his chance to go on the attack and deflect the heat. 'Isn't one entitled to ask a colleague about a personal issue? Such as . . . such as the recommendation of a dentist?'

'Is Anna having dental work?' Carl asked.

Ulf looked at his watch. He would leave the question unanswered, as if it were simply too unimportant to merit a response. 'I have to go,' he muttered. 'I have to meet somebody.'

He left the office and began to make his way downstairs. The incident had disturbed him. He had now decided that he would have to speak to Anna and say, in the most general terms, of course, that notes left about the office could be intercepted by colleagues who had no business reading them. He would not say anything about the inscribed kiss, but if it had meant anything, then she would know what he was talking about. On the other hand, if it had been a casual, meaningless gesture, then she might wonder why he was so concerned that others might read an office note. People were always writing memos to one another and then, if they were physical rather than electronic, leaving them on other people's desks. Anna might reasonably ask why that should be a matter for concern, and if she did then he would have to say something about the kiss. It would be embarrassing, but he would have to do it.

He went out of the front door of the office and crossed the road to the café. There was no meeting – that had merely been an excuse to leave – and with nothing better to do, he decided to spend half an hour or so in the café, reading the newspaper or perhaps mulling over the implications of the news of Signe's disappearance.

The café was not busy, and he found a table at the window. Somebody had conveniently left on the table a copy of the *Sydsvenska Dagbladet* and he began to browse this while he was waiting for his coffee. There were the usual items: the crimes and the threats of crimes, the wringing of hands, the advice of politicians and civic leaders. It had not been like this before, but that was in the time of innocence. Now it was all very different.

Ulf sighed. Why could people not live together in harmony? Why did people think that berating and assaulting others should do anything but make everything worse for everybody? His eye fell on an advertisement inserted by the university. A new master's course was being offered in community relations. He read the short paragraph extolling the usefulness and topicality of this course. He wondered whether it would help, or whether it was no more than an aspiration – a course in what might be, but wasn't. But at least they were trying; at least they were not instituting a new master's programme in cynicism and indifference.

He turned the page. Journalistic gloom was replaced by levity, with a photograph of the latest piece of mouse-related street art. Malmö had been transfixed by the appearance of tiny constructions, created at floor level by anonymous artists, purporting to be the premises of local mice. There had been a restaurant, and people had left cheese outside it for the real mice that had started to frequent the premises; now there was a bookshop for the more literate mice. He looked at the picture, and smiled.

Tiny books filled the miniature, real glass windows of the pint-sized bookshop; a bench stood against a wall; within a recess a bookcase stood replete with special offers. A restaurant, or a night-club, or a patisserie – it was difficult to tell – was next door. In the foreground, a few fallen leaves showed the scale.

Ulf suddenly wanted to cry. He did not know why he should feel like this; he was not given to lachrymose moments, but now he felt the urge simply to cry. It was something to do, he thought, with the fact that this was a tiny, ordered world – a world in which there were none of the things he had read about on the previous page. Or it could be that this little construction was all about civilisation, and the desire to create an *urbs*, a place where civic life may be led, ordered and courteous. Or it was the architecture, which was on such an unthreatening scale and so human, while at the same time being exactly the sort of thing that a mouse architect might be expected to create.

On impulse he reached for the note in his pocket. He opened it and read it for a third time. *Who am I fooling?* That was the question he used to ask himself as a young man, and had found it a valuable corrective to any of the common dishonesties of this life, the excuses one gives oneself for not doing the things one ought to do. *Who am I fooling?*

And now that question seemed so very apt. He was denying to himself that he loved Anna. There, he had said it. He had said that he loved her. And he did. He did.

Yet he could not; he simply could not. Anna was married to Jo. She had two young daughters who presumably loved both their parents. They were a family; he was not. How could he contemplate, even for the briefest of moments, breaking up all that? How could he look Jo in the face and admit that he would take away his wife, his companion of so many years, the mother of his children? The answer was that he could do none of this, and that this love that he had, for the very first time, acknowledged would have to be suppressed, denied, hidden away, as so many impossible loves have had to be through all time – loves that would not work, loves that were frowned upon, loves that could blast apart a social or personal order.

He fingered the note, as if it were a talisman. A letter from a lover is always like that, he thought. It carries the sympathetic magic of the hand that wrote it; *that* hand. He read it one last time, and then tore it into several pieces, and then tore those pieces up until the note was no more than confetti.

And that was the point at which Carl appeared, as if from nowhere. 'I thought you said you were meeting somebody,' he said, staring pointedly at the fragments of the note still in the palm of Ulf's hand.

Ulf said nothing as he closed his fist around the fragments of paper. 'Have you seen this?' he said to Carl. 'It's a mouse bookstore.'

Carl looked at the photograph. 'Strange,' he said.

'What does it make you feel?' asked Ulf.

'Strange,' repeated Carl.

Ulf gestured towards the empty chair at his table. 'Why don't you sit down, Carl? Then we can talk.'

Carl accepted the invitation. 'Talk about what?' he asked.

'Everything that we would each like to say,' said Ulf, 'but that we are too embarrassed to put directly.'

Carl's eyes widened. He looked again at Ulf's clenched fist. 'That note: what was in it?'

Ulf drew in his breath. He would make a clean breast of it. He could do nothing but that now. 'Anna put a kiss at the end – you know, an x. It was probably meaningless, but . . . ' He faltered.

'You like her, don't you?' said Carl.

Ulf nodded. 'I like her, but I can't like her, if you see what I mean.'

Carl looked away. It was clear to him that Ulf was telling the truth. At first he was silent, but now he spoke. 'What are you going to do?'

'Nothing,' said Ulf. 'It can't be.'

'I can see that,' said Carl. He leaned forward and put a hand on Ulf's shoulder. 'Let me tell you something, Ulf: you are the best, kindest, funniest person I know. You are also the most truthful.'

Ulf was not sure whether there was ironic reproach in that accolade. Truthful? Earlier on, he had lied about the content of the note, but Carl, of course, did not know that. Or did he? If he had read the note while Ulf was out of the room, then he himself had behaved reprehensibly, even if he had not actually lied to Ulf.

Ulf decided to ask him. 'Did you read the note?' he asked.

Carl hesitated, and his gaze, until that moment focused on Ulf, slipped away. Ulf knew, and he breathed a silent sigh of relief. They were moral equals now – both as bad as one another.

'Unimportant,' said Carl.

Ulf raised an eyebrow. One did not fend off an unwelcome question by simply saying it was unimportant. That was not for Carl to judge; it was for Ulf himself.

But Carl was not going to answer. He took his hand off Ulf's shoulder and clasped the fist in which Ulf held the note. 'Give that to me.'

Ulf opened his fist to reveal the fragments. Carl took these, scooped them up, and then dropped them to the floor. 'There,' he said. 'Gone.'

CHAPTER ELEVEN

Hormones Come into It

Ulf's life, normally so settled and so ordered, had now become markedly more complicated. What had been the Bim Sundström case had now become the Signe Magnusson investigation, and had, in the process, transformed itself from a case of the suspected non-disappearance of a non-existent person to one involving the actual disappearance of a real person. He had yet to find the time to devote to that issue and left Anna to make preliminary inquiries by herself. Carl had also played a role, and the two of them had so far confirmed one thing: Signe was nowhere to be seen.

Then he had Martin to worry about; the vet had advised him to give the dog plenty of attention, but the demands of work had been such that this had been left to Mrs Högfors. He felt bad about that; Martin was his responsibility and he believed that he should not palm him off on his neighbour, no matter how obliging she might be. And, of course, there was also that business with

Anna and her note. He would have to watch that situation very closely and be on his guard; affairs started so easily and yet were so difficult to extricate oneself from. As far as his relationship with Anna was concerned, Ulf felt that he was standing at the brink of waters that were both deep and dangerous. He would have to be extremely careful or he would find himself embroiled in a situation from which there would be no easy escape. So he would have to do something that up until now he had never had to do: he would have to fall *out* of love. And he was not sure how to do that, at least not how to do it deliberately.

Now, to make matters worse, a case had been referred to him by no less a person than the Commissioner of Police himself, a barely glimpsed, remote and quasi-apocryphal figure. Very few people in the Criminal Investigation Authority had ever met the Commissioner; indeed, there were those who denied his existence, saying that he was no more than a cypher for the shadowy police management committee that answered to the government on policing policy. Others said that he existed, but that he was a recluse who found social interaction disturbing and who ran the department by fiats dictated to a few hand-picked officers who were allowed to enter his presence.

Neither of these views was correct. Police Commissioner Ahlbörg did exist; he was certainly not a public man, preferring to work quietly in the background, but he was considered by those who knew him to be a painstaking administrator, a scrupulously fair boss, and an astute defender of the force's interests. He did not choose to appear in public or to be seen very much by those who worked below him because he felt that it was not necessary for him to do this. He was by nature a delegator and was quite happy to let people get on with their jobs without his breathing down their necks. Privately, he and his family led a model life. He helped with Swedish-adjustment classes for refugees, while his wife, Anita, was an accountant who voluntarily did the accounts of two local charities. Their two clear-eyed sons had co-founded an aero-modelling club for disadvantaged youths. They were well liked in the suburb in which they lived, where very few, if any, people knew that their mild and rather pleasant neighbour was in fact the Commissioner of Police.

That morning, when Ulf arrived in the office, Erik hailed him from the other side of the room. 'Important message for you, Ulf,' he shouted. 'Ahlbörg wants to see you. Pronto.'

Ulf laughed. 'Ha ha, Erik. It's not the first of April, you know.'

Erik was the person in the office who most enjoyed the first of April and the opportunities it gave to play practical jokes on his colleagues. They were forewarned, of course, and most of his efforts had been spotted immediately. Thus the memo he had circulated earlier that year that all detectives were to be equipped with a false moustache, in the case of men, or false eyelashes in the case of women, had been greeted with no more than tolerant groans. More successful, though less inventive, had been the trick he had played on Anna, putting two spoons of sugar in the coffee that she normally took unsweetened.

'Ha!' he had exclaimed as he saw her grimace at the taste. 'April fool!'

Ulf had pointed out to him that this was not really a proper April fool prank. 'There has to be deception, Erik. You have to give somebody a piece of news that is false, but just believable. Something like that.' He thought quickly. 'But it mustn't actually be true – such as this morning's news about the fishing ban.'

Erik frowned. 'What fishing ban?'

Carl had been listening. 'Haven't you heard, Erik?'

Ulf glanced at Carl. 'The Riksdag has approved a ban on recreational fishing. It's going to be outlawed. It's something to do with the fish lobby.'

Erik dropped the file he was holding. 'They can't,' he stuttered. 'They can't do that!'

'It does seem a bit extreme,' said Ulf. 'But they've said they'll review it next first of April.'

At this point Anna, sensing Erik's distress, had brought the deception to an end. 'Ulf's joking,' she said. 'Don't worry, Erik – nobody's going to ban fishing.'

'Yet,' said Ulf. 'But give them time.'

But now, Erik made it clear he was not joking. 'I took the call,' he assured Ulf. 'I noted down the extension. I'm not making this up. They said you had to phone and make an appointment the moment you came in. Here it is.' He walked across the room to give Ulf the slip of paper. Ulf dialled the number and scribbled on a notepad before replacing the receiver.

'Looks like you're right,' he said. 'I'm to report to Ahlbörg at eleven-thirty.'

'See,' said Erik. 'I told you.'

Anna was concerned. 'I hope it's nothing you've done,' she said.

'Or failed to do,' said Carl.

Ulf was puzzled. 'I can't think of anything.'

Carl wondered whether it was something to do with the Gustafsson case. 'That statement you gave to the court,' he said. 'It was pretty sympathetic to Hampus Johansson, wasn't it? Ahlbörg – if he exists – might think that you were sending out the wrong message about knife crime.'

Ulf thought this unlikely. 'Nobody at Ahlbörg's level will have noticed that case. They have bigger fish to fry.'

Erik looked up, but only briefly.

Anna tried to reassure Ulf. 'I suspect it's nothing very important,' she said. 'It's probably some new initiative in staff communication. He probably has to speak to every section head once a year, just to show that channels of communication are open. You know how they're always going on about channels of communication.'

That was some comfort to Ulf, but he still felt a degree of trepidation when he made his way over the Carolibron Bridge to the imposing building that was the headquarters of the Police Southern District. He had rather unwisely drunk two cups of strong coffee, and his nerves were jangling. He was not sure what to call the Commissioner, and he wondered if there was some etiquette that he should know but did not. If he simply called him Mr Ahlbörg it might sound as if he were deliberately playing down the Commissioner's exalted rank, and yet if he called him Commissioner it might sound like Commissionaire, which was a different matter altogether. Or *sir*: it was always possible to call him *sir*, but then there were plenty of other senior officers who would merit that, and this might not be quite respectful enough for an officer of his status. Of course, these days people used first names in so many circumstances, and Ulf had read of companies where surnames were banned on the grounds of excessive formality. The problem with that, though, was that not only was it unlikely, but Ulf also did not know what the Commissioner's first name was; as far as he could make out, nobody knew that.

By the time he was ushered into the Commissioner's office, Ulf had worked himself up into a state of heightened anxiety. But he was immediately reassured when the Commissioner, beaming with a smile of welcome, arose from his desk to greet him.

'I'm so sorry about the short notice,' said Ahlbörg, after he had shaken Ulf's hand. 'It's very good of you to drop everything and come over here.'

Ulf breathed a sigh of relief. 'It was no trouble, sir. Any time.' The *sir* slipped out, and seemed entirely natural.

'Please,' said Ahlbörg. 'It's Felix.' He paused, before smiling again at Ulf. 'And you're ...'

'Ulf.'

'Of course. I noticed that when I saw your name. Both mean wolf in Old Norse, don't they?'

Ulf nodded. 'Some people find my name repetitive,' he said.

Ahlbörg laughed. 'Names are odd, aren't they? Some people talk about nominal determinism, but I find it a bit of an odd idea, frankly. Do you think one's name can be one's destiny?'

Ahlbörg returned to his side of the desk as he asked the question. As he did so, he gestured for Ulf to sit.

'I'm not sure about nominal determinism,' Ulf said. 'Although I did once arrest a motorcycle thief by the name of Vroom.'

The Commissioner laughed. 'And you read about dentists called Drill, and so on. Personally, I think it's coincidence – nothing more than that.'

'I agree,' said Ulf.

'Mind you,' Ahlbörg continued, 'I've often wondered about criminal types, you know. I know many people would look askance at me for saying this, but I've certainly observed a relationship between physical appearance and criminality. There are some people who just look the part, don't they?'

'There was that Italian criminologist, wasn't there?' said Ulf. 'Lombroso.'

Ahlbörg raised a finger. 'Yes, indeed. Now that's a thing, Ulf:

how many members of this police force would know about Cesare Lombroso? I can answer that myself – precious few. Perhaps just you and I in the entire district.'

Ulf said nothing. He had relaxed now, and the Commissioner's demeanour had ruled out the possibility that this was a disciplinary interview; unless, of course, the Commissioner was a nasty cop behind a nice cop's façade ... Clichés might be clichés, but they existed for a reason.

'I'll get to the point,' Ahlbörg said. 'I need an officer to deal with a very sensitive matter. That's why I've called you in.'

Again, Ulf felt a flood of relief. This was routine. He crossed his legs. He could sit back and enjoy the meeting now.

'I'm at your service ... Felix.' It was still an effort to use the first name, but he had to. It would be rude to revert to *sir*.

'There's a small town not far from where we are,' Ahlbörg began. 'It's not an important place – a bit off the beaten track. A farming place mostly, but pretty enough to get some visitors in the summer. A couple of hotels and a spa. There's a marina too. That sort of thing.'

Ulf waited.

'The spa happens to be run by a cousin of mine. They used to own a hotel and then, about ten years ago, they made it into a health spa. They get people going out there for detoxification. You know, the carrot cure, or whatever happens to be fashionable at the time.' He paused. 'Are you vegetarian, Ulf?'

Ulf replied that he was not. He was sympathetic, though, to vegetarianism and was in general eating far less meat than he used to.

'You're on the right track,' said Ahlbörg. 'My wife and I have cut right back. A bit of chicken now and then, and we eat fish of course, but not much red meat.'

'Red meat has a pretty large environmental footprint,' Ulf said. 'All those forests in South America being cut down so that they can ranch cattle.'

'Exactly,' agreed Ahlbörg. 'And that means more methane.'

Ulf remembered his last conversation with Blomquist, and the discussion of methane in the vet's waiting room. That made him think of Martin, and his troubles.

'Methane is definitely an issue,' Ulf said. 'Even dogs contribute methane.'

The Commissioner nodded. 'My sons have a dog. They've been very good about looking after it. I think looking after an animal is quite good training for a child, don't you?'

'Yes,' said Ulf. Then he added, 'My dog's been depressed, I think. The vet gave him something called clomipramine.'

This seemed to pique the Commissioner's interest. 'Has it made a difference?' he asked.

'Yes, I think so,' said Ulf. 'I was told that I would have to wait for a while before he picked up, but he seems less down in the mouth now.'

The Commissioner appeared pleased. 'Isn't it remarkable what modern pharmacology can do?' He looked out of the window. 'Sometimes I wonder if it wouldn't be a good idea to put something like that in the drinking water. It would make our job a whole lot easier – if not do us out of a job altogether.'

Ulf laughed. 'You could suggest it. The press would be grateful to you on a slow news day.'

The Commissioner winced at the mention of the press. 'Actually, that brings me back to the question of my cousin. One of the reasons why I asked to see you is my worries about the press. We have to be so careful, you know – the slightest thing and they're off. Discretion is required.' He looked searchingly at Ulf. 'I've heard that the Department of Sensitive Crimes is known for its discretion.'

Ulf assured him that he knew all about confidentiality. 'It's our stock in trade, sir.'

'Felix.'

'Yes, Felix. We're ultra-discreet. Not even any pillow talk. Nothing.'

The Commissioner said that that was what he liked to hear. 'You see, Ulf,' he went on, 'I need somebody to find out why somebody seems intent on ruining my cousin's business.'

Ulf raised an eyebrow. He had not expected to be asked to do a personal favour – something unofficial. There were rules about that and he would have thought that the Commissioner, of all people, should know about those.

His doubts were anticipated. 'Oh, no. I'm not asking you to do something on the side,' said the Commissioner. 'This will be a perfectly proper criminal investigation.'

'The crime being?' asked Ulf.

'The crime, I suspect, is malicious interference in trade. That's in the penal code, section whatever it is – I forget the numbers of these things. If you maliciously set out to interfere improperly in my business, you commit a crime. That makes it a matter for the police.'

Ulf said that he understood.

'And it's sensitive because the local police have proved to be hopeless at dealing with it. They say there're no grounds for suspicion that a crime has been committed.' The Commissioner paused. 'Now I could instruct them to investigate more thoroughly – I could overrule them. But the problem with that is that if I did so, and it got out that I was doing it to help a cousin, I'd be accused of exercising improper influence for a personal reason. You see my difficulty?'

Ulf said that he did. 'I'll take care of it,' he said. 'Leave it with me. Just give me the address of the spa and I'll handle the whole thing.

The Commissioner arose from his seat. 'I'm very grateful, Ulf. And report to me, will you, if . . . when you find something.'

They shook hands and the Commissioner began to show Ulf out of his office. 'What was the name of that stuff they're giving your dog?' he asked.

'Clomipramine.'

'Interesting,' said the Commissioner. 'Do you think it works on cats?'

'Possibly,' said Ulf. 'I don't really know, though.'

'Because we have a cat as well as a dog,' said the Commissioner. 'The cat belongs to my wife – I'm not really a cat person, you see. But the cat is very difficult. Antisocial, in fact. It takes a swipe at you from under a chair as you walk past. Draws blood sometimes.'

'You could try,' said Ulf. 'But sometimes cats just have nasty natures, don't you think? And you can't do much about a personality disorder. Cats are psychopaths at heart.'

The Commissioner looked disappointed. 'How long do cats tend to live?'

'They can last for a long time,' said Ulf. 'Twenty years in some cases.'

The Commissioner sighed. 'We all have our burdens in this life, don't we?'

'Yes,' said Ulf.

They shook hands again and Ulf left the office. When he returned to his own desk, the email from the Commissioner's assistant had already arrived, giving the name of the spa, its address and a telephone number to call if he needed directions to find it.

It was almost lunchtime when Ulf returned to the office. Carl had already left to eat his sandwich lunch in a nearby park, while Erik, taking his lunch at his desk, was paging through an angling magazine.

'You survived,' said Anna as Ulf walked into the room.

Erik looked up from his magazine. 'Does he really exist?'

Ulf smiled. 'Yes, I survived – and he does exist. He's charming, in fact. Polite. Interested. Everything you'd want a police commissioner to be.'

Anna was eager to hear the details. 'What did he want? Are you getting a promotion? Are *we* getting promotions?'

'Or early retirement?' added Erik.

'No,' said Ulf. 'Nothing was said about that.'

'So?' pressed Anna. 'Why did he get you over there?'

Ulf crossed to his desk. 'I'm sorry,' he said. 'I can't talk about it.'

Anna and Erik both stared at him in incomprehension. 'But we're colleagues,' said Anna. 'We tell one another what's going on. Otherwise ...' She shrugged her shoulders in a way that implied the collapse of sensitive crime work in Malmö, perhaps in all southern Sweden.

'Yes,' said Erik. 'There are no secrets here.'

Ulf was not to be swayed. 'I gave the Commissioner my word that I would not discuss the case with anybody. Sorry, but that means you.'

Anna shrugged. 'Very well, if that's the way it's to be.'

'I really am sorry,' explained Ulf. 'I'd love to tell you, but I just can't. Put yourself in my position – you'd do exactly the same.'

Ulf's appeal had its effect. Mollified, Anna suggested that they go for lunch in the café together where she would tell him about the latest developments in the Signe Magnusson case. 'Something odd has been going on,' she said, as they prepared to leave the office. 'I don't know what it is, but it's definitely fishy.'

Erik glanced up, but then returned to his magazine.

'There's been something odd about it from the beginning,' agreed Ulf.

In the café across the road there was no table at the window and they were obliged to seat themselves at the back. A straggling group of students, noisy and bound up in themselves, had taken the best places and were drowning out conversation at neighbouring tables with their laughter. Ulf looked at them with an air of slight regret.

'Were we like that?' he asked.

Anna glanced up from her scanning of the menu. 'Yes, I think we were. Nothing changes, really.'

'And yet,' said Ulf, 'when you're at that stage you have no idea that you yourself will change, have you? When you're twenty, you can't imagine your forty-year-old self.'

'What's that English poem?' Anna mused. 'Gather ye rosebuds while you may . . . '

'Old time is still a-flying . . . '

She was impressed. 'I didn't think you knew much poetry.'

'I don't,' said Ulf. 'We were made to learn poetry at school. I rather enjoyed it – others didn't. Strindberg, Erik Axel Karlfeldt; some German poets, too; some Shakespeare. Some of it stuck. But not much.' He remembered something. 'Oh yes. Homer. We read Homer.'

'In Greek?' she asked.

'No, Swedish. Homer sounds rather good in Swedish – it

could be an old Norse saga, if you changed the names. Lagerlöf's translation. I remember thinking of the Odyssey as taking place in the Stockholm archipelago. At that age, I couldn't really imagine Greece.' He paused as he looked down at the menu. 'Tell me about Signe. Bring me up to date.'

Anna leaned forward; there was a woman at the table next to them who had been eavesdropping on their conversation about poetry, so she lowered her voice as she spoke. 'Right. She was reported missing five days ago. A young woman by the name of Linnea Ek, a student at the university, reported to the local police that her friend had failed to turn up for a meeting. They were both something to do with the university's amateur dramatic club and the meeting had been set up for some time. It was an important meeting, apparently, and she thought it most unlike her friend not to show up.

'She tried calling her on her mobile – to no avail. The phone was switched off, and still is. Then she tried her parents, but they're in Japan apparently. We've been in touch with them subsequently – they're very anxious, as you can imagine. They could throw no light on the matter.'

Ulf asked about Signe's other friends, and, in particular, Bim.

'I spoke to her,' said Anna. 'She was worried at first that I was coming to raise the matter of her own recent behaviour, but she relaxed a bit when she realised that this had nothing to do with that. She said she thought it most unlike Signe to go off without telling anybody. Apparently, she reports her movements obsessively on social media. You can effectively track her from her online posts.'

'And have there been any?' asked Ulf.

Anna said there had not. 'That's the most worrying thing,' she said. 'But listen to this: several hours after my interview with

Linnea Ek, she called me back and said that she had been thinking about it all and had an idea that she wanted to run past me.

'Actually, the idea was a suspicion. When she told me she looked rather worried. She said that it had suddenly occurred to her that Bim might know more about the matter than she was letting on. She said that Bim and Signe had had a major falling-out over Signe's coming to us to report on the disappearance of that imaginary boyfriend. Bim believed that Signe had stolen that selfie from her, and was not ready to forgive her for it. She more or less suggested that Bim had killed Signe in some unknown place and in some unspecified way.'

Ulf snorted. 'Unlikely. A little dispute amongst a few imaginative young women. This doesn't smell of homicide.'

'Yes,' said Anna. 'But there's something else: Linnea said that on the day Signe disappeared, she had received a text from Bim saying they had to meet. That was just before the amateur dramatic meeting that she didn't turn up to.'

'How did Linnea know that?' asked Ulf.

'Signe texted her.'

'And where were they to meet?' asked Ulf.

'Signe didn't say.'

Ulf thought for a moment. 'And Bim? What does she say about that meeting?'

Anna leaned even further forward. The woman at the next table had inclined her head slightly, to be able to hear better. 'Here's another interesting thing: Bim denies all knowledge of the meeting with Signe. She flatly denies it.'

Ulf groaned. 'Lies,' he said. 'Somebody's lying.'

Anna agreed. 'Yes, but who? This seems to be one of those cases where you have A saying x and B saying y.'

'I like you when you're algebraic,' said Ulf – and immediately regretted it. It was a flirtatious remark – describing somebody as algebraic was undoubtedly to cross a line. You would not normally describe an *ordinary* friend as algebraic, and then say that you liked her that way.

He saw the effect on Anna, and his regret deepened.

'Algebraic?' she said, half coyly. 'Well, I'm very happy to enter into any equation.'

Ulf floundered in his attempt to extricate himself. 'I wasn't being personal, Anna. I was simply referring to your use of symbols.' He paused, and then added, 'That's all, really. Just that. Nothing else.' He put an emphasis on the words *nothing else* that they would normally not have had. They were not an afterthought; they were the thought itself.

She was looking at him intently. 'I thought you said you liked me. I thought that was what you meant.'

'But of course I like you. I wouldn't be having lunch with you if I didn't like you. Algebra has got nothing to do with it.'

She lowered her eyes to the menu, and he saw that she was blushing. There was nothing he could do about that; she had picked up his message of disengagement, *if* that was the message, and he was not sure about that. It was geometry, rather than algebra. The geometry of this situation was wrong: there was a triangle, with Jo and Anna as two points of the diagram and himself as the third. He did not want to be involved in that sort of arrangement, because it was a triangle that had ended his marriage – an involuntary triangle – and he did not want a repetition. Anna was married. It was as simple as that. He could not become responsible for jeopardising a marriage.

She looked up. 'Ulf,' she blurted out. 'I value your friendship – you know that.'

147

His reply was measured. 'Of course.'

'But I do think – I've always thought – that we should keep our friendship as just that: a professional one.'

He caught his breath. This was not what he had expected. After her remark about equations – which surely was pretty unambiguous – he thought that it would be for him to put the brakes on the situation. But now she was acting as the one who was intent on calling a halt. Was that to save face?

He knew what he had to do. Ulf was gentlemanly, and he knew that a gentleman in these circumstances would assume the role of the proposer and would apologise and take a step back. That was what a gentleman would do. And although he knew that nobody talked about being a gentleman any more, the concept still existed and was waiting to be rediscovered. Perhaps it had just been renamed and was still operating somewhere under the burden of the new language of relationships, the language that stressed self-determination and personal space. That was not all that different from the code of gentlemanly conduct that had previously prevented men from inappropriate conduct in their relations with women. The things that men were now supposed not to do were precisely the things that gentlemen were not meant to do anyway – so what was the difference? Were we simply becoming old-fashioned again, as societies tended to do when they saw the consequences of tearing up the behavioural rule book?

Ulf had never reflected on where his values came from, but had he done so, the answer would have been obvious. His father, Ture Varg, had been the doorman of a famous, old-fashioned hotel. He was a self-taught man who spent his spare time reading in an effort to make up for the education that family misfortune had prevented him from getting. He was well known to the hotel's clientele and in the wider city, much appreciated for his courtesy and charm. In his professional role, he wore a stovepipe hat that he doffed to all who entered. He wore grey kid-leather gloves and a long frock coat on which two small military medals were pinned. He sang in a choir that performed Swedish folk songs. He never spoke harshly or rudely to anyone.

That was where Ulf came from, and now, intuitively and automatically, he knew what his father would do.

'I'm very sorry,' he said. 'I spoke out of turn. Forgive me; it was my fault entirely. I was forgetting that some things simply cannot be, no matter how much one might wish otherwise.'

Anna seemed to recover remarkably quickly. It was a relief to her, he thought. 'Of course,' she said. And then repeated, 'Of course.'

Ulf pointed to the menu. 'What are you going to have?'

Anna pointed to an item at the top of the handwritten menu. Although describing itself as a café, and although much of its business was in the serving of coffee to office workers, this was really a bistro with a carefully prepared, if small, selection of classic dishes. 'Jansson's Temptation,' she said. 'When did you last have that? Ten years ago?'

Ulf licked his lips. 'I loved that. My mother sometimes made it on a Sunday evening.'

It was a simple dish, consisting of onions, potatoes, anchovies and cream. It was *echt* comfort food.

'Or Gubbröra,' Anna said, pointing to another item.

'Both,' said Ulf with delicious irresponsibility. 'Jansson's Temptation first, and then Gubbröra.'

The waitress came to take their order. As regulars, they both knew her, and they listened as she complained about the students. 'You know what I'd like to say to them?' she said. 'I'd like to go up to them and say: what gives you the right to sit about in cafés laughing your heads off when other people have to go to work? You know how long they'll stay in here? Three hours at least. And the government pays them to study, doesn't it? They get all that money to sit about in cafés and make a din.'

'Would you like us to arrest them?' asked Varg. 'We could, you know? For sitting about. It's there somewhere in the penal code.'

The waitress laughed. 'Somebody will believe you one of these days, Mr Varg.'

Their order placed, Ulf steered the conversation back to Signe. 'Why was the matter referred to us?' he asked. 'A missing student – and they usually turn up – is hardly a sensitive crime.'

'Her father's a diplomat,' explained Anna. 'He's the Swedish representative on a number of anti-terrorism initiatives. Hence . . . '

Ulf raised a hand. 'Enough said.'

'Although I don't think this has anything to do with terrorism.'

'No?'

Anna glanced at the woman at the next table, who had now given up her attempt to listen to their conversation. A reproachful glance came in return.

'I think,' Anna continued, 'that this has nothing to do with anything political and everything to do with some silly goings-on between three young women. Boys are probably involved somewhere in the background – especially after that ridiculous business of the imaginary boyfriend. Hormones come into it, I think.'

'Don't they always?' said Varg.

'Possibly. Anyway, I don't think that Signe has been the victim of anything. She hasn't been kidnapped or murdered. She's probably just gone off in a huff because of a row with her friend Bim. Or ex-friend, I should say.'

Ulf fiddled with the menu. 'So this is all just collateral damage resulting from a bust-up between Signe and Bim?'

Anna nodded. 'Yes.'

'So, what do we do now?'

Anna spread her hands. It was a gesture of defeat in the face of uncertainty. 'Heaven knows,' she said.

CHAPTER TWELVE

Being Swedish Is Not Always Easy

On his return to the office, Ulf was told by Erik that Blomquist had telephoned him and wanted him to return the call. As he sat down to dial the number, Ulf felt the effect of the Jansson's Temptation – the lingering taste of anchovies, always given to repeat itself, was accompanied by a heaviness in the stomach that, although not unpleasant, was hardly conducive to work. He would have liked a siesta; he would have liked to stretch out on a sofa and think about anything other than a telephone call to Blomquist.

Blomquist answered quickly. 'You aren't busy, are you?'

Ulf resented this. There was a widespread belief in the police force that those in special offices – such as the Department of Sensitive Crimes – occupied virtual sinecures, with very little to do.

He could not help himself and replied snappily, 'Fairly busy.' He added, 'As always,' which was not true, of course, but seemed merited in the circumstances. He could, of course, tell Blomquist that he was preparing for a major case assigned to him by no less a person than the Commissioner, but confidentiality prevented that. And it was also true that he did not have much preparation to do; but that was irrelevant – the point was that Blomquist had no business insinuating that the Department of Sensitive Crimes was underemployed.

Blomquist revealed what he wanted. He had been, he said, on regular duty on the street when he had been approached by Hampus Johansson. 'You'll remember him, won't you? The man who stabbed Malte Gustafsson? I gave you the information and—'

Ulf cut him short. He had anticipated that Blomquist would take the credit for Johansson's arrest, but in fact it was he, Ulf, who had had the idea in the first place that the crime had been committed by somebody of short stature. But he was not going to get involved in an argument with Blomquist about that, so he simply replied, 'Yes, your response to my initial query was very helpful, Blomquist.' And before Blomquist could say anything else about who had done what in bringing Hampus to justice, he added, 'What does he want?'

'He wants to see you. He's very ... well, I suppose you'd describe him as distraught.'

Ulf sighed. 'We can't reverse convictions. We're not a court of appeal.'

Blomquist said that it was nothing to do with the conviction. 'It's the sentence, Mr Varg – his community service sentence.'

'But that's the court's affair,' said Ulf. 'We don't decide who has to do what. You must know that, Blomquist.'

'It's very difficult for him, Mr Varg. He feels you're the only one who can help. He has a lot of respect for you, you see.'

Ulf looked up at the ceiling. He had felt sorry for Hampus – everybody in that courtroom had felt that way. And he was a kind man, possibly the kindest man in the entire Swedish police service, and he found it difficult to refuse a heartfelt request – such as this obviously was. Yet at the same time there were limits to what you could do. The world was a place of sadness and strife, of selfish behaviour and disagreement, of oppression and injustice; and efforts to remedy that, to set right the scales of justice, sometimes seemed like patching up a crack in a dam wall with sticking plaster. But you had to do what you could, and, more specifically, what your role in life expected of you. And he was a detective; he was a member of the Malmö Criminal Investigation Authority, and that meant there were souls within his care … yes, he thought *souls*, because that old-fashioned word said so much more than the word *person*. A soul was something more than that – a soul had feelings and ambitions and private tragedies. A soul weighed more than something that was not a soul.

These thoughts were a reminder of duty, of what he had to do simply because he was Ulf Varg. 'Of course I'll see him, Blomquist,' he said at last. 'And thank you again for what you did in that case. We couldn't have solved it without you.'

Blomquist's pleasure was evident down the telephone line. 'Anything I can do, Mr Varg. Anything. Any time.' And then he added, 'I know how busy you people are.'

The conversation ended with the arrangements. Blomquist would come to the office within the next half-hour and they would drive together, in the Saab, to the dance studio where Hampus taught. As Ulf hung up, he pictured the studio where that extraordinary meeting with Hampus had taken place. He saw the revolving mirror-ball, that cheap dispenser of glittery light that seemed *de rigueur* in those tawdry dance places. He saw the sprung floor, with its pliant boards and its dusting of French chalk …

French chalk. French chalk. For some reason this resonated with him, but he could not remember why.

Hampus was playing the piano when they arrived. Two couples were on the dance floor – two instructors with their clients. The instructors were women, the clients, two middle-aged men, one in a loose-fitting white suit, the other wearing jeans and a seersucker jacket. Hampus, who did not see them arrive, was perched on a piano stool, his legs far from touching the floor or the pedals of the piano; his limited reach meant that he had to twist from this side to that as the music ascended or descended.

The instructors noticed them enter but continued dancing. One was counting out loud to her pupil as she guided him through the steps; the other was demonstrating the correct position of the arms as she moved the man in the seersucker jacket through the steps. Blomquist beamed with pleasure as he watched the dance, tapping a foot against the floor in time to the music. 'I just love dancing,' he whispered to Ulf. 'My wife and I go out dancing whenever we can. We dance a lot.'

Ulf nodded. 'Yes,' he said. Letta had been keen on dancing, he less so.

'Our daughter's turning into quite a good little dancer,' he said. 'Ballet, though – not ballroom.'

Ulf smiled. 'Very nice,' he said.

'You know there's a ballet school up in Stockholm?'

Ulf watched the dancers. Blomquist talked too much, he thought; he really did. What was wrong with silence? 'I've heard of it.'

'The Royal Swedish Ballet School. They take quite young children, I believe. We couldn't send Svea up there just yet – she's only eight, you know. Eight's too young, don't you think? You can't make up your mind about a career – and ballet really is a career – if you're eight.'

The pace of the music increased; Hampus twisting from side to side more energetically now to reach the higher or lower notes. The floor creaked as the dancers moved. Ulf saw the French chalk, a thin white layer on the wood, striated by the dancers' feet.

'I went to ballet lessons myself when I was a boy,' said Blomquist. 'Just for a year or two. I gave them up because I was being teased.'

Ulf glanced at him. 'I can't quite see it, Blomquist.'

Blomquist grinned. 'Oh, I think I was quite good, Mr Varg. Perhaps I could have continued. I might have become a professional ballet dancer rather than a policeman.' He paused, as if imagining the contrast. 'Life's odd, isn't it? You make a decision that could dictate the whole course of your life, and you don't know at the time that it will do that, do you? You don't.'

'No, I suppose you don't.'

'You never did ballet, Mr Varg?'

'No, Blomquist. I never did ballet.'

'You might have been quite good, you know. Some surprising people are quite good at ballet.'

Hampus was reaching the end of the tune. With a final flourish he concluded, and then closed the piano lid with a bang. The man in the seersucker jacket said, 'Ah!' loudly – an exclamation of satisfaction. His instructor patted him on the shoulder in congratulation – a dance well danced.

Hampus turned around and saw Ulf and Blomquist. Slipping off his stool, he walked quickly across the floor and shook hands with Ulf.

'Thank you for coming, Mr Varg,' he said. 'I hope you haven't been waiting too long.'

'I enjoyed watching,' Ulf replied. 'And you're a fine pianist, Mr Johansson.'

Hampus made a self-effacing gesture. 'No, I'm not really, Mr Varg. I play very functionally.'

'I see that you can't reach the pedals,' Blomquist observed. 'That can't help.'

Ulf glanced at Blomquist. Hampus frowned, and then rubbed his hands together as if to restore the circulation.

'Couldn't you have some device to extend the pedals?' Blomquist went on. 'Some sort of lever device?'

Hampus stared fixedly at the floor. 'I don't know. Maybe.'

'You wanted to see me,' said Ulf.

'Yes,' said Hampus. 'I was going to go to your office. I didn't expect you to come down here, but Mr Blomquist told me that you didn't have much to do and wouldn't mind.'

Ulf glanced at Blomquist again, who looked away, lifting his gaze to the static mirror ball. 'I see.' He looked again at Blomquist. He was unrepentant, he noticed. Sometimes it was difficult to be as tolerant as he wanted to be; but then, thought Ulf, the whole point about high ideals is that they *are* high. Being Swedish was not always easy, but you had to do your best, and hope that you didn't slip, and become ... well, Mediterranean in outlook. It was so easy, such a beguiling option, to shrug your shoulders and behave as your immediate emotions dictated. And how comfortable it must be to sit in the sun and smile, and say the world will look after itself, and that its problems will resolve themselves tomorrow, or even the day after that.

Ulf became businesslike. 'Well, here I am, Mr Johansson. What's the trouble? Mr Blomquist tells me you're not happy with your community service arrangements.'

157

Hampus nodded. 'Certainly not. Very unhappy.'

Ulf spread his hands in a gesture of acceptance. 'But that's the whole point about a court sentence, you know. The people who get it are usually not very happy. In fact, some of them are downright unhappy.'

'That's what I said,' Blomquist interjected.

Ulf asked Hampus what his assignment was.

'I've been assigned to work at an army base,' said Hampus. 'I was told that I would be given general duties. Eight hours a week.'

Ulf said he thought that sounded reasonable enough. 'Some people doing community service get very unpleasant tasks, you know.' General duties in an army base did not sound too onerous to him.

Hampus looked at Ulf defiantly. 'This is. This is very onerous.'

'Tell me, then,' said Ulf. 'What do they make you do? Carry heavy things? Peel potatoes in the cookhouse?'

'Potatoes are best eaten unpeeled,' interjected Blomquist. 'The skins contain a lot of the real nutritional material, you know. You shouldn't peel potatoes.'

Ulf threw Blomquist a dismissive glance. 'I know that, Blomquist,' he said. 'But does the army?'

'You'd think they would know by now, Mr Varg. The army should keep up to date with these things. Soldiers need a balanced diet – just the same as everybody else.'

Ulf turned back to Hampus. 'So, what do they make you do, then?'

Hampus hesitated. 'They haven't told me yet,' he answered.

Ulf frowned. He was beginning to feel irritated by Hampus. The dance instructor was lucky to have been let off so lightly by the court – he could easily have ended up in prison – and it ill became him now to complain about his community service assignment. What was wrong with being allocated to an army barracks? A pickpocket of Ulf's acquaintance – a habitual thief whom Ulf had arrested on several occasions during his early days in the police – had recently been given one hundred hours of general duties in the sewage works, and another, a public drunkard and indecent exhibitionist, had been sentenced to fifty hours of cleaning up at the fish market, a malodorous job involving the disposal of rotten fish heads. The army would be nothing like that.

'So how do you know you won't like it?' asked Ulf.

'Because I was warned about it,' said Hampus. 'Somebody who comes for dance lessons is married to one of the sergeant majors up there. He told her that they've planned something very unpleasant for me. He didn't tell her what it was, but he said he would never do it himself – even if they offered to promote him.'

Ulf sighed. 'That's not enough,' he said. 'That doesn't give me grounds to interfere.'

Hampus looked at him imploringly. 'He said I might not survive. That's what he said.'

Ulf raised an eyebrow. This was different. Was the army planning to use Hampus on some sort of dangerous combat mission? 'You mean that you might be obliged to fight?' he asked.

Hampus nodded. 'That's what it looks like.'

Ulf glanced at his colleague, who shrugged.

'They're short of men,' Blomquist said. 'Maybe it's their way of recruiting – they get community service people.'

'That's ridiculous,' retorted Ulf. 'Absurd.'

'Defence spending cuts,' ventured Blomquist.

Ulf looked at Hampus, who was staring back at him, waiting for

159

his response. He trusts me, thought Ulf. He expects me to protect him. And at that point, the urge that had prompted Ulf to join the police all those years ago once again tugged at his heart. If there was an injustice – or an abuse of power – then he felt compelled to set it right. And there was an abuse of power here – a major one, perhaps – and he would not dodge it.

Ulf found himself thinking of what he would do. He knew that one could go back to the court and get a community service order varied, but that this could take time. The last time he had been involved in that particular procedure, it had taken two months. Hampus did not have two months; he might not even have two days. It was almost unbelievable that the army should behave in this way in the twenty-first century. If they wanted to take risks with their own men, that was their affair, although he imagined that they were careful to train them properly. But to take a complete outsider and put him into combat was breathtakingly irresponsible. Hampus was now looking imploringly at Ulf. 'Could you speak to the colonel?' he pleaded. 'Ask him not to make me do whatever they've been planning. I'll do anything – anything that a civilian can do. Even peel potatoes – gladly.'

'You shouldn't,' said Blomquist. 'There are minerals in potato skins. It's pointless to get rid of the best part of—'

Ulf interrupted him. 'I think you have a very strong case,' he said.

'So you'll do it?' asked Hampus eagerly.

'Whatever they have in mind,' Ulf said, 'sounds unacceptable. I'll go to the base and insist on seeing the colonel.'

'Good,' said Hampus. 'Thank you.'

'And if he won't deal with it immediately,' Ulf continued, 'I shall speak to the Commissioner of Police and ask him to intervene.' He paused. 'I know him, you see.'

Blomquist looked sharply at Ulf. 'You know him? You know Ahlbörg?'

Ulf did his best to sound casual. 'As it happens, I do.'

'Wow!' exclaimed Blomquist, and then, his voice dropping, he added, 'What's he like?'

'Very pleasant, actually,' Ulf replied. 'Felix is—'

Blomquist's eyebrows shot up. 'Felix? You know his first name?'

Ulf's manner remained casual. 'He asked me to call him that. It wasn't my idea.'

'Felix,' mused Blomquist. 'And what did he call you? Ulf?' He laughed at the sheer unlikelihood.

'Yes,' said Ulf. 'He called me Ulf.'

Hampus looked up sharply. 'Is that your name? Ulf?'

'Yes, I'm Ulf.' And then, with a smile, 'I don't mind if you call me that, if you like.'

'So both your names mean *wolf*,' said Hampus. 'You're Wolf Wolf.'

'It's a common enough name,' said Ulf. 'There are other names that refer to animals.'

Blomquist frowned. 'Not many. You don't come across many people called "Dog" or "Horse", do you?'

Ulf felt himself becoming irritated. Both Ulf and Varg were perfectly good names and somebody called Hampus was hardly in a position to question the names of others. Hampus ... what a ridiculous name that was – not that he would ever dream of drawing attention to it.

Blomquist ploughed on. 'Remember the story of the boy who cried wolf? Remember that one?'

Ulf did not reply. He turned to Blomquist. 'What about you, Blomquist? Doesn't Blomquist mean "flower branch"?'

161

He did not wait for an answer, continuing, 'Anyway, we don't need to discuss names. When are you next due at the base?'

'Tomorrow,' said Hampus. 'Unless they call me in before then. They said I might have to come in at short notice if there's an emergency, but they didn't tell me what sort of emergency it could be. An invasion, maybe.'

Ulf looked at his watch. 'I could try to get over there later this afternoon. Otherwise, I'll go first thing tomorrow.'

Hampus gave him a look of gratitude. 'You've been very kind to me, Mr Varg,' he said. And then, to Blomquist, 'And you, too, Mr Blomquist.'

In the Saab, on the way back to the office, Ulf made known his views on the army. 'They think they're above the law,' he said. 'That sort of conduct – exposing a civilian to risk – is downright criminal.'

'I couldn't agree more,' said Blomquist.

'I won't take no from that colonel,' Ulf continued.

They turned a corner and Blomquist indicated where he would like to be dropped off. Before he alighted, though, he turned to Ulf and said, 'That missing girl – the one they sent a notification out on . . .'

'Signe Magnusson? Yes?'

Blomquist looked at his fingernails. 'I could have some information about her.'

Ulf frowned. 'Well? Have you seen her?'

'No, not seen her. But it so happens that I go to a coffee bar not far from my place. Not too often, but now and then. They serve really good coffee, you see – Central American stuff. You know, it's amazing the difference the origin makes.'

'Yes, it's important,' said Ulf. 'But what about this place? What's it got to do with the girl? Did she go there?'

Blomquist said that she did not. 'One of the baristas is a young guy called Loke. He's from Gothenburg. He used to play semi-professional football, but he hurt his knee and had to give it up. That's hard luck, you know. You get a knee injury and that's your career finished. Over. Pretty hard luck.'

'Yes,' said Ulf. 'It must be tough. But what about this Loke?'

'He was her boyfriend,' said Blomquist.

'Ah.'

'Yes, or should I say *one* of her boyfriends.'

Ulf waited for Blomquist to continue. It was difficult to hurry him on, he felt, and it was best just to let the natural stream of consciousness play itself out. There were people like that – Mrs Högfors, Blomquist, one or two others.

'You see,' Blomquist went on, 'apparently Signe Magnusson had two boyfriends. She had the barista, this Loke, and then she had some guy who worked in a tax office somewhere. Both at the same time.'

'Two-timing,' muttered Ulf.

Blomquist looked disapproving. 'It's unusual to find a woman doing that, you know. Men, yes, but women ... The problem is, I suppose, that women are becoming more like men and two-timing goes with the territory. Do you think society's becoming more androgynous, Mr Varg?'

'I think so, Blomquist. But tell me: did the young men know about this situation?'

Blomquist looked amused. 'They didn't. Loke said he had no idea at all until a girlfriend of Signe's told him. She came specially to see him and gave him the news.' He paused. 'And she told the other boy too.'

163

Ulf asked who the informant was.

'It was the girl in the photograph with the guy who didn't exist,' said Blomquist. 'Quite a coincidence, wouldn't you agree, but that's who it was.'

CHAPTER THIRTEEN

Pericarditis

The soldier at the barracks gate, unpersuaded by Ulf's official identity card, insisted on searching the Saab.

'Nice old car,' he said as he rummaged around in the glove compartment. 'Not the sort of car a terrorist drives.'

Ulf smiled good-naturedly. 'Well, if you aren't allowed to profile people, then how about profiling their cars?'

The soldier grinned. 'Impossible. No profiling in any circumstances. Those are the orders.'

'Including police officers?'

'Yes, including police officers. You see, I can tell that you're not a terrorist wanting to blow us up, but I might be wrong, mightn't I? So it's best for me not to trust my instincts.'

Ulf agreed that this was so. But as he got back into the Saab, now declared safe after its cursory examination by the soldier, he thought: what has happened to trust? What sort of place have we become? They were painful questions, and for that reason people avoided asking them. And he would be no exception. He had a job to do and he would do it, correctly, and, in so far as he could, with compassion. The rest would have to be left to History, whatever History was. Was it what people used to call God, or Providence, or even Fate – all of which were, by their very nature, unquestionable by mortals, and certainly by any member of the Sensitive Crimes Department of the Malmö Criminal Investigation Authority? Even Mr Ahlbörg, the Commissioner, on his distant Parnassus, had to carry out the unfathomable will of those above him, in their remote fastness in Stockholm; and they, in spite of all their power and authority, had to heed the diktats of even higher authorities in Brussels and at the European Court in Luxembourg. Under such structures, immense and unchallengeable, he thought, we live our small lives, doing the routine things we are expected to do, trying to convince ourselves that we are in control of our destiny and that our views count for something. And if it was like that for him, then how much worse was it for somebody like Blomquist, several steps below him in the hierarchy, or for Martin, even lower still, in that layer of society occupied by dogs, where obedience to a human master is all and where freedom is rationed or excluded. Martin . . . He was making good progress now, and Mrs Högfors had reported positively on her latest walks with him. He had chased some prematurely fallen leaves with what had struck her as real interest; prematurely, because the autumn was a long way away still; there was still light, and warmth and the things that dogs appreciated.

Ulf smiled as he parked the Saab. He had much to be grateful for, in spite of his limited freedom, in spite of being a small part of a great and complex machine. Not the least thing to be grateful for was the fact that he was who he was, living where he was: he was

Swedish, at a time in history when there were many worse things to be than to be Swedish; and even if there was a small number of people who would happily blow him up simply for being Swedish, then there were many, elsewhere, who lived their lives under the threat of whole armies, with generals and air forces, and all their costly and destructive paraphernalia directed against them. The misfortune of others, thought Ulf, is our misfortune too – its ripples spread a long way, touch the lives of all of us.

A sign at the edge of the car park said *Commandant's Office*. Ulf went in the direction indicated, past an ordered flowerbed, the plants laid out in neat rows by a military-minded gardener – but with weeds pressing in from the edge, Ulf noted. Then, beyond the flowerbed, was a circle of stone from which sprouted two flagpoles, at the top of one of which was the Swedish flag, and of the other a regimental flag of some sort – private symbols of soldierly association: a bugle, a drum, a lance. The flagpoles had been white, but were no longer: here and there the paint had blistered, exposing the dark wood below.

Then Ulf was at the office, a square, impassive building of three storeys, built in an indeterminate period, in front of which various official-looking cars, gleaming and beflagged, were parked. The colonel did not keep him waiting, and within a few minutes of his arrival, a smartly attired female corporal, her skirt pressed in starched lines, her two chevrons of rank golden and gleaming, ushered him into a large office at the front of the building.

This was the office of Colonel Bååt Püke Téörnflychte, commanding officer of the Carl XII Gustav Infantry and Semi-Mechanised Base, aristocrat, bon viveur, and decorated veteran of several NATO peacekeeping ventures in the Balkans, Afghanistan and elsewhere. The colonel, a man in his mid-fifties, was at the height of his career; he was not interested in being a general, as that would have too seriously restricted his ability to pursue his other interests, and would have resulted, too, in excessive scrutiny of how he discharged his duties. Being a colonel was just right: he could run the base as he wished, surrounded by the genial and supportive company of the officers' mess, with plenty of time for the parties and official receptions in which he took such delight. Life was quiet, and comfortable, and he wanted to keep it that way. Of course, every so often one of the men went off and did something stupid – committed a crime involving a civilian, or something of that sort – and would need to be dealt with outside the framework of military discipline. Those cases were distasteful, as they involved the civilian police authorities, and that, he thought, as he greeted Ulf in his office, was what this detective had come about. A murder, perhaps? Or could it be something involving those missing stores of dynamite? The colonel had been concerned right from the beginning that those could end up in the wrong hands – a safebreaker's, perhaps – and that would lead to all sorts of questions about security. Perhaps that was what brought this . . . what was he called? Ulf Varg – unlikely name – to his office. We would see.

The colonel came from behind his desk to shake Ulf's hand. He led him to the side of the room where two easy chairs had been placed on either side of a table. The table bore copies of various foreign military magazines and armament catalogues: *High Tech Weaponry*, cheek by jowl with *The Modern Infantryman* and *Special Forces Review*.

He saw Ulf's eye fall on the magazines.

'Light reading, hah!' said the colonel.

Ulf pointed to *High Tech Weaponry*. 'I suppose everything is pretty complicated these days.'

The colonel spoke in an elaborate, plummy drawl. It was not an accent one heard very often, thought Ulf. It was as if it had been dredged up from a black-and-white film of the thirties. 'Immensely,' he said. 'The days of simply pulling the trigger are over, hah! We have to read the instruction manual every time we fire a shot.'

'I was reading that the battles of the future will be fought by electronic proxies,' said Ulf. 'Drones and robots – that sort of thing.'

The colonel gave a toss of his head. 'I read something similar myself, somewhere or other. That won't leave much for fellows like me to do, hah!'

He looked at Ulf pointedly, as if challenging him to disagree. Ulf returned the stare, noting the colonel's very light blue eyes, and his unusually pink face. Drink, he thought. Food. Other things.

The colonel was clearly not one to beat about the bush. 'I assume, Mr Varg, that you are here about one of the men doing something or other. Let me apologise in advance: we try to choose our men very carefully, and by and large we make the right choices. But these days . . . ' He shrugged. 'You'll know what I mean – we don't have the choice that we used to have. Young men don't fancy the military life.'

'Of course the reintroduction of national service will make a difference,' said Ulf.

The colonel made an equivocating gesture. 'We'll see,' he said. 'I don't look forward to getting today's eighteen-year-olds. Look at them, Mr Varg, just look at them. Scruffy bunch, hah! High on drugs and electronic gizmos in equal measure.'

'I'm sure you'll be able to lick them into shape.'

'We'll have a go. But, frankly, I'm not sure if it'll be worth it.

In the old days, everything worked very well because our young men were tough, Mr Varg. We – that's the officers – handed them over to our senior NCOs and let them get on with it. We officers had a somewhat better life in those days, I can tell you. When I was a subaltern, I went to a party every single night, would you believe it? Marvellous parties – bags of girls, champagne flowed like water – and lots of time for watching polo or whatever. Some of us raced vintage cars. My old mess had a Bugatti that we took in turns to take to various rallies. We went down to Belgium once, Mr Varg – raced her there on some God-awful track. Dreadful circuit. You ever been to Belgium, Mr Varg?'

Ulf nodded. 'Yes, but not for some time.'

'Dreadfully dull place, hah! But wonderful food. Lashings of it. Oysters, lobsters, hundreds of different varieties of pâté. Useless forces, of course, but I gather their army catering corps is second to none. Soldiers all overweight as a result. The Belgian army can't run to save their lives, I believe. They'd resist an invasion for five minutes and then it would be time for lunch and game over, hah!'

'It's not about one of your men,' Ulf said. 'Or at least, it's not about one of your men causing trouble for civilians.'

The colonel looked puzzled. 'So, what is it, then?' He stopped. 'I'm sorry, that sounded impatient. I was just wondering.'

Ulf took his notebook out of his pocket. There was nothing in it that was relevant to what he had to say, but it gave him a sense of psychological security to have the familiar leather cover between his fingers. 'I believe you have community service clients working here.'

The colonel stared at him. 'Clients?'

'That's what the social workers call them,' said Ulf.

The colonel's face reddened. 'Clients? Hah! Criminals, you mean.'

170

Varg smiled. 'You could call them that. I wouldn't dissent. After all, they have done something criminal in order to get here.'

'Exactly,' said the colonel. 'Robbery. Fraud. Drunken assault, sexual hanky-panky … You won't find my men doing much of that, but these low-grade characters they send us – hah! I'll tell you something, Mr Varg – some of these characters are real pond life. We've got five or six at the moment, and one of them, would you believe it, actually stabbed some poor fellow in the back of the knee. The back of the knee, hah! What a cowardly thing to do! If you stab somebody, I always say, never do it in the back. Do it in the front, like a man!'

Ulf remained silent.

'I've sorted that chap out, I can tell you.' The colonel lowered his voice. 'I can trust you to be discreet, Mr Varg, can't I? And we're on the same side, I assume – law and order, you know what I mean. Stability … This fellow who stabbed the other fellow in the back of the knee is hardly fit for society, in my view. Wouldn't be missed, so to speak – like a lot of the riff-raff we come across.' The colonel grinned. 'So I thought up a terrific assignment for him. Just the ticket for a chap like him.'

Ulf spoke carefully. He tried to smile. 'What exactly is it, Colonel?'

The colonel smiled. 'Can't tell you, I'm afraid. Hush-hush stuff. Terribly sorry, but I can't tell you – you not being army, you see.'

Ulf did not react. He sat back in his chair and gazed at the pictures on the walls. There were photographs of the colonel against varied backdrops. He was in the desert, his head sticking up out of an armoured personnel carrier. He was sitting on a tree trunk in a jungle somewhere, his shirt stuck to him with perspiration. There were several photographs of the colonel playing polo, and one in

171

which he was even wielding a cricket bat. 'You people do get about, don't you?'

'That's one of the perks,' said the colonel. 'We certainly see the world.'

There was another photograph that caught Ulf's attention. This was of the colonel in what looked like an army mess. There were cases on the wall displaying large silver trophies; there were officers standing in front of a bar, a glass in each hand.

'And I gather that some of your messes have very fine chefs,' remarked Ulf.

The colonel suddenly became animated. 'They certainly do. We have one of the best officers' messes in the country right here. I'm actually President of the Mess Committee. I rather pride myself on our standards.'

Ulf waited for a moment or two. Then he said, 'So lunch can be quite an affair, I suppose.'

The colonel rose to the bait. 'Lunch? My goodness, it can be pretty good.' He paused, glancing at his watch before continuing, 'You wouldn't fancy a bite to eat, would you? They'll be serving lunch in a few minutes and I'm feeling slightly peckish, truth to tell.'

Ulf replied immediately. 'That's very civil of you, Colonel.'

'I believe that our cook has been experimenting with rack of lamb,' the colonel said. 'Fancy trying that?'

'I love lamb,' said Ulf.

'Good. Well, let's make our way over to the mess and see what's going on. We can talk over lunch, of course.' He looked inquisitively at Ulf. 'What did you want to discuss, by the way?'

Ulf shrugged. 'Nothing in particular,' he said. Behind his back he crossed the index finger and forefinger of his right hand. It was a childish thing to do – he had always done that as a boy when he told a lie. Some old habits die hard; some not at all. 'I'm just interested in seeing how your end of community service works.'

'Good,' said the colonel. 'I can show you some of what we do, even if I can't show you the lot. The hush-hush stuff remains under wraps, I'm afraid.'

'Of course,' said Ulf. 'But there are plenty of other things we can discuss.'

'Of course there are,' said the colonel. 'Do you play polo by any chance?'

Ulf crossed a finger again. 'No, but I'm very interested in it.'

'Are you now?' said the colonel. 'That's wonderful. We can talk a bit about that too.'

'I look forward to it,' said Ulf – and crossed his fingers once more.

'You know something,' said the colonel. 'Polo is beginning to catch on in Russia.' He shook his head in disapproval. 'Mind you, they're the most dreadful cheats – they really are. No sense of fair play – none at all.'

They left the colonel's office and walked a short distance to a low-roofed building on the other side of the parade ground. Two miniature cannons, knee-height and made of polished brass, stood on either side of the front door.

'Those don't work,' said the colonel, pointing to the cannons. 'But we love them. The regiment stole them from the Germans at the end of the war. Hah!'

Inside, a uniformed attendant spirited Ulf's overcoat off to an unseen cloakroom. Then the colonel led him into a large rectangular dining room down the middle of which a polished mahogany table ran from one end of the room to the other. This was laid

173

with six places at the far end – gleaming silver, starched white table napkins and glittering crystal.

Once seated, the colonel showed Ulf the printed menu. *Officers' Mess*, it was headed. Beneath the heading the menu read: *Lunch, Wednesday: Potage d'Asperges; Rack of Lamb with Rosemary and Red Wine Sauce; Tiramisu; Coffee and Petits Fours.*

The colonel nodded towards the menu. 'You see?' he said. 'I told you we'd get a very good lunch.' He reached for a small bell in the middle of the table and rang it. 'This will summon the steward,' he said. 'He will bring us a bottle of wine. Any preference?'

Ulf, who never drank at lunchtime, demurred. 'A very small glass for me,' he said. 'Whatever you choose, but I'm driving.'

'All the more for me,' the colonel said cheerfully. 'I have only to get myself to the other side of the parade ground. Not difficult. Hah!'

The steward appeared and the colonel ordered a bottle of Medoc. 'Goes well with lamb, I'd say, wouldn't you?'

'Yes,' said Ulf. 'You can't go wrong with Medoc.'

'No,' said the colonel. *'Bordeaux, toujours Bordeaux,* I always say.'

When the steward appeared with the opened bottle of wine, the colonel gestured for Ulf to be served first and then took the bottle from the steward and filled his own glass up to the rim. Toasts were made and the meal began.

The colonel had drained his first glass of Medoc by the end of the soup course. He replenished his glass and downed that too before the rack of lamb arrived. That required a third glass, but given the voluminous nature of the crystal glasses, the bottle was now virtually empty.

'Please don't hold back,' said Ulf politely. 'Would you allow me to buy the next bottle?'

174

'Absolutely not,' said the colonel. 'That's against mess rules. I'll sign for everything.'

The steward was summoned and another bottle of Medoc appeared. By this stage, the colonel's face had turned from pink to red. His speech was still quite clear, but seemed to have loosened up considerably. He was now talking about other NATO powers and was giving Ulf his assessment of their capacities. 'The French aren't bad,' he said. 'And some of them are pretty good. But they're difficult soldiers to command. Dreadful. Constantly complaining and making strange noises of disagreement – *bof* and *pouf* and so on – when you give them an order. They also gesture a lot. Watch them marching. They gesture a lot with their hands while they march. Very odd.

'Of course, they have their Foreign Legion. I visited them down in Corsica once – Camp Raffalli, just outside a place called Calvi. Full of bandits and desperadoes from all over. They give them false names when they sign up. But they're pretty effective. You put a platoon of legionnaires in somewhere and – *pouf* – trouble over: opposition all dealt with. Just like that. Pretty effective. Rather like the Gurkhas that the British use. They frighten the wits out of the other side with those kukris of theirs.'

The colonel took another large mouthful of wine. 'Now, the Italians. Oh dear, such charming people, mostly – apart from the thirty-three per cent of the population engaged in organised crime. Lots of style, and fantastic uniforms – really very smart. Even their carabinieri are dressed every bit as smartly as our generals, if not even more so. Wonderful chaps to have on show but a bit flaky when it comes to the business. Their heart isn't really in it, you see. The Italian army loves sitting about drinking cappuccinos. Their Alpini, of course, have those wonderful hats with feathers in them.

I envy them that. That must give the Russians something to think about, I'd say.'

And so it continued. After they had eaten their rack of lamb and were waiting for the tiramisu, Ulf decided the moment was ripe to continue his inquiry.

'These people you get for community service,' he said. 'These . . . '

'Riff-raff,' said the colonel, now beginning to slur his words. 'Yes, what about them?'

'You mentioned somebody who had been convicted of stabbing someone in the back of the knee.'

'Yes,' said the colonel. 'Very short fellow. You could trip over him if you weren't watching your step. Ridiculous.' He paused. 'I wish I could tell you what I have planned for him.'

'You could, you know,' said Ulf.

The colonel shook his head, and then tapped the side of his nose in a gesture of confidentiality. 'Sorry. No can do.'

'But I'm a serving officer of the Department of Sensitive Crimes,' said Ulf quietly. 'We're very careful about confidentiality, you know.'

The colonel looked thoughtful. 'I suppose you're a sympa-thiser,' he said.

'Naturally,' said Ulf, wondering what it was he was expected to sympathise with.

'You see we should stop handling these people with kid gloves,' said the colonel.

'Absolutely,' said Ulf.

The colonel leaned towards him. Ulf noticed that his nose was now almost glowing, small red blood vessels being visible on the sides of the nostrils. Yet he still seemed hesitant, and Ulf decided to pour him another glass of wine.

'Very fine Medoc, this,' said the colonel appreciatively.

'This community service man,' Ulf prompted.

'Oh, him. Yes, well, I've got a little surprise for him,' said the colonel. He laughed. 'His community service should go with a bang, I'd say. Hah!'

Ulf waited.

The colonel took another sip of his wine. 'Bomb disposal,' he whispered. 'I've put him on bomb-disposal duty. How's that? That'll teach him to stab people in the ankle.'

'Knee,' said Ulf.

'Yes, knee – wherever. The point is that a few days in bomb disposal will sort him out.' The colonel reached for his glass. 'I had a very good man in bomb disposal, but he lost his nerve and asked for a transfer. I gave it to him because I thought he deserved a change. But when I looked around for volunteers, nobody else stepped forward. Not a soul, which shows what the country has become, I'm afraid. Then I thought: this nasty piece of work, this knee-stabber would be ideal. So that's where he's going. Hah!'

'But he's had no training,' Ulf pointed out. 'Bomb disposal is a very skilled business, isn't it?'

'A bit,' said the colonel. 'But we have pretty good manuals, you know. He can read up before he tries his luck.'

Ulf sat back in his chair. 'I don't think you should do it,' he said. 'You can't put innocent civilians into bomb-disposal units.'

'Innocent?' the colonel retorted.

'Or guilty,' said Ulf evenly. 'They're still civilians.'

'Nonsense,' said the colonel. 'It'll do him good. And frankly who cares if he blows himself up? Serve him right.'

Ulf persisted. 'No, Colonel, you shall not do it.'

The colonel stared at Ulf. The earlier bonhomie of the lunch seemed to evaporate. 'Excuse me, Mr Varg, you are not in command here. I am. Now, how about some tiramisu?'

'No thank you,' said Ulf. 'But in respect of this man, you are not to expose him to any danger. Give him a job peeling potatoes or painting things. And if you don't, I shall report you. I shall report you for recklessly endangering life. You said it yourself – your own words. You said you were happy for him to blow himself up.'

'Report me?' said the colonel, his voice rising – unsteadily. 'I am a serving officer of His Majesty's forces – who will believe your word rather than mine?'

Ulf smiled. 'A tape recording might help,' he said. And with that he withdrew the small recording-pen device tucked into his top pocket. 'It makes very good recordings,' he said. 'And it was very silly of me to leave it on. I must remind myself to turn it off – I really must.'

The colonel stared at him for a moment, and then broke into a grin. 'Fair enough,' he said. 'I'll put him in the kitchens.'

'Thank you,' said Ulf.

'Not at all,' said the colonel. 'Now, did I ever tell you about a month I spent on secondment in northern India? Those Indian army messes are superb – just superb. Tiger heads on the wall. Fantastic curries; kedgeree for breakfast and so on. Most agreeable company and remarkable horsemen. They have some camel-mounted units too, you know. They look marvellous, with their long lances decorated with flags. Wonderful, quite wonderful.'

When he left the base, Ulf telephoned ahead to suggest to Anna that as his return to the office would more or less coincide with the afternoon coffee break, they should meet in the café before he came up to the office. She agreed: he had left her a message about Blomquist's revelations, and she was keen to discuss this with him.

'This case is getting no simpler,' she said over the phone. 'I'd like your input.'

'Sometimes the most complicated cases are in reality the simplest,' said Ulf.

There was a brief silence. 'The most complicated . . .' she began, and then, 'Ulf, what exactly does that mean?'

Ulf was not sure. 'That's the point,' he said. 'Meaning is not always apparent.'

He drove back, parked the Saab, and made his way to the café. It was not busy, and he was able to get his preferred table at the window. He felt proprietorial about that table, resenting those who were sitting at it when he came in, as if they had no right to be there. That feeling, though, amused him, as might any unjustified conviction or sense of entitlement. Tables in cafés were common property and nobody had a greater right than anyone else to occupy them; and yet, and yet . . . there were subtleties in the claiming of space; we staked out our territory on beaches, small squares of sand to which we felt entitled to return after our swim; we created all sorts of unseen boundaries, temporary and informal, by leaving our possessions on seats and benches – a jacket left on a chair made a claim every bit as specific and discouraging as a notice of legal title. This is *mine* – I'm coming back. Don't think of sitting here.

Anna arrived five minutes later. 'Good,' she said. 'You've got our table.'

Ulf told her he had just been thinking of that. 'It's not really ours,' he said.

'It should be,' said Anna. 'We've been coming here for years.'

Ulf looked out of the window. 'Possession,' he mused. 'Don't

179

they say that possession is what counts?' He transferred his gaze to Anna. 'So, who owns Sweden?'

'I don't know what you mean.'

'The people who owned it in the past, or the people who are here right now?'

She looked at him cautiously. 'Nobody likes to talk about that, do they?'

He agreed – they did not. 'I think it's a mixture,' he said. 'The past has its claims, but it has to recognise that there's a different present.'

'And behave in a civilised manner?'

Ulf nodded. 'Precisely.'

'Behave Swedishly?'

Ulf laughed. 'Exactly. Behave Swedishly.'

'Which involves?'

That was difficult, thought Ulf. And yet he knew what Swedish behaviour was, and could recognise it when he saw it. 'Being civil to other people, I suppose.'

Anna became businesslike. Social philosophy was all very well, but there was a job to be done. 'And that leads me to the matter in hand,' said Anna. 'Blomquist's information.'

Ulf asked her what she felt. Did the fact that Bim had betrayed Signe to her two boyfriends make a difference to her view of the case?

Anna frowned. 'Two boyfriends . . . What's she thinking of?'

Ulf shrugged. 'I've never understood how people can do that. Or *why* they should want to.'

'Variety,' said Anna. 'You get fed up with somebody but you don't want to end things with him. Somebody else comes along who makes you feel good. It's understandable, I think.'

'But would you do that yourself?' asked Ulf. The question came out spontaneously, and he immediately regretted it. She could always take his question the wrong way – as an invitation, or suggestion – in spite of their conversation of a few days ago.

She did not, and Ulf felt relieved. 'I wouldn't,' she said. 'But then, most people say they won't do things … until they do them.' She looked at him, and for a few moments they held each other's gaze.

Ulf felt he had to bring the moment to an end. He was about to say what he thought he would not say, and so he had to stop. 'Give me your thoughts,' he said, 'about what's been going on. If Bim has—'

She held up a hand. 'Hold on, let's look at it in terms of who wants what. Or rather, what we *think* people want.'

'Then reverse it,' suggested Ulf. 'Because often what we think people want turns out to be the opposite of what they actually want.'

'Or, indeed, who they are in the first place – just in case we're looking in the wrong place.'

Ulf reflected on this – Anna was right. When Blomquist had first mentioned Bim's role, he had immediately thought that this provided a clue to Signe's disappearance. They knew nothing about these boyfriends, but if a young woman disappeared, the first person whom one might wish to interview was usually the boyfriend, especially if, as in this case, the couple had become estranged. Here, of course, there were two young men who might feel strong resentment against Signe, and in Ulf's view if anything had happened to her, then they would be prime suspects.

He suggested this to Anna. 'The two boyfriends – what do you think?'

'Possible,' she said. 'Remember that case we had three years ago

181

when that make-up artist went missing and was eventually found up north ...'

'... under the permafrost.'

'Yes, under the permafrost,' said Anna. 'That was the boy-friend's doing, wasn't it? He worked up at the research station. He discovered she was having an affair with that television producer – the wildlife man, the one who made that film about the reindeer.'

Ulf remembered the case well. He had spent two weeks up north, accompanied by Carl on that occasion as Anna could not leave the children back in Malmö. He remembered the digging – the sound of pneumatic drills hammering away against the silence of the tundra, and then the discovery, and the thought that always occurred to him in such circumstances that this was the moment when the end of somebody's world was confirmed: not the world of the victim so much as the world of those left behind, the relatives. It defeated him that anybody could ever bring such a result about if they knew, or could imagine, the heartbreak of the victim's family. Of course the people who did these things were usually deficient in moral imagi-nation – they could not see what it would be like because they simply lacked the capacity to do so. Expecting them to understand – and to empathise – was like expecting a blind person to see a rainbow.

Ulf signalled to the waitress to take their order. 'So you think we should bring those young men in?'

'Yes,' said Anna. 'We'll need to get Blomquist to give us the details. Did he tell you which coffee bar one of them works in?'

Ulf said that he had not. 'Blomquist likes to keep things to himself. I think he resents being excluded from the investigation.'

'But it's none of his business,' Anna pointed out.

Ulf said that Blomquist did not see it that way. 'I think he feels frustrated. He's tried twice to get into the Criminal Investigation

Authority but was refused on both occasions. Somebody said they thought he was dyslexic.'

'That shouldn't be a bar these days.'

'No,' said Ulf. 'You'd think not. But I was told that on his application, he wrote that he wanted to get into the AIC rather than the CIA. I suspect that didn't help.'

Anna smiled. 'Poor Blomquist.' She looked at her watch. 'Could we get him to come in here – if he's free?'

'Can't do any harm,' said Ulf, taking his phone out of his pocket. As he dialled the number he told Anna about the results of his visit to the colonel.

'Hampus is off bomb-disposal duty,' he said. 'And I don't think the colonel will try that one again in a hurry – thanks to my recording pen.'

Anna was surprised. 'You have a recording pen?'

Blomquist's phone was ringing. Ulf took his pen out of his breast pocket and showed it to her.

'Where are the controls?' she asked. 'How do you play something back?'

Ulf smiled as he took the pen back from her. 'You don't,' he said. 'It can't record at all.' He paused, slipping the pen back into his pocket. 'Not that the colonel was to know that.'

'Hah!' said Anna.

'That's what the colonel kept saying. It was a pronounced mannerism he had.'

'I hope I don't say *hah* too much,' said Anna. 'You'd tell me if I did, wouldn't you?'

Ulf reassured her that he would notify her of any irritating mannerism, but that he felt she very rarely said *hah*. Anna thanked him. 'It's good that we can talk so freely,' she said.

'Yes, it is.' But he thought: I can speak freely to you about everything, except the one thing that is really important. I can't speak to you about that. I can't tell you how I feel about you because I cannot allow myself to feel that way. That is forever closed to me. Forever.

Blomquist blew over his coffee. 'Too hot,' he said. 'These people always serve their coffee far too hot. It's bad for the lining of the stomach.'

'You're right, Blomquist,' said Ulf. 'I find I get heartburn if I drink things too hot.'

'Heartburn is very unpleasant,' said Blomquist. 'Mind you, did I tell you what happened to me four or five months ago?'

Ulf began to say that perhaps some other time, but Blomquist had already started.

'I woke up,' he began. 'It was about midnight, I think. No, hold on, it was more like one in the morning, maybe even a bit later. My wife is a very sound sleeper – she'll sleep through a thunderstorm right overhead – and I didn't wake her up. But what a pain I had in my chest – somewhere there, over the sternum. I had some of those antacid tablets, and I took one; maybe even two, I forget, but it made no difference.

'It was worse when I lay down, and so I spent the rest of the night – morning, actually – sitting in a chair in the living room. Eventually, at six or so, I realised that this wasn't going away, that this wasn't heartburn. So I woke up my wife and she drove me to the emergency department up at the hospital. They took one look at me and I could see they thought: heart attack. So they hooked me up to an ECG machine, and you know the result? They said the pattern was typical of classic pericarditis. You know what that is? Pericarditis?'

184

Anna said that Jo had explained it once, but she had forgotten what he'd said. One of his colleagues had it, he said.

'Well, it's inflammation of the pericardium,' said Blomquist. 'It's caused by a virus in most cases. You breathe it in or it's on food or whatever, and it goes to the pericardium. An anti-inflammatory relieves it. They gave me that and I was fine. But I was told not to exert myself for six weeks.' He paused. 'That's pericarditis for you.'

Ulf and Anna stared at Blomquist, who stared back at them.

Eventually Ulf said, 'Most unpleasant.'

'Yes,' said Anna. 'I'm glad you recovered, Blomquist.'

'That young barista you spoke to,' Ulf said. 'I think we should have a word with him.'

Blomquist took a tentative sip of his still-steaming coffee. 'Why?'

Ulf resisted the temptation to tell the policeman that it was not for him to question the direction of an investigation being carried out by the Sensitive Crimes Department.

'Because we think he – or the other boyfriend – could have a motive for harming Signe. One of them may have something to do with her disappearance.'

Blomquist considered this for a few moments, and then shook his head. 'No,' he said. 'It won't be one of them. Or certainly not the barista.'

'How can you be so sure?' asked Anna.

'Because of the way he told me,' answered Blomquist. 'If he had done something to her, he wouldn't have volunteered the information. He knows I'm in the force; I often go in there in my uniform.'

Blomquist waited for them to absorb this before he continued, 'If you would like my opinion, that young woman has disappeared of her own free will.'

'In order to put heat on Bim?' prompted Ulf. 'Bim told her boyfriends of her two-timing. She had a score to settle with her.'

'But Bim had a score to settle with *her* too,' Anna interjected.

'Yes,' said Blomquist. 'Both of them would love to do something to get the other into trouble.'

'So which one did it?' asked Ulf. 'Bim or Signe?'

Blomquist shook his head. 'That's too binary. There's another factor in the equation.'

Anna looked unconvinced. 'What?'

'Linnea, the girl who reported it.'

Ulf had not anticipated this. 'Why did she get involved?'

'Because of something the barista told me.'

Ulf and Anna were silent as they waited for Blomquist to explain.

'He said to me that he used to go out with Linnea – before he became a member of Signe's stable. I had the impression that Signe had prised him away from Linnea.'

Ulf was listening intently. 'And she – Linnea – didn't like that?'

'Presumably,' said Blomquist. 'Who would?'

'So Linnea had a grudge against Signe, and Bim and Signe had a grudge against each other?'

Blomquist took another sip of his coffee. 'That's a bit cooler now. You know, one of these days somebody's going to scald their tongue and make a big song and dance about it.' He took another sip. 'Grudges? Yes. Definitely.'

It took a bit of effort on Ulf's part, but he felt they needed to know what Blomquist would do. 'So who should we speak to, Blomquist?'

'Linnea,' said Blomquist, without hesitation. 'Because she's the one who's been hoping that we would take action against Signe when she turns up. She's hoping, I imagine, that

Signe will be punished for wasting police time with her non-disappearance.'

Ulf and Anna spoke in perfect unison. 'Non-disappearance?'

'That girl's around,' said Blomquist. 'She's just pretending to disappear. She'll be staying with Linnea, I imagine, because she – Signe – may have no idea that Linnea has a grudge against her. Of course they may both be enjoying the spectacle of Bim being investigated by us. *Schadenfreude*, as the Germans call it.'

'You really think Signe will be with Linnea?' asked Anna. 'Isn't that just a bit too predictable?'

Blomquist shrugged. 'When you do what I do,' he said, 'you get used to the predictable. Everything I see, more or less, is predictable. You might not see that in your position ...' He looked at them challengingly. 'But it's often clear to me. Often.'

They stood outside the door of Linnea's apartment, one of a number in a block of student dwellings. *Ek* proclaimed a piece of cardboard in the name slot outside. Ulf rang the bell, glancing at Anna and Blomquist as he did so. He was eager to locate Signe, but he did not want to find her as a direct result of information from Blomquist.

'I suspect we're wasting our time,' he said. 'Even if the bird was here, she'll have flown the nest.'

Blomquist seemed confident. 'I doubt it,' he said.

There came the sound of a bolt being drawn inside, and the door was opened. Linnea stood before them, dressed in a kimono and wearing large sheepskin slippers. Her face fell when she saw who was standing on her doorstep.

'Ms Bengtsdotter. And ... and ...'

'We're colleagues of Ms Bengtsdotter,' said Ulf. 'Malmö Criminal Investigation Authority.'

'And police,' Blomquist added.

Linnea had regained her composure. 'I'm sorry,' she said. 'This isn't convenient. Please come some other time.'

Ulf shook his head. 'That won't be convenient for us. Sorry.'

Linnea glared at him. 'This is definitely the wrong time for me,' she said. 'It's just the wrong time. Believe me.'

'Studying?' asked Anna. 'Surely that can wait. We won't need much of your time.'

Linnea turned to her. 'No. Not studying. I've told you: this is *not* a good time.'

'You're going to have to explain,' Blomquist said. 'Tell us why we can't come in.'

Linnea drew in her breath. 'All right,' she hissed. 'Since you ask, I'll spell it out for you. I'm having sex, that's why.'

All three were taken aback, but it was Blomquist who recovered first. 'Oh yes?' he said. 'In your slippers?'

She narrowed her eyes. 'What's wrong with that? Just because you people are so . . . so *conventional*.'

Ulf had to laugh. 'Your generation thinks you invented sex,' he said.

And then Blomquist, without any warning, pushed roughly past Linnea. Taking advantage of her surprise, he walked quickly down the short corridor into the apartment's living room. Ulf called out after him. 'Blomquist, we don't have a warrant.' But it was too late.

Linnea turned to rush after him, and Anna and Ulf followed. Once in the living room, they saw that there was another person there, sitting in an easy chair, fully clothed, and looking embarrassed.

'Well, well,' said Ulf. 'Here you are, Signe.'

Blomquist turned to Linnea. 'Your partner, I take it.'

Linnea was crimson with embarrassment. 'I was only joking,' she said. 'I'm not a lesbian.'

'Who said you're a lesbian?' asked Signe. 'What do these people want?'

'We want to talk to you,' said Ulf.

Signe's surprise seemed unforced. 'Why? I've done nothing wrong.'

'Where have you been?' said Ulf.

'Here.'

'All the time?'

Signe shrugged. 'The last few days. A week probably.' She looked at Linnea. 'It's been about a week, hasn't it, Linnea?'

Linnea did not answer.

'Since you broke up with your boyfriend ... boyfriends?' asked Anna.

Signe looked down at the floor. 'Yes,' she mumbled. 'I felt I should ... get out of the way.'

'Because they were angry?' Anna pressed.

Signe took a few moments to answer. 'Yes, you could say that. But maybe also because I just couldn't face them. I felt so bad about everything.'

Ulf turned to Linnea. 'Did you talk to Signe about reporting this?'

Before Linnea could answer, Signe blurted out, 'Reporting what?'

'That you were missing,' said Ulf.

This brought an immediate reaction from Signe. 'Me? Me missing?' she exclaimed. 'I've been here all the time. I haven't been missing.'

Now they all turned to face Linnea, who had sat down heavily on a sofa, her head sunk in her hands. 'I feel very ashamed of myself,' she said. 'I didn't see it turning out like this.'

Anna exchanged glances with Ulf.

'Tell me,' Ulf said to Signe. 'Has your phone been switched off all this time?'

Signe said it had. 'I didn't want the boys to get in touch,' she said. 'I just couldn't face it.'

'And what about your parents?'

Signe made a dismissive gesture. 'They're away. They're in Japan.'

'Oh, you stupid, stupid young woman,' muttered Ulf.

'What was that? What did you call her?' said Linnea.

'Stupid,' said Blomquist, stepping up to stand within a few inches of her. 'And that's what *I* call you too. Stupid.'

Anna felt that there had been sufficient calling of names, cathartic though it had undoubtedly been. 'You're going to have to come with us, Linnea,' she said.

'And me?' asked Signe.

Ulf shook his head. 'I don't think you've done anything wrong. But if I were you, I'd phone your parents immediately. Don't worry about time zones. Just call them straight away and tell them you're fine. Explain to them why you haven't been in touch.'

'What, now?'

'Right now,' said Ulf firmly. 'This instant.'

Blomquist was staring at Linnea. 'You're a very stupid young woman,' he muttered again. 'You'll be lucky to get community service.'

Anna said, 'Let's not anticipate too much.'

'I'm just informing her. There'll be a vacancy in bomb disposal, I think.'

Ulf tried to keep a straight face. 'Possibly deserved in this case,' he said under his breath.

'Bomb disposal?' asked Linnea.

Blomquist nodded. 'You'll soon find out,' he said.

'Peeling potatoes probably,' said Ulf.

Blomquist looked disappointed. 'You'd think the army would be more enlightened about food values.'

Linnea looked confused – and miserable. 'I'm really sorry,' she said. 'I only did it because Bim asked me to.'

Ulf frowned. 'Hold on,' he said. 'Bim asked you to? Bim?'

'Yes, she wanted you to think that Signe had staged her disappearance to spite her. Then she would be arrested. She didn't think you would arrest me.'

'But you were the one who made the false report,' Blomquist pointed out.

Linnea looked away. 'Maybe,' she said. 'But Bim was the one who thought it all up.'

'This is ridiculous,' said Ulf.

Anna drew Ulf aside. 'Do we really need to take this any further?' she whispered.

Ulf hesitated. He glanced at the two young women, looking at one another in confused misery. He made up his mind. There was mercy for the guilty – at times – and mercy, too, for the plain silly.

'Listen,' he said. 'All three of you have been very foolish – to put it mildly.'

'I'd say stupid,' suggested Blomquist.

'That too,' agreed Ulf. 'But we shall draw a veil over the whole affair if we receive undertakings from all of you that this nonsense stops right here. No more going to the police with any ridiculous stories. No more squabbling over anything – and I mean, anything. Understand?'

191

They stared at him in an incomprehension that turned fairly quickly into delight.

The officers did not stay, but made their way back to the Saab. Blomquist was smiling. 'Well,' he said. 'Solved that one.'

Ulf said nothing. He was not sure that they had solved anything. In fact, he was not sure about whether they had really got to the bottom of whatever it was that they had been investigating.

'Do you feel confused?' He intended the question for Anna, but from the back seat Blomquist answered as well. Anna said, 'Yes, completely.' And Blomquist replied, 'No, not at all.'

Ulf did not take the matter further. They dropped Blomquist off at his police station and then, at Anna's request, Ulf drove her to pick up her two daughters from their swimming club, since her own car was being used by her husband. Ulf had met the girls before, and they were not inhibited in their breathless account of the afternoon's practice races. Ulf listened with only half an ear; he was thinking about the visit to Linnea's flat. There was something he had spotted, but of which he had not really taken much notice. Now it came back to him: a pair of men's shoes beside a chair. They had not really registered, but now they did. What were they doing there?

In a break in the girls' narrative, he said to Anna, 'That flat . . . '

'Yes, what about it?'

'There was a pair of shoes next to a chair.'

'Yes,' she said. 'I was going to talk to you about that. I noticed them – I wondered whether you'd seen them too.'

Ulf looked in the driving mirror. The two girls in the back seemed absorbed in a magazine. 'What do you think?' he asked.

'There were men in there.'

He gave her an enquiring look. 'Men?'

'They were two left shoes,' said Anna. 'I noticed that. I thought it a bit odd. If there were two left shoes, then there must have been two right shoes somewhere. Two pairs of shoes – four legs – two men.'

'So what were two males doing in that flat – and why were they hiding them from us?'

Anna thought the answer obvious. 'Because there was something going on,' she said. 'And they didn't want us to find out what it was.'

Ulf sighed. 'I knew it,' he said. 'I knew there was more to this case than meets the eye.'

'You're right,' said Anna. 'But I don't think there's much we can do about it – mainly because we don't know what *it* is.'

'Of course it may be none of our business,' Ulf pointed out. 'After all, we can't sort out all of the world's problems.'

'True,' said Anna. 'Our role as detectives is strictly circumscribed.'

'We're not miracle workers,' Ulf said.

'Nor avenging angels.'

They drove on. Ulf looked up at the sky. He felt a curious, indescribable happiness, and was not sure why he should feel this. Was it because he was in Anna's company – or was it because of something quite different? He could not tell, but he remembered learning, years ago, that the important thing with happiness was simply that you should feel happy; it did not matter, the philosophers said, if you did not understand the reason why you felt happy, as long as the happiness itself was there. That was all that counted.

And then he thought: what if the shoes belonged to Signe's two boyfriends? What if they'd been there, in the house, when they called round? Blomquist said he had spoken to one of them, but that was a few days ago. What role did they have in all this?

'I'm thinking of remote possibilities,' he said to Anna.

'Don't,' she said. 'Just don't.' Then she added, 'Because the remote often becomes less remote if you think about it. And that just complicates life.'

He would need to think about that, he told himself. Later. Not now.

CHAPTER FOURTEEN

Lycanthropy

The following morning, Ulf prepared to leave for the small country town in which he was due to begin his investigation into the matter with which Commissioner Ahlbörg had entrusted him. He had arrived in the office early, in order to be able to leave before ten. Carl was already there, and had been at his desk for a good hour when Ulf came in. Anna would arrive a bit later, as would Erik, who was usually last in and first to leave.

'Message for you,' said Carl. 'A motorcycle courier brought it. It must be important.'

He handed Ulf the brown envelope and watched as he opened it. 'Commissioner Ahlbörg?'

Ulf nodded. He read the handwritten letter with growing dismay. 'I know that we want to limit the number of people who know about this,' wrote the Commissioner, 'but I've been feeling a bit concerned about your undertaking this without back-up. Perhaps I'm being a bit too careful, but I feel that you should have somebody from the uniformed branch with you – just in case. Better safe than sorry is my policy, as you may already know. So I have asked somebody to be allocated to you and I understand there's an officer by the name of Blomquist who will be coming with you. Please impress on him the need for the utmost discretion. Warmest wishes, Felix Ahlbörg.'

Ulf became aware that Carl was watching him, and now his colleague's curiosity got the better of him. 'Bad news?' he asked.

Ulf crumpled the letter into a ball and tossed it into a wastepaper basket. Then, thinking better of it, he retrieved it, folded it, and tucked it into his pocket.

'No,' he replied to Carl. 'Neither here nor there.'

That was not true. The attachment of Blomquist to this otherwise intriguing and sensitive mission was not good news at all as far as Ulf was concerned. He would now have a drive of almost an hour with Blomquist going on about steroids and potato skins and all the other things he liked to talk about. And at the other end, he imagined that the policeman would want to tag along with him, offering his insights at every turn and generally making what would otherwise have been a pleasant and interesting day in the country into an irritating chore.

Carl had guessed that the letter concerned the private task that Ulf had spoken about a few days earlier and about which they had managed to extract no information at all. 'You're going off some-where today?' he asked.

Ulf nodded. 'Yes.'

Carl waited a few moments before posing his question. 'Where?'

'The country,' said Ulf tersely. 'And I'm to take Blomquist. That's what that letter was about – that's all.'

Carl raised an eyebrow. 'Blomquist?'

*

196

The traffic was light and the Saab, to which Ulf occasionally extended the compliment of having an inner life, seemed pleased to be on the road. The last time Ulf had driven the car any distance, it had developed a mysterious rattle somewhere in the engine compartment, but this seemed now to have disappeared. The part in question, he told himself, had either settled down or fallen off altogether; an old car was like an old body – various provinces of the central system revolted but could be pacified by nothing more than sympathy and a spot of oil. Many parts were superfluous to the main purpose, which was to get the chassis from one point to another; if that had to be done without operating windows or heating systems or any of the other optional extras, then so be it, and tomorrow there would be something fresh to worry about.

Blomquist was in a cheerful mood. They had been authorised to spend up to three days on the inquiry, staying at the Commissioner's cousin's spa. This was an unusual arrangement, as the acceptance of free hospitality was against departmental rules, but it had been specifically approved of by the Commissioner himself, 'given the special circumstances of this sensitive case'.

'I've never stayed at a spa before,' said Blomquist, as Ulf drove through the last vestiges of the Malmö traffic. 'I take it there'll be a gym.'

'Bound to be,' said Ulf. 'People go to these places for the sake of their health. Exercise is all part of that—'

He got no further. 'Oh, you don't have to tell me that,' Blomquist interrupted. 'I follow the High Intensity Exercise Programme. Have you heard of that?'

Ulf wished that he had not referred to health, but it was too late now. Sighing inwardly, he said, 'No, tell me about it, Blomquist.'

'Well,' said Blomquist, 'there have been a lot of studies that . . .'

Ulf allowed his mind to wander as Blomquist explained about high intensity exercise. Like Blomquist, he was pleased to get out into the country, and Abbekås, their destination, seemed like a pleasant coastal town, just short of the better-known and more popular beaches of Skåne. He knew that he would have to work, and that this was not a holiday, but the weather report was encouraging and there would be plenty of fresh air and sun. He had contemplated bringing Martin, and had established that the spa was happy to accommodate dogs, but he decided that it would be better for him to be in the familiar surroundings of Mrs Högfors' apartment while he was having his treatment. Progress had been made, and he would not want to jeopardise that with a sudden change of surroundings.

Ulf was not at all sure how he would proceed with this case. All that he knew so far was that there had been what the Commissioner called 'unfortunate incidents' at the spa, and that these had been picked up by online reviewers. It was very easy to frighten people, and apparently this had been happening. Since the incidents had started, the spa's room occupancy had tumbled and two of the staff had been laid off. He was curious about the incidents – he wondered whether these were acts of vandalism. There were so many ways one could interrupt the smooth running of a hotel and the peace of mind of the guests: interference with the hot water system, noise in the middle of the night, fights in the bar, the adulteration of food – a piece of rotten fish or meat tossed into the soup – could easily have the desired effect.

' . . . the problem with sunblock,' Blomquist was saying, 'is that if you apply too much of it, and too often, you won't absorb the necessary vitamin D. But then, if you use too little, there's the prospect of sun damage. Apparently in Australia, where there's a hole in the ozone layer, you have to be really careful. They take sun hats very seriously in schools out there – if a child doesn't take a sun hat to school, then no time in the playground. It's the only way. A friend's aunt, you know, got badly burned when she was in South America. She's normally very careful, but she forgot to put sunblock on one day and they were pretty high up where they were staying – six thousand feet, I think, and so the sun's rays at that level are particularly dangerous . . . '

South America, thought Ulf. He liked the idea of travel and had done a certain amount himself, but for some reason he had never been very far south. In fact, when he thought of where he had been, without exception his journeys were northern ones: he had, of course, been to Finland and Norway – Denmark, being just over the water, did not really count as travel in Ulf's view. And the same applied to the Baltic countries, to the countries known as the *ias* – Estonia, Latvia and Lithuania. Ulf liked Tallinn, which he viewed as a sort of eastern Sweden, and he felt that there was an unspoken bond of sympathy between those who lived in the shadow of Russia. He had been to Scotland, too, and Iceland, and, for three glorious weeks, in the second year of their marriage, he and Letta had hiked in Nepal. He remembered the thinness of the air, and the cold at night, and the sky that seemed to him to sing, it was so vast and light and, at that altitude, so close to the touch.

' . . . you see,' said Blomquist, 'what you have to watch are those areas that seem to attract the sun – your nose, for instance: you have to watch your nose. Then there are the ears. If you go to a derma-tologist and he or she – I have a lady dermatologist, you know – if he or she carries out a general inspection, then it will include the tops of the ears. Have you seen sailors? Yachtsmen, I mean, because professional sailors, merchant seamen, I mean, usually keep out

199

of the sun – but yachtsmen, take a look at their ears. No, I'm not joking, just look at the tips of their ears and you'll often see sun damage ...'

All north, thought Ulf; all north. And then there was North America – he had been there first when he was a student at Lund and he had bought a cheap ticket. But that had been to Canada, and when he got there he seemed to go north, as if drawn by instinct. He had been up to Yellowknife, where he had worked for a month as a barman, and then, with the proceeds, had gone off on a month of travels. He had been determined to see the United States, but he ended up only seeing the northern tip of it: Minnesota and Wisconsin. He had been given a good welcome there, because of the Scandinavian population of those northern states, but before he knew it he had been obliged to return home. So he never got to New Orleans, as he had hoped to do, because north had claimed him once again. One day he would go. South America. Perhaps India, or even Australia, where he had a distant female cousin who lived in Darwin and who had once turned up in Malmö and invited him to visit her in the friendly way of Australians. 'Stay as long as you like,' the cousin had said. 'In fact, stay for the rest of your life – lots of people do. They never go home.' What would that be like, he wondered. Warmth. Sun. He would have to be careful about sun exposure, of course, as Blomquist had said ... And other things too. He had asked the cousin about crocodiles, and she had replied that they did have them around Darwin but that she had very rarely seen one in the wild, although they had once been on a picnic and there had been one in the river and they had all moved well away from the bank, just to be safe. She had a friend, she said, who knew somebody who had almost been eaten by a saltwater crocodile, but he had been drunk at the time and it was often the case that people who fell foul of crocodiles had drunk too much at the time of the incident.

'Crocodiles,' he suddenly said.

Blomquist, who had been talking about the danger of tanning salons, was arrested mid-sentence. 'Crocodiles?'

'Yes,' said Ulf, 'I was just thinking. You were talking about sun, weren't you? Or at least you were a few minutes ago, and I thought about crocodiles. Have you ever seen a crocodile, Blomquist?'

'In a zoo,' Blomquist replied. 'Just lying there. He was doing nothing particular. You know, they're cold-blooded – I think – and they need sun to get them going. Apparently, if they're cold they can't harm you very much, although, frankly, I wouldn't care to test that, would you? What about a wolf? Have you seen a wolf, Mr Varg?'

'No. Not really.'

'Well, we don't get them down where we are,' said Blomquist. 'They're up near that place, what's it called? Skinnskatteberg. Apparently, there are about three hundred wolves in Sweden, which isn't bad, bearing in mind there were none about fifty years ago. People are odd about wolves, aren't they? Do you know that dogs are descendants of wolves – all dogs, even those ridiculous little dogs you see in the parks. Wolves. Imagine how embarrassed a real wolf would be if he knew that he was cousin to a shih-tzu? Of course, we shouldn't think animals have feelings like us – I don't think they can be embarrassed, do you? My daughter's cat is incapable of feeling anything very much, I can tell you – and certainly not embarrassment . . . '

Ulf looked at his watch. The miles were passing, but in a strange cloud of facts and warnings and unilateral, unanswered observations. What would it be like, he wondered, to do a long train

201

journey with Blomquist – say, on the Trans-Siberian Express, or one of those trains that cross Canada? Day after day of Blomquist on every conceivable subject . . .

He thought of Blomquist's wife: how would she have greeted the news that he was to be away for up to three days? With relief, he imagined. He smiled privately. But then he reminded himself that Blomquist had somebody who loved him, and who presumably appreciated him for what he was – a loyal, good husband, who provided for his family without complaint. Mrs Blomquist would be proud of him, he thought, and she would attribute his lack of promotion so far to the fact that his superiors did not understand him, or to jealousies within the force, or something of that nature. Our shining heroes are never held back by their own limitations; it is usually the work of others.

The spa sat in its own large grounds off the main road into Abbekås. The town was only a short walk away, but a feeling of rural tranquillity had been encouraged by stands of birch trees planted by a previous owner. These trees not only masked the buildings from the road and from neighbours, but also provided a haven for colonies of small birds. As Ulf parked the Saab, the sound of birdsong could be heard coming from the birch trees, while from somewhere inside, music – Mozart, he thought – drifted across a wide, carefully trimmed lawn. There was a cluster of deckchairs in the centre of this lawn, draped with towels, but unoccupied, it seemed, by any of the spa's guests.

Their arrival had been observed from the main building, a sprawling red-roofed construction with the air of a domestic house that had been extended in a haphazard way by a series of owners. A door opened, and a man in white trousers and a green, open-neck

202

shirt strode out to greet them. This was Baltser Björkman, proprietor of the spa and husband of Angel. Baltser was a man in his early fifties, fourteen years the senior of Angel, who now followed him out onto the lawn to greet the visitors.

'Felix told me you were coming, Mr Varg,' said Baltser after he had shaken hands with Ulf. 'And your colleague, of course, Mr . . . '

'Blomquist,' said Blomquist.

Baltser smiled. 'Of course, of course.'

Angel joined them. As introductions were made, Ulf glanced appraisingly at her, wondering how it was that these two had ended up together. It was a line of thought that often occurred to him when he met couples. Sometimes it was obvious enough why one person married another: identity of interest, similarity of background – factors of that sort explained a great deal of mutual human attraction. Ulf had also observed that people often went for somebody who looked like them. This conclusion would surprise many, he believed, but every time he put it to the test, it seemed to be confirmed. And then Dr Svensson himself had supported the theory with chapter and verse from one of his professional journals in which an article on the subject had appeared. Finnish researchers, Dr Svensson revealed, had examined extensive collections of wedding photographs going back decades and had concluded that the parties often looked remarkably similar. Tall, dark-haired men married tall, dark-haired women; people with prominent cheekbones chose those with a similar feature; noses were attracted by noses of a similar shape – and so on.

Ulf had been interested to discover that his own observations appeared to be borne out by empirical research, although when he mentioned this conversation to Carl and Anna, they had been unimpressed.

'I don't look at all like my wife,' said Carl. 'She looks very different.'

'That's because she's a woman,' remarked Anna dryly. 'By and large, though not always, men tend to marry people who look like women.'

'You know what I mean,' said Carl. 'People can look the same, but different. Features are nothing to do with gender.'

'I don't look at all like Jo,' said Anna, adding hurriedly, 'Not that I wouldn't like to. Jo's a good-looking man.'

'I don't think he is,' said Erik, who had been following this conversation from the other side of the room. 'No offence, of course, but I don't think he is. And anyway, these people who did that research – didn't it occur to them that all Finns look the same?'

Carl shook his head. 'Look the same? The Finns?'

'Yes,' said Erik. 'It's well known. Look at a bunch of Finns and I challenge you to tell the difference. They're a good-looking people for the most part, but nobody can ever tell one from the other. They're all just … Finnish, really.' He paused. 'And so it's not surprising that they found people married people who looked like them – they didn't have much choice.'

But now, glancing at Angel and then again at Baltser, Ulf felt that any theory of similar types would, in this case, be challenged. And that led him to another conclusion, not one based on any information – he had only met them a few minutes ago – but one that had come to him on the basis of immediate intuition: Angel did not like her husband.

It was an extraordinary thought to have so soon after meeting somebody. And yet it had come to him quite forcefully. He had no idea why he should think this – on the face of it, it was absurd to jump to such a conclusion on the basis of no evidence at all. But there was a current of animosity between these two, and it emanated from her; there was no doubt about it.

As they walked into the spa to collect their keys, Ulf reflected on his rushed and surely unreliable assumption. It had to be unreliable, he told himself, because any belief based on nothing – as this one was – was open to that fundamental objection. But why should he think it? That puzzled him.

Carnality, he thought. Some people *ooze* carnality. They seem to be made for it. They are intensely sexual beings. That is what they think about; that is what they do. He glanced again at Angel, walking beside him. She was strikingly attractive, even if in a slightly blowsy way. She was what Ulf's mother would have called *the barmaid type*. Bless you, Ma, he thought; bless you for all your strong opinions and colourful categorisations; bless you for all the respects in which you were misguided, or just plain wrong, and for all you wanted in this life and never got.

He looked again at Angel. Her blonde hair, shoulder length, had been tied back with a red ribbon. A red ribbon stood for carnality – of course it did. And her blouse was tight – deliberately so. You don't wear clothes that are tight unless you want to get out of them at the first opportunity – everybody knew that. And her jeans were close-fitting and even her shoes looked several sizes too small for the feet that were within.

And then he glanced at Baltser. He was a tall, well-built man, with a pleasant enough smile, but ... Ulf looked again. He was hairy. Not only were his wrists and the tops of his hands covered in fine black hair, but his cheeks were also hirsute. And his mouth ... when he opened his mouth, the teeth were very prominent – he was not buck-toothed in any way, but the teeth were definitely larger than normal. Ulf suppressed a shudder. There was something about

205

Baltser that was physically repulsive, at least to him. And that, he decided, was a view shared by Angel: she was also repulsed by her husband's physical appearance – and Ulf could see the reason why. These two were physical opposites – walking exceptions to the rule of spousal physical similarity.

Ulf did not invite Blomquist to take part in his first meeting with Baltser and Angel. This was not because he wanted to exclude him from the investigation ... No, it was, he had to admit to himself; of course it was. But he felt justified in not having Blomquist there because the other man's presence could distract him from what he had to do, which was to allow his own sense of what was happening to develop. He did not want Blomquist waffling away, as he undoubtedly would do, preventing him from picking up the nuances. And there would be nuances, Ulf decided; they would be there, under the surface, and they would affect his assessment of what was happening.

Initially he spoke to Angel, whom he found behind the reception desk in the foyer. She suggested that they move to the office, where she invited him to sit down while she leaned against a desk at the side of the room. 'Baltser will be along in a few minutes,' she said. 'He's just checking the plunge pool. But in the meantime ... '

She left the sentence hanging.

'We could talk,' supplied Ulf.

'Yes. We could talk. He – I mean Felix – said you might help us work out what's happening.'

Ulf nodded. 'Yes, if you could fill me in on the details.'

Angel was sizing him up, Ulf noted; her glance, superficially casual, was penetrating.

'We've had a series of negative reviews,' she said. 'Guests

have complained of noises at night. One or two claimed to have seen things.'

Noises, thought Ulf; things.

'Noise in general?' he asked. 'Bad sound insulation?' That could be a problem in hotels, he knew: what happened in the next-door room was not always what one wanted to hear.

'No,' said Angel. 'Strange noises outside – or so they said. Howling, according to some of them.'

'Shouting?'

Angel smiled. 'No, they said howling.' She paused to let this sink in. 'Odd, isn't it?'

'And you have no idea what this was ... or rather, who was howling?'

Angel shrugged. 'I'm a very sound sleeper,' she said. 'I go out like a light and re-emerge the next morning. It would take a thunderbolt to wake me.'

'And what about the things that people saw? Or claimed they saw?'

Again Angel shrugged. 'They weren't very specific. One said that they saw a movement in the bushes beside the lawn. Another said there was a face at the window. It was all very general. Some creature, apparently.'

'A dog?' asked Ulf. 'Perhaps a stray?'

Angel said that she thought this was unlikely. 'There are no big dogs around here,' she said. 'The farmer over that way' – she pointed out of the window – 'keeps a couple of largish dogs, but they're very well controlled. He always shuts them up at night, he says, and they don't wander anyway.'

It was at this point that Baltser entered the room. He nodded politely to Ulf before sitting down behind the desk. Ulf noticed that Angel seemed to ignore his arrival, avoiding eye contact with her husband.

'Your wife was telling me about the guests hearing things,' said Ulf.

Baltser sighed. 'People complain. But now all we get is complaints. Bookings are right down.'

'What do you think is happening?' Ulf asked.

The question was addressed to the room in general, but it was Angel who answered. 'I think the place might be haunted,' she said. 'There might be one of those ... what do you call those things? Polter ... '

'Poltergeists,' said Ulf.

'Yes, one of those.'

Baltser shook his head. 'Nonsense,' he said. 'Ghosts don't exist.'

Angel gave him a sharp look. 'How do you know?' she asked. 'If you've never seen one, how do you know they don't exist?'

Baltser frowned. 'I can't see how to answer that question,' he said.

Angel clearly felt that her point had been made. 'Well, there you are.'

Ulf asked whether they felt there was anybody who might be pursuing a vendetta against them. No, there was not. Or what about a competitor who might want to put them out of business? No, the other hotels in the area were all doing perfectly well and would have no interest in damaging them.

'It's all very odd,' said Angel. 'If you can find anything out, I'll be very pleased.'

Ulf thought that she spoke without much conviction. She was indifferent to the problem, he decided; she did not care.

'Yes,' agreed Baltser. 'It would be very helpful.' He looked

208

down at his hands. 'I don't think we can carry on much longer losing money.'

'No,' said Ulf. 'Nobody can, I suppose.'

'Unless you're the government,' said Angel. 'You can just borrow indefinitely if you're the government.'

Ulf thought this was probably true. Governments seemed to operate in a world where the plain facts of economics did not apply. And yet surely profligacy caught up with everybody sooner or later – even if you were a government. And where did all that money come from? Who were the people who lent it to governments?

After this exchange, nobody spoke for while. Then Ulf broke the silence. 'I suppose I should just look around,' he said. 'And then perhaps I'll hear – or even see – something tonight.'

'That's possible,' said Angel. 'It seems to be happening most nights.'

She left the desk against which she had been leaning and made for the door. Ulf noticed that she paid no attention to Baltser, whose eyes followed her as she crossed the floor. He hates her, he thought.

When Ulf returned to his room, he found Blomquist waiting outside the door, now wearing his uniform.

'I thought I might make some enquiries in the town,' the policeman said.

Ulf smiled. 'I'd better fill you in,' he said. 'So that you know what to enquire about.'

Ulf told him what he had heard from Angel and Baltser. 'I suspect that this is all about some unbalanced local having a bit of fun,' he said. 'Or it might be a previous employee – somebody with a grudge.' He paused. He did not imagine there was much point in Blomquist wandering about asking questions. It would keep him busy, he supposed, and that was a worthwhile goal. 'What exactly did you propose to do in the village? What can you ask about?'

'Build up a picture,' Blomquist replied. 'Get the feel of the place. Put my ear to the ground. That sort of thing.'

'No harm in that,' said Ulf. 'But for now, I propose to sit in the sauna for a while. Then take a dip in the plunge pool, I think.'

Blomquist looked concerned. 'Be careful of the plunge pool,' he said. 'Infection. Those things harbour all sorts of germs.'

'I'll be careful,' Ulf reassured him.

'And the water can get too hot,' Blomquist continued. 'People scald themselves.'

'I'll watch the temperature,' said Ulf. 'Shall we meet for dinner, then?'

He felt that he had to say that. He knew that dinner with Blomquist would involve his sitting there listening to the other man going on about something or other, but he had to be friendly. And, for all his irritation with his colleague, Ulf's fundamental kindness won out, as it invariably did, and he would not want Blomquist to pick up on his irritation.

Ulf was relaxed when he went into the spa dining room that night. There were a few other guests, although most of the tables were unoccupied. Blomquist was already seated, and he waved across the room to Ulf as he came in.

'The curious thing about these places,' said Ulf as he sat down, 'is that they make you feel better almost immediately.'

'Psychological,' said Blomquist.

'I suppose so. Mind you, a sauna always lifts the spirits.' He glanced at the menu. 'What about you, Blomquist? A successful nose about the town?'

It was as if this was the question for which Blomquist had been waiting. 'Very,' he said, beaming. 'I made good progress. In fact . . .' He hesitated. 'In fact, I think I've found out what's going on.'

Ulf was not prepared for this. 'But we've just arrived . . .'

Blomquist leaned forward. 'I found a very useful source,' he said. 'They're always helpful, those people.'

'Which people?' asked Ulf.

'Librarians. They know everything.'

Ulf said nothing.

'A very charming woman,' Blomquist continued. 'I found myself outside the library, and so I went in and introduced myself. She was impressed with the uniform – you could see that – and she told me all I needed to know.'

Ulf waited.

'I said that we were staying at the spa. She told me that she knew the owners, Baltser and his wife.'

Ulf was not sure where this was going, but Blomquist explained. 'You can find out a lot about people from the books they read, you know.'

'Oh yes?'

'Take Erik, for example – that man who works in your office. He reads books about fish. That tells you he's interested in fish.'

Ulf smiled. 'He tells you that himself. Quite often, in fact.'

Blomquist persisted. 'I said, I imagine they're keen readers. But she'd asked for some special titles recently that the library had been obliged to borrow on the inter-library loans system.'

Ulf was on the point of saying that this was irrelevant detail, but something prevented him from dismissing Blomquist's long-winded account.

'She's been reading books on lycanthropy,' said Blomquist. 'That's what the librarian told me, anyway.'

For a few moments Ulf said nothing. Man into wolf: it was a strange obsession – one of those myths that for some reason seemed to engage people's imaginations even if it was an altogether fanciful notion. At length Ulf said, 'Are we to take it that her husband is a werewolf?'

Blomquist was silent.

'Well, Blomquist, is that what you are seriously suggesting?'

Blomquist looked away. 'I'm not accusing anybody of anything,' he said. 'I'm just reporting to you what I was told.'

Ulf made light of the information. 'Frankly, I think all one can conclude from that is that Angel is interested in paranormal nonsense. Plenty of people are. Aliens and ESP and all that stuff. People lap it up.'

'Perhaps,' said Blomquist. 'But what if Baltser *is* a werewolf?'

'There's no such thing,' said Ulf.

Blomquist shrugged. 'I've just reported what I heard,' he said. 'I'm not saying that I believe in werewolves.'

'Just as well,' said Ulf. 'I'd hate to have you committed. I assume that the psychiatric wards are full of people who believe in were-wolves and the like. Don't go down that path, Blomquist.'

'Let's just see,' said Blomquist. 'Let's just see what happens tonight.'

'Nonsense, Blomquist. It's just nonsense.'

'Some may not think it nonsense,' said Blomquist. He nodded in the direction of the office once more. 'Did you see his wrists? Did you see how hairy they were?'

'I did,' Ulf answered. 'But look, Blomquist, there's no such thing as a werewolf. And what has this got to do with anything?'

'The howling?' Blomquist said. 'The movements in the bushes?'

'But that's ridiculous. Even if it is Baltser – which is highly unlikely – why would he scare his own guests?'

'Because he can't help it,' said Blomquist. 'If you start turning into a wolf, you can't stop yourself.'

This was too much for Ulf. 'Oh, really, Blomquist! This is all utterly fanciful. You haven't been drinking, have you?'

Blomquist looked affronted. 'Certainly not.'

There was reproach in his voice, and Ulf immediately apologised. 'I'm sorry. I didn't mean that. It's just that ... well, werewolves don't exist. They just don't.'

'They exist, Mr Varg. You may think you know better, but go and speak to people in the country. Find out what *they* think.'

'I don't care what people believe,' said Ulf. 'They swallow all sorts of things. I wouldn't base my own views on the curious views of others.'

'Well,' said Blomquist. 'That's as may be. But I think I'm right about this, you know.'

There was now a note of resentment in his voice. 'You did ask me to tell you what I found out, Mr Varg. That's what I've done.'

Ulf felt guilty. 'I know, Blomquist – I know. And I'm sorry – I didn't mean to sound dismissive.'

Blomquist was pacified. 'Well, we can see what happens tonight,' he said. 'I'll be next door. I'll wake you up if I hear anything.'

'And I shall do the same for you,' said Ulf.

Ulf dreamed of Letta. For some time after her departure he had dreamed of her regularly – almost nightly, he thought. The dreams were confusing, as are the dreams we have of those who have died: they are with us, they are still there, but also they are not, because they have died. So it was with Letta: she was still living with him in his dreams, but she had also left him; all he had to do was to tell her that she had made a mistake and she would realise that, and come back to him, but he was mute in the dream, unable to find the words that would effect her return. And then he would wake up to feelings of regret, and loss, and sadness.

In this dream he was engaged in a conversation with her in a place he did not recognise. She was sitting in a car, and he was speaking to her through the wound-down window. There was another man at the wheel, but he could not make out who it was. It must be her new man, he thought – although he was hardly new, as Letta had been gone for four years now. She had left him for a stage hypnotist – a Dane who had lived in Sweden for fifteen years and who earned his living through a combination of stage shows and work as a hypnotherapist, helping smokers who were desperate to give up their habit, or those whose social confidence needed boosting. Ulf had met him on only one occasion, after Letta had gone. He had done his best to make the occasion a civil one – he saw no point in being at daggers drawn with Letta, and he still loved her, of course. He had steeled himself for small talk and the scrupulous courtesies of a dreaded meeting, and by and large the encounter had not strayed beyond those. But then the other man had said, 'We are all unhappy, you know – everybody, everybody.' Ulf had waited for him to say more, but he had not, and Ulf had resisted the temptation to say that destroying the marriages of others hardly added to the sum total of human happiness.

Ulf awoke suddenly, and for a few moments he had difficulty in remembering where he was. But when he remembered, he quickly shrugged off the vestiges of sleep. Something must have woken him – some sound, presumably – but now there was nothing.

Then he heard it. It was faint, as if coming from some distance away, but it was quite identifiable. Something, some person or animal, was howling.

Ulf slipped out of bed. He had left his shirt and trousers ready on a chair, and now he put these on in the darkness. He did not want to switch on a light, as that might warn the creature – if that was what it was – that somebody was up and about. So he fumbled with his belt and his shoes before quietly opening the door onto the corridor outside.

He gave a start. Blomquist had obviously been woken by the same sound, and was waiting for him – in uniform.

'Did you sleep in that?' Ulf whispered, gesturing to the police top with its badges and buttons.

Blomquist did not answer, but pointed down the corridor. 'It's coming from somewhere over that way,' he said, his lowered voice barely audible.

They made their way down the corridor in the darkness and then out onto the lawn. The chairs in the middle of the grass were black shapes in the night, like grazing sheep. Above them, a cloudless sky had traces of light, as they were on the cusp of full summer and its white nights.

They heard the howling again. This time it was louder, and it was easier to tell the direction from which it came.

'Over there,' whispered Ulf, pointing to a cluster of bushes on the far side of the lawn.

They both began to run, and as they did so, Blomquist began to blow loudly on a whistle. Ulf stopped in his tracks, taken by surprise by the whistle. Whatever it was that was howling must presumably have been surprised as well, as there was a commotion in the bushes, a movement of branches and leafage, and a harsh, truncated yelping sound. Then silence.

Blomquist now produced a flashlight and played the beam over the dense undergrowth. 'You are under arrest!' he shouted.

Nothing happened.

Ulf sighed. Ridiculous Blomquist!

'Whom are you arresting?' he asked. 'The bushes?'

Blomquist pointed with the flashlight beam. 'Whoever's in there.'

'Then let's take a look,' said Ulf.

Ulf parted the branches while Blomquist moved the flashlight beam around the ground before them. There was nothing to be seen – just branches and twigs and leaves. Ulf began to walk back towards the building.

'He got away,' said Blomquist.

'So it would seem,' said Ulf. 'And I assume you believe it was him – Baltser?'

'Of course it was,' said Blomquist. 'Unless there's another were-wolf in the vicinity.'

'Oh, really!' Ulf exploded. 'Get a grip on yourself, Blomquist. Those things don't exist.'

Blomquist fought his corner. 'Well, why don't we go and knock on their door and wake him up – if he's in. He won't be, I suspect, because he will have been out being a werewolf.'

Ulf agreed, if only to exclude what he thought of as Blomquist's quite unreasonable supposition. 'It won't tell us anything,' he said. 'But if it'll keep you happy, we might as well.'

'It will,' said Blomquist.

Angel had pointed out their flat earlier on. This was tacked onto the edge of the main building, like an architectural afterthought. It was in darkness now, although a small external light glowed dimly near the front door.

Ulf rang the bell. Somewhere inside, he heard a chime, and then silence. He pressed the button again.

A light was switched on and the door opened. It was Baltser. He was fully dressed.

Ulf stared at him. Baltser's eyes appeared unfocused, as if he were looking over their shoulder into the darkness beyond. He seemed confused.

'I just wanted to check that all was well,' said Ulf.

Baltser said nothing, but stood in the doorway, swaying slightly.

'Are you all right?' asked Ulf.

Again Baltser did not respond, but suddenly put his hand up to his face, as if to feel his features.

'Should we get a doctor?' muttered Blomquist.

A light was switched on behind Baltser, and Angel appeared. She was wearing a dressing gown and had something in her hand that Ulf could not quite make out.

'Everything's fine,' she said, taking Baltser by the elbow and pushing him gently back into the room. 'Was there a noise?'

'Yes,' said Ulf. 'We heard howling.'

This did not seem to interest her very much. 'Well, I think we should all get back to bed,' she said. 'We can talk in the morning.'

With that she closed the door.

Blomquist turned to Ulf. 'See?' he said. 'See? It's him. And she must know it.'

Ulf was unsure what to say. Unlike Blomquist, he did not believe that there was anything paranormal happening here, and yet the

217

expression on Baltser's face had been quite chilling. It had been one of anguish, he thought.

The next morning, Ulf was out of bed a good hour before breakfast was due to be served. He found Angel already at her desk at reception, examining the booking register.

'We need to talk,' Ulf said.

Angel looked up. Her gaze, Ulf felt, was flirtatious. 'Any time,' she said.

There was nobody about. Ulf drew in his breath. 'I've reached the conclusion that your husband is the person causing the disturbances,' he said.

She showed no reaction. 'Really,' she said. And then, in the same flat tone, she added, 'That's not true.'

'Why was he fully dressed when we rang your bell last night?'

Angel took the question calmly. 'He hadn't gone to bed yet.'

'It was one-thirty.'

Angel shrugged. 'Some people don't go to bed until three. He's a night owl.'

'Or a night wolf . . . '

'What?'

Ulf looked away. 'Nothing.' And then he continued, 'He seemed confused.'

'He had dropped off in his armchair,' said Angel. 'Sometimes he does that. He drops off to sleep for a while before he finally goes to bed. If you wake him up then he's a bit fuzzy – who wouldn't be?'

'So he was with you all the time?' asked Ulf.

'Yes. I told you. We were both in our flat.' She paused. 'You're barking up the wrong tree, Mr Varg. If there was somebody in the garden last night it wasn't my husband.'

218

Ulf tried another tack. 'Are you interested in lycanthropy?'

He watched her. She did not reply immediately. But then, when she did, her reply was disarming. 'Funny you should ask. Yes, I'm doing a course in folklore – one of these correspondence courses. I have an essay to write on popular myth. Wolves play quite a big part in those, you know.'

Ulf met her gaze. She was telling the truth, he thought. What she said was perfectly feasible, and his instinct – cautious though he was about trusting his intuition – was to believe her. Baltser was not a werewolf – how could anybody be anything that simply did not exist? – and whoever it was who was creating these disturbances was still there. He and Blomquist would have to be quicker next time if they were to catch him in the act. But they still had two nights before they were due to return to Malmö and it was, he remembered, a full moon that night. A full moon was a real temptation to a werewolf – not that they existed, of course.

Ulf decided to explore the area that morning. There was nothing for him to do at the spa and, rather than spend the day waiting for the evening, he thought he would take the Saab for a brief drive along the coast. He had initially contemplated doing this by himself, but on reflection he decided to invite Blomquist to accompany him. Blomquist showed an almost pathetic need for approval. That could be irritating, as such needs often are, but it was easy enough for Ulf to be kind to him, and after all it would cost him nothing. No doubt on this drive he would be regaled with lengthy Blomquist stories, full of odd diversions and non sequiturs, but it would be unfriendly, he felt, to leave Blomquist to entertain himself.

'We can get a bit of lunch somewhere along the coast,' he said. 'And then be back by mid-afternoon.'

'A very good idea,' said Blomquist. 'I don't know this part of the country at all.'

They set off, following the coastal road through a series of small resorts. It was a fine day, with broad sunshine and only the hint of a breeze. 'Who needs to go off to Italy for a holiday,' said Ulf. 'We have all this right here in Sweden.'

'True,' said Blomquist. 'Mind you, there's a lot to be said for going to Italy. I went, you know, a few years ago. My wife and I flew to Milan and then we went by train down to Rome. You know what we saw there?'

Ulf shook his head. 'Let me guess, though. The Pope?'

Blomquist burst out laughing. 'Right first time. Or almost. We didn't quite see him, but had we been in St Peter's Square a few minutes earlier, we might have. There was a big crowd, you see, and when I asked somebody what was going on, they said that the Pope had just gone past on a bicycle.'

'A bicycle?' exclaimed Ulf. 'No, surely not.'

'That's what I thought,' said Blomquist. 'But that's what he said. He was a Dutchman, I think – this fellow I asked.'

'I think he might have been pulling your leg,' said Ulf.

'I don't think so,' said Blomquist. 'And I suppose it's possible, isn't it? Didn't one of them play tennis? John Paul II, I think. He played tennis, I think.'

'Yes, but that's rather different, isn't it? Somehow that seems the sort of thing a pope might do. But ride a bicycle through St Peter's Square? It's hardly in keeping with the dignity of the office. I don't think any pope would do that, Blomquist – I really don't.'

After they had been driving for about half an hour, they came to a sign beside the road that announced *Sunshine Beach 400 metres.*

Ulf slowed down. 'Should we take a look?' he asked. 'These dunes seem rather attractive.'

Blomquist nodded his assent. 'Perhaps we might have a stroll along the sand,' he said. 'We could get a bit of fresh air into our lungs.'

They followed a rough track that led off into the dunes. It was bumpy, and at one or two points the underside of the Saab scraped along the sand. Ulf slowed down to walking pace.

'There,' said Blomquist, pointing to a parking area beside the track.

There were several cars already parked in the small, tree-lined enclosure, but there was room for the Saab. Ulf nosed it into a parking place and he and Blomquist got out. Between them and the sea, which they could hear nearby, was a ridge of dunes, largely covered with wispy reed grass.

'Let's take a look,' said Ulf.

A narrow path wound its way through the dunes in the direction of the sea. A short distance along this, a small sign, standing at something of an angle, gave information about the beach. Ulf pointed to this, and he and Blomquist made their way over towards it.

Nudist beach, the sign said. *Members of the public are asked to respect the privacy of users of this beach. No radios; no dogs; no consumption of alcohol.*

Blomquist chuckled. 'Look where we've ended up, Mr Varg. A nudist beach.'

Ulf smiled. 'Well, it's the weather for it.' And then he added, 'Not for you and me, of course. I wasn't suggesting that we should . . . '

'No, of course not,' said Blomquist. 'But what does this sign mean? Respect their privacy? Does that mean we can't go any further?'

Ulf said that he did not think that. 'I suspect it probably means no photography. And no, well, looking.'

'Or not too much looking,' suggested Blomquist. 'No staring. That's different from just looking. Staring is . . . '

'Looking intently,' offered Ulf. 'Or looking in the wrong places.'

They fell silent. Then Blomquist ventured, 'I still want to take a look at the sea.'

'Not stare at it?' asked Ulf.

'No, just look. After all, they don't own the beach. Beaches belong to everybody, don't they?'

Ulf said that he thought that was the case. 'I think we can go and take a quick look at the sea – and then come back. We don't need to hang around.'

'No,' said Blomquist. 'You first, Mr Varg.'

They continued to walk along the path. After a short distance, it climbed over the ridge of a dune, the windswept sand crumbling away under their feet.

'Coastal erosion,' said Blomquist. 'They need to plant more of this grass. It binds the sand.'

'Yes,' said Ulf.

'There are some countries that are being blown away, you know,' said Blomquist. 'Many people don't know that, but wind erosion is really serious.'

'Yes,' said Ulf. They were almost at the top of the dune, and his attention was drawn by an umbrella top he could see in a hollow ahead. He pointed to this, and he and Blomquist stopped.

'Nudists,' whispered Blomquist. 'Look.'

A man and a woman were lying half in, half out of the shade provided by the umbrella. Being in the hollow, they could not see

Ulf and Blomquist, even though they themselves were afforded little privacy from anybody approaching on that path.

Then the man moved, rolling out from the shade and into the sun. The woman followed, and it was at this moment that Ulf gave an involuntary gasp. The woman was Angel.

Blomquist saw her too, and pointed mutely.

'That's Angel,' whispered Ulf. 'From the spa.'

'Yes,' Blomquist whispered back. 'And who's he?'

Ulf shrugged. 'Heaven knows.'

'What are they doing?' asked Blomquist.

The man was applying sunscreen to the woman's back, rubbing it in with wide, sweeping movements.

'Sun protection,' said Ulf.

'Very important,' whispered Blomquist. 'You know, if you don't use that stuff you can get serious skin damage. But there's something else to bear in mind. Vitamin D. Sunblock can prevent you getting the necessary—'

Ulf interrupted him. 'You've told me this already, Blomquist. In the car.'

Blomquist looked puzzled. 'Did I?'

'Yes, you did. You told me about how sunblock can prevent the body making vitamin D.'

'Well, it can,' said Blomquist firmly. 'And that couple down there should be careful. Mind you, I suppose nudists have better vitamin D levels than most of us, wouldn't you say?'

Ulf tapped Blomquist on the shoulder. 'Look,' he said. 'They're getting up.'

The man, having suddenly looked at his watch, had said something to the woman. She answered him and then, reaching for a towel, stood up.

'They're leaving,' whispered Ulf. 'We'd better turn back.'

'But we were going to take a look at the sea,' Blomquist protested.

Ulf pushed him gently. 'Come on, Blomquist. We don't want her to see us.'

'I don't see why—'

Ulf cut him short. 'There's a reason, Blomquist. That's her lover – pretty obviously.'

'So?'

'So that may throw some light on what's going on at the spa. It's relevant information.'

They made their way down the track and were back in the car by the time Angel and her companion appeared. Their car was parked some distance away from the Saab and so they did not see the detective and his colleague watching them. Nor did they notice when the old Saab slipped out of the parking place and followed them, discreetly, down the track and onto the main road. Angel was at the wheel; the man in the passenger seat beside her.

Making sure that he did not lose sight of the couple, but careful not to get too close, Ulf followed Angel's car into the traffic.

'I want to see where she goes,' he said to Blomquist. 'I think that could not only be relevant, but very relevant.'

Blomquist looked thoughtful. 'You don't necessarily know that he's her lover,' he mused.

'Oh come on, Blomquist. A man and a woman lying naked on a sand dune . . . let's not be too naïve.'

'But nudists are odd,' Blomquist persisted. 'They could just be friends. Presumably nudists have ordinary friendships – unclothed friendships, so to speak.' He paused. 'When I was a boy, there was another boy who brought a nudist magazine to school to show it

224

around. It had photographs of nudists playing ping-pong. I've never forgotten that.'

Ulf smiled. Blomquist was almost quaint – in a slightly irritating way: ping-pong, nudists, vitamin D. 'As well you might not,' he said. 'But usually nudists do these things in big groups, rather than *à deux*.'

'He might just be a relative,' said Blomquist. 'You can't exclude that, can you?'

Ulf sighed. Would he have to spell it out? 'I don't think so, Blomquist. There was an aspect of the situation that indicated otherwise. Perhaps you didn't notice.'

'Notice what?' asked Blomquist.

'That particular aspect.'

'What aspect?'

'Suffice it to say,' Ulf replied. 'Suffice it to say that there was an indication of . . . Well, really Blomquist, I don't think we need to go there.'

'Where?' asked Blomquist.

Ulf said nothing. So much communication between people, he thought, depends on what is not said rather than what is said. Yet there were people – and Blomquist was clearly one of them – who seemed unable to pick up the unarticulated clues that conveyed our meaning. They needed things to be spelled out; not just alluded to, but made brutally clear. And yet poor Blomquist, for all his failings, only wanted to be helpful; only wanted to be appreciated as a colleague; only wanted his efforts to be recognised. But he would never make a proper detective if he failed to observe the glaringly obvious.

'Where?' repeated Blomquist. 'We don't need to go where?'

Ulf sighed. *There* was not a place, it was a metaphor. Or was it,

225

more correctly, a metonym? Without thinking, he muttered, 'It's a metonym.'

Blomquist looked puzzled. He hesitated for a few moments, as one might do when anxious about displaying ignorance. Then he said, 'You may think I'm ignorant, but I don't know what a metonym is.'

'I don't think you're ignorant,' Ulf reassured him.

'I don't have as much formal education as you do,' Blomquist went on. 'I know you went to university. I didn't have that opportunity.'

Ulf swallowed. He felt acutely embarrassed; he had not intended to make Blomquist feel inadequate, but that was exactly what he had done. He should not have said anything about metonyms – it was grossly insensitive on his part. What could one expect if one were a senior detective in the Department of Sensitive Crimes and one went on about metonyms to members of the uniformed branch? It was a form of flaunting of superior knowledge that Ulf, by deepest instinct, would never consciously engage in.

'I didn't know about metonyms myself,' Ulf said quickly. 'Not until recently, that is. Then I read about them.'

Blomquist looked out of the window. 'I thought you might have learned about them at university.'

'No. We didn't. I studied criminology, you know. And a bit of philosophy.'

Blomquist continued to gaze out of the window. 'I never had the chance to study philosophy.'

Ulf kept his eyes fixed on the road ahead and the car they were following. It seemed to him that Blomquist was verging on self-pity now, and there was no reason why he should pander to that. Self-pity was almost always unattractive, and it did Blomquist no favours to indulge him.

226

'You can't really say that, Blomquist,' he said briskly. 'Anybody can study philosophy at any time. There are plenty of courses you can take. You can even study philosophy online, you know.'

'My English isn't good enough,' said Blomquist.

'There are courses in Swedish,' countered Ulf. 'Plenty of them. You don't need English to study philosophy.' He paused. 'How about enrolling on one of those courses? You could become quite knowledgeable, don't you think? You could be quoting Aristotle to me next, eh, Blomquist!'

'I'm not sure who he is,' said Blomquist.

'He was a Greek philosopher,' Ulf explained. 'He lived . . . ' He hesitated. When had Aristotle lived?

Blomquist turned to face him. 'So?' he said. 'When did Aristotle live?'

'I'm afraid I don't know,' said Ulf. 'A long time ago, though.'

'Anyway,' said Blomquist. 'What's a metonym?'

'It's a word you use to refer to something else. So if you say, "The White House is under pressure," you don't mean that the actual building is under pressure – you mean the administration that works in the building is under pressure. That's a metonym.'

'So why don't we go there?' asked Blomquist.

'Where?'

'The place you said we shouldn't go to. The metonym.'

Ulf's grip on the steering wheel tightened. 'I suggest we move on,' he said. 'Metaphorically.'

Blomquist pursed his lips. 'I've been thinking of those nudists back there,' he said. 'What do you think drives people to take their clothes off, Mr Varg?'

'I suppose they want to get back to a more natural state of being,' said Ulf. 'Clothes are an encumbrance, after all.'

227

Blomquist smiled. 'I've just remembered something,' he said. 'When I was a boy we used to play a game of thinking of people without their clothes. We did this with teachers, mostly. We'd whisper, "In the bathroom," and that would be a signal for all of us to imagine the teacher with no clothes on. Then we'd start to laugh, of course, and the teacher would say, "What are you people laughing about?" And of course we couldn't reply. It was very funny.'

Ulf raised an eyebrow. 'Children,' he said. 'We were all childish once.'

'Mind you,' Blomquist continued, 'I still do it from time to time. I find it helps.'

'You think of people with no clothes on?'

Blomquist was taken aback by Ulf's surprise. 'Why? Don't you?'

'Not these days,' said Ulf. 'Maybe when I was much younger. A boy, perhaps.'

'I don't see what's wrong with it,' said Blomquist, somewhat peevishly. 'It's not harming anybody.'

'No,' said Ulf. 'I'm not being judgemental. I'm just a bit ... well, surprised. That's all.' He made a mental note to tell Anna. He would have to warn her, he thought, that if she saw Blomquist looking at her in a peculiar way, she should be aware ...

The car in front slowed down. They were now not far from their hotel and Ulf wondered whether Angel was driving directly back there, without dropping off her lover first. Would she do that? Was Baltser aware of this man's existence? Was this an open marriage of the sort one read about occasionally – prevalent, it would seem, among a certain set of advanced thinkers and artists, people for whom conceptions of marriage and fidelity were risibly bourgeois and conformist?

The car now indicated it was about to turn off the road. Ulf slowed down further, keeping well back from their quarry. And then, as the car made the turn, Blomquist read the sign at the turning: Hotel Lillebäck. *Sea Views. All facilities. Home cooking.*

The side road onto which Angel and her companion had turned was no more than a brief track, ending in front of the hotel. From where they had pulled in on the main road, Ulf and Blomquist were able to watch unobserved as the man alighted from the car, waved to Angel, and then disappeared through the hotel's main door. As he did so, Angel started her car again and began to make her way back to the main road. This was the signal for Ulf to pull away quickly and head back to the spa. Neither he nor Blomquist said anything for a short while, but as they neared their hotel Ulf revealed to his colleague what he thought was happening.

'That's her lover,' he said. 'We know that. We can also conclude that he runs the Hotel Lillebäck. That we know.'

'Yes,' agreed Blomquist. 'We know that. But what does it tell us?'

'It means,' said Ulf, 'that Angel might have split loyalties – in hotel terms, that is. So, imagine that you're close to the owner of the Hotel Lillebäck . . . '

' . . . close enough to go to a nudist beach with him . . . '

Ulf grinned. 'Yes, that close. And further imagine that you don't like your husband . . . '

'Are you sure of that?' asked Blomquist.

Ulf assured him that his assessment of relations between Baltser and Angel was correct. 'Unexpressed feelings,' he said. 'Unexpressed feelings will out. I saw them. Those two are not friends.'

Blomquist shook his head. 'I've never been able to understand how people can stay together when relations become that sour. How do you feel when you wake up and see a head you don't like on the pillow next to you?'

'Regretful?' suggested Ulf. 'Trapped? Resigned?' He thought of all the ways that so many people felt about life. Life was a matter of regret – how could it be anything else? We knew that we would lose the things we loved; we knew that sooner or later we would lose everything, and beyond that was a darkness, a state of non-being that we found hard to imagine, let alone accept.

Blomquist sighed. 'I knew a boy at school who was always unhappy. Nothing was right for him. And when I saw him later – in adult life – he was still miserable. He had done none of the things he'd wanted to do. He was in the wrong job. He was living in the wrong place, and he had married the wrong girl. Everything was wrong.'

'That's very sad,' said Ulf.

'Yes,' said Blomquist. 'I remember his father's car very vividly. He used to come to collect his son – this boy was called Lars – from the school gate. The car was an old Saab – much older than yours – much older. A Saab 92. It had that lovely sweeping back that those cars had. It was rounded, too. People called it a feminine car because of its curves. It was very beautiful.'

'Ah,' said Ulf. Saabs were beautiful – or had been.

Blomquist looked wistful. 'It was one of the originals, you know. It was made back in 1950. They started production in 1949.'

'1949?'

'Yes,' said Blomquist. 'The engine was two stroke, and it was mounted transversely. It used the thermosiphon method.'

'Ah,' said Ulf. He wondered what a thermosiphon looked like, or had. 'A thermosiphon?'

'Yes. A thermosiphon works by letting cold liquid sink and hot liquid rise. That's how it circulates fluids.'

Ulf tapped the steering wheel with his fingers. They were now almost back at the spa. 'Blomquist,' he said. 'How do you know all this?' He wanted to say *why* do you know all this, but he did not.

Blomquist shrugged. 'I just do.' And then he added, 'I thought everybody knew about the Saab 92. Didn't you?'

'No,' said Ulf. 'I did not. But I do now, obviously.'

For a few moments Blomquist was silent. Then he said, 'Of course, knowing a lot of stuff might make me suitable for detective work, rather than staying in the uniformed branch. I would have thought that might be taken into consideration, wouldn't you?'

Ulf decided that he should give no encouragement. There was no point in raising hopes that would only be dashed later on.

'No,' he answered. 'The force doesn't work like that, Blomquist. There are lots of other factors involved.'

'Such as?' challenged Blomquist.

'Experience. Manpower needs at the time. A hundred things, actually.' He paused. 'But look, we were talking about what somebody in Angel's position might do. Let's accept that she doesn't like Baltser. Let's accept that she's having an affair with the Lillebäck man. Let's imagine that our Lillebäck friend would like to buy a better hotel because his own hotel is having a rough time of it. In such circumstances he might look around for a hotel that's going on the market cheaply because ... '

' ... because bookings have been slow,' interjected Blomquist. 'Because there have been strange goings-on and people are put off ... '

'My thoughts exactly,' said Ulf.

'So she – Angel, that is – knows her husband is a werewolf ... '

Ulf corrected him. 'Alleged werewolf, please. Werewolves don't exist, you see, but I believe there are people who behave like werewolves for some reason or other.'

231

'All right,' said Blomquist. 'Alleged werewolf. So she does nothing and lets him go out and howl and so on – knowing, of course, that this will hasten the sale of the spa ...'

'... to her lover. Yes.'

Ulf nodded silently. He was parking the car now, and their conversation would soon come to an end.

'So what do we do?' asked Blomquist.

'We report back to the Commissioner. We tell him.'

'Can we have a sauna before we go?' asked Blomquist. 'We've come all this way to a spa and I haven't had a sauna yet.'

'You may,' said Ulf. 'I won't.'

'You should,' protested Blomquist. 'It opens the pores. It gets impurities out.'

Ulf shook his head. 'No thank you, Blomquist.'

Blomquist persisted. 'Impurities are bad for you, you know.'

'I know,' said Ulf. 'I'll try to avoid them.'

'You should consider colonic irrigation,' said Blomquist.

Ulf switched off the engine. He wanted to get back to Malmö.

Ulf invited Blomquist to accompany him to see the Commissioner the next morning. It was the least he could do, he felt. For all his faults, Blomquist deserved his share of whatever credit there might be for solving an otherwise obscure and difficult case. And if the Commissioner should choose to express satisfaction at the result, then it was only right that Blomquist should be there to receive part of the praise.

They were early, and had fifteen minutes or so to wait before they were admitted to the Commissioner's office. Blomquist spent the time adjusting his tunic, making sure that the creases in his trousers were correctly aligned, and speculating as to what the

Commissioner might say. 'He certainly won't ask me to call him Felix,' he said. 'You're different – you're already on first-name terms with him.'

'Just be natural,' said Ulf. 'The Commissioner's a very informal man.'

'I'll try,' said Blomquist.

When they went in, they were given a warm welcome. 'So you're Blomquist,' said the Commissioner, shaking Blomquist's hand. 'I've heard good things of you.'

Blomquist beamed with pleasure. 'I do my best, sir.'

'Please,' said the Commissioner, 'call me Commissioner.'

They sat down. 'Now,' said the Commissioner, 'tell me what you found out up there. Did you get to the bottom of it?'

Ulf nodded. 'We did,' he said. 'We have an idea what's going on. And it isn't very pleasant, I'm afraid.'

'I didn't think it would be,' said the Commissioner.

Ulf realised that there was no avoiding this difficult situation. 'I'm afraid there is something abnormal about your cousin's behaviour,' he began.

The Commissioner frowned. 'In what respect, may I ask?'

'Pathological behaviour,' said Ulf. 'You see, the cause of the disturbances – which are real enough, by the way – is him. He's the one causing all this, but he doesn't know about it, I think. It's a medical issue, really.'

The Commissioner had raised a hand. 'Hold on, Ulf, hold on. You said *he*. It's she.'

'No,' said Ulf. 'Angel is not the one causing the disturbances. It's him – it's Baltser.'

'Yes, yes,' said the Commissioner. 'But he's not my cousin – *she* is.'

233

Ulf swallowed hard. 'She? Angel?'

'Yes,' said the Commissioner, smiling at the confusion. 'I thought I explained: she's my cousin, not him.'

Ulf thought hard. His task had suddenly become more difficult. Now he had to explain that the Commissioner's cousin was engaged in an underhand plot – possibly criminal – to deprive her husband of his spa, all for the benefit of herself and her lover.

He did his best, and the Commissioner listened gravely. At the end, Ulf and Blomquist waited while the Commissioner rose from his chair and went to stand in front of the window.

'One thing that interests me,' he said, 'is how you found out about my cousin's relationship with this other man – this Lillebäck person. How can you be sure they're lovers?'

Blomquist intervened. 'We saw them together,' he said. 'And they had no clothes on.'

The Commissioner's eyes widened. 'Well, I suppose that's fairly conclusive.'

'Actually,' said Ulf, 'they were lying together on a—'

The Commissioner held up a hand. 'Please, Ulf, spare me the details.'

'It's just that—'

The Commissioner interrupted him once again. 'You've been very frank with me,' said the Commissioner. 'And the news you've given me is not exactly palatable.'

'No,' agreed Ulf. 'It isn't.' He had tried to make a full disclosure, but the Commissioner himself had prevented him from doing so. His conscience was clear in that respect.

'So what I'm facing here,' the Commissioner continued, 'is a situation where my cousin is behaving very badly and an innocent man is the victim. That's what it boils down to, doesn't it?'

234

'Yes,' said Ulf. 'I think it does. What's more, the innocent man is ill. He needs help, I think.'

'Of course he does,' said the Commissioner. 'And it behoves me, too, to deal with my cousin.'

Ulf looked at the floor. 'That's for you to decide, sir . . . Felix.'

'Yes,' said the Commissioner. 'I shall. And I shall act appropriately.'

The Commissioner was looking intently at Ulf. 'It would be most embarrassing for me if news of this were to get out,' he said. 'There are journalists who would love this. *Police Commissioner's Cousin in Attempt to Steal Werewolf's Spa* – that sort of thing. Can't you see the headlines?'

'Yes,' said Ulf. 'I'm afraid I can.'

'So it would be helpful, shall we say, for not a word of this to be breathed – to anyone.'

Ulf inclined his head. 'We are very discreet, Felix.'

'Of course you are,' said the Commissioner.

Now he turned to Blomquist. 'I gather, Blomquist, that you have in the past requested transfer to the plain-clothes department.'

'That's correct, Commissioner,' said Blomquist.

The Commissioner stroked his chin. 'Now let me see . . . How about a transfer to the Sensitive Crimes Department – Mr Varg's unit. Will that do?'

'It would do very well,' said Blomquist. 'When? Could it be with immediate effect?'

'Of course,' said the Commissioner. 'As of now. Right now.'

Ulf stared fixedly at the floor.

'And as for you, Ulf,' continued the Commissioner, 'we've been thinking of putting you up a rung or two on the ladder. Same job title – same office and all that – but a salary increase, of course.'

Ulf thanked him, but there was something he needed to say. 'We're a bit crowded in the office, Felix. I'm not sure where we'll be able to put Blomquist.'

'The floor below,' said the Commissioner. 'He can go in with the typists. I was having a look round there the other day – there's plenty of room.'

At least that was some relief for Ulf. He turned to Blomquist and managed a smile. 'Welcome aboard, Blomquist,' he said.

CHAPTER FIFTEEN

Nihil Humanum Mihi
Alienum Est

'This is a very strange story, Dr Svensson,' said Ulf. 'In fact, I feel a certain embarrassment in mentioning it to you.'

The psychotherapist made a diffident gesture. 'Please don't be concerned about that,' he said. '*Nihil humanum mihi alienum est*, Mr Varg. Nothing human is foreign to me. In other words, I suppose, I've seen it all.'

'I thought that too,' said Ulf. 'We both see – or, in your case, hear – things that would shock most people. And yet this . . .'

'I do assure you, Mr Varg, nothing would surprise me about humanity – nothing.'

'But this is quite incredible.'

'Is it? Try me.'

Ulf, sitting in Dr Svensson's consulting room at the end of

his regular session with the psychotherapist, began to recount Baltser's story. He did not mention his real name, nor the place, nor the connection with the Commissioner; having given his word that the story would go no further, all of that was cut out. And he had explicit permission from the Commissioner to find out whether anything could be done for Baltser, and how that might be arranged. In his view, that permission justified this conversation.

'I met a man, you see,' Ulf began, 'who looked in some respects like a wolf. Hairy hands and face – that sort of thing.'

Dr Svensson listened impassively.

'And he had big teeth too,' said Ulf.

Dr Svensson's eyes widened slightly.

'We talked quite normally during the day,' Ulf continued. 'But at night I'm convinced we heard him howling like a wolf.'

Dr Svensson took off his spectacles and polished them with his handkerchief. 'Very interesting,' he said. 'And then?'

'When I went to check up that he and his wife were all right, he seemed dishevelled and a bit confused. I'm pretty sure that he had been out in the bushes, howling like a wolf.'

Dr Svensson asked if that was all.

'It is,' said Ulf.

Dr Svensson folded his hands. 'This is less unusual than you think,' he said. 'I'm not saying that it happens a great deal, but it is something that we are aware of.'

'You aren't telling me you believe in werewolves,' said Ulf.

'No,' said Dr Svensson. 'As you know, I am a rationalist. I believe in reason and in a scientific explanation for everything. So I don't believe in werewolves.'

'I'm glad to hear it,' said Ulf. 'And yet I must say I was rather taken aback. If I did believe in them – which of course I don't – I can imagine myself being extremely frightened. It was the look in his eye, I think. It was extremely disturbing.'

Dr Svensson nodded his agreement. 'Of course it was,' he said. 'Psychotic illness is very harrowing. I remember when I first encountered it as a medical student – well before my psychiatric studies. I remember being appalled by the sheer awfulness of it – the misery. People don't necessarily know about that.'

Ulf listened as the psychotherapist explained the features of lycanthropy. 'Clinical lycanthropy is a very peculiar condition,' he said. 'It refers, of course, to more than the belief that one is a wolf – it can include any delusional belief about being an animal of any sort. There have been cases of people believing they are cows and there is even a very rare form of it, ophidanthropy, where you think you've become a snake. The belief can be very strong. It's no good saying to somebody *You are* not *a wolf.* That won't work.'

'No?'

'No. Because the point about a delusion is that you really believe it.'

Ulf asked about the cause.

'It could be hysteria or affective disorder,' said Dr Svensson. 'Or it could be something organic – something to do with frontal lobe or limbic system lesions. I'd be inclined to look for an underlying condition – possibly schizophrenia, possibly depression, and treat it accordingly.' He paused. 'This poor man – will somebody help him get treatment?'

'I think so,' said Ulf. 'His wife's cousin is in a position to intervene.'

Dr Svensson looked at Ulf. 'You know, Mr Varg, your life is a very interesting one – far more interesting than mine.'

Ulf sighed. 'Sometimes I wish it were simpler. Sometimes I wish I had a simple, nine-to-five job.'

'Do you think you'd like that?'

'Probably not,' said Ulf. 'I'd get bored, I suppose.'

'I think you would,' said Dr Svensson. 'You need the occasions of good, as we all do – even if we don't have a name for them.'

'I don't know what I need,' said Ulf. 'Somebody to love, maybe. And I don't have her. Or rather, I can't have her.'

Dr Svensson was gentle. 'Because you know it would be wrong?'

'Yes,' said Ulf. 'Because it would be wrong. It would destroy too much.'

Dr Svensson sighed. 'I can't tell you how many people I have had here in this consulting room, in that very chair you're sitting in, telling me about their need for love.'

'And you can't do anything about it?'

'I can't. And nor, in many cases, can they. It would be nice, though, to be able to wave a wand and bring them the resolution they're looking for.'

'Resolution?' asked Ulf.

'Yes, resolution. I thought you, as a detective, would understand resolution. Your work is all about that, isn't it?'

'Sometimes,' said Ulf. 'But then sometimes not.'

After his session with Dr Svensson, Ulf returned to the office. Anna was engaged in paperwork, but was only too ready to take a coffee break. So she and Ulf went to the coffee house over the road. Their preferred table was occupied by a group of noisy students, and so they retreated to the back.

'So you sorted everything out?' she asked.

Ulf nodded. 'I think so.'

Anna knew that he was not at liberty to say much more, and she did not try to press him. But she did ask whether he had learned anything in the process. 'Something about lycanthropy,' said Ulf. 'And a bit about nudists. And, oh, Saab 92s and vitamin D – that was Blomquist's contribution.'

'Nothing much, then,' said Anna, smiling.

He loved it when she made these witty understatements. He loved it so much. But then he remembered the conversation about metonyms, and about not going there. He could not go *there*. He could not. *There* was forbidden territory – the apple tree in the innocent garden, except that there was a snake in the garden – there always was, whether the snake was a metonym or a real serpent.

'What about you?' he asked. 'What have you been up to in the last few days?'

Anna sipped her coffee. She thought, I should answer: *thinking about you*. But she could not do that. So she said, 'The girls had a swimming competition.'

'Oh yes?' said Ulf. 'And how did they do?'

'They lost,' said Anna. 'They came last.'

Ulf looked sympathetic. 'That's a pity. But then we all lose sooner or later, don't we?'

'We do.'

'And at work?' Ulf asked. 'Anything happen?'

'You won't believe this,' said Anna. 'You won't believe it but that boy – the one who works in the coffee bar – was reported missing by his parents. He lives at home, you see.'

Ulf stared at her. The shoes in the flat . . .

'So I went straight to that flat – the one where we saw the shoes. I found him straight away. And the other boy too.'

'Both of them?'

'Yes. And they had no clothes on – neither of them did.'

'How strange,' said Ulf.

'I told him to get dressed and go and assure his parents that he was all right.'

'The best thing to do,' said Ulf. He shook his head. 'Young people!'

'We were just the same,' said Anna.

'We didn't take our clothes off,' said Ulf. 'Or not as often as they do.'

'Oh well,' sighed Anna. 'No good crying over . . . '

Ulf finished the reference for her: ' . . . spilt milk,' he said.

They were both silent. It was time to go back to the office. Neither wanted to. But they had to.

That evening, when he returned to his flat, Ulf showered, changed, and then knocked at Mrs Högfors' door to collect Martin. His neighbour had been making blueberry jam, and she gave him a jar of it for his store cupboard. 'You spoil me, Mrs Högfors,' he said. And she said, 'You deserve it, Mr Varg. And if a widow can't spoil a man like you, then what is there left for her to do, I ask you?'

He asked her about Martin's day.

'He's definitely on the mend, Mr Varg,' she said. 'There's no doubt about it. He chased a squirrel today, which is something he hasn't done for a long time. And his bark is coming back – he sounds more confident.'

'I'm delighted to hear that, Mrs Högfors,' said Ulf.

He took Martin out for an evening walk. He did not have to cajole him – the dog came willingly, and seemed to be interested once more in the sights and smells of the park. Ulf felt happy – Martin had been away in a strange land, and now he was back.

Had I been Catholic, he thought, I would have lit a candle to St Francis, in gratitude for the return of my dog; but I am not; I don't believe in any of that – although perhaps I wish I did, perhaps I would take comfort in at least parts of it. And what was wrong in believing in St Francis, who was gentle, and beloved of animals, when there was so much wrong with the world? If you can't find one sort of love, Ulf thought, then perhaps there are others out there, to hand, ready to do for you what love has always done for people. Perhaps it was there.

He looked down at Martin, who was trotting beside him on one of the paths in the park. 'You're a good dog, Martin,' Ulf said.

Martin, being deaf, did not hear. But then he looked up at Ulf, who on impulse, said, articulating carefully and moving his lips very clearly, *Wolf.* He did not know why he said it, but the word just came to him.

Martin gazed at him, struggling to read his master's lips against the light. But then he succeeded, and to Ulf's astonishment, the dog sat down, raised his head in the air, and howled.

Ulf stood quite still. Then he bent down, patted Martin reassuringly on the head, and took him back along the path by which they had come – which is, of course, the path that you can always trust to take you back to where you belong.

Continue reading for an extract from the next instalment of the Detective Varg series . . .

THE
TALENTED
MR VARG

ÄLEXANDER
McCALL SMITH

CHAPTER ONE

Enlarged Pores

Ulf Varg, of the Department of Sensitive Crimes, drove his faded silver-grey Saab through a landscape of short distances. Southern Sweden lay before him, parcelled out into farms that had been in the ownership of the same families for generations. Here and there, dots of white amid the green, were the houses of the people who worked this land. They were settled people, of long memories and equally long jealousies, whose metaphorical horizons stopped where the sky met the land, which sometimes seemed only a stone's throw away; who had never gone anywhere very much, and who had no desire to do so.

He thought of the life these people led, which was so different from his own in Malmö. Nothing was particularly urgent here; nobody had targets to meet, nor reports to write. There would be no talk of outputs and inputs and communicative objectives. Most people worked for themselves and no other; they knew what their neighbours would say, about any subject, as they had heard it all before, time upon time, and it was all as familiar as the weather. They knew, too, exactly who liked, or disliked, whom; they knew who was not to be trusted; who had done what, years back, and what the consequences had been. It would be simple to be a policeman here, thought Ulf, as there were no secrets to speak of. You would know about crimes almost before they were committed, although there would be few of those. People here were law-abiding and conformist, leading lives that ran narrowly and correctly to the grave – and they knew where that grave would be, right next to those of their parents and their parents' parents.

He opened his car window and took a deep breath: the country air bore notes of something floral – gorse, he thought – or the flowering trees of an orchard that ran beside the road. Trees were not his strong point, and Ulf could never remember which fruit tree was which, although he believed that he was now in apple-growing country – or was it peach? Whatever it might be, it was in blossom, a little later than usual, he had heard, because spring had been slow in Sweden that year. Everything had been slow, in fact, including promotion. Ulf had been told – unofficially – that he was in line for advancement within Malmö's Department of Sensitive Crimes, but that was months ago and nothing had come of it since then.

It had been a bad idea to spend the anticipated rise in salary in the purchase of a new living room suite, especially one that was upholstered in soft Florentine leather. It had been ruinously expensive, and when his salary remained obstinately the same, he had been obliged to transfer funds out of his savings account into his current account in order to cover the cost. Ulf hated doing that, as he had vowed not to touch his savings account until his sixtieth birthday, which was exactly twenty years away. Yet twenty years seemed such a long time, and he wondered whether he would still be around then. The world was imperilled, its fragile eco-system hopelessly compromised by human greed and short-sightedness. Twenty years on, it was quite possible that not only would he not be here to make use of his savings, but neither would anybody else. We borrowed the world, he thought, and that which is borrowed must eventually be returned.

Ulf was not one to dwell on such melancholy reflections about our human situation. There was a limit to what one could take on in life; his job was to protect people from others who would harm them in some way – to fight crime, even if a rather odd end of the criminal spectrum. He could not do everything, he decided, and take all the troubles of the world on his shoulders. Who could? It was not that he was an uninvolved and irresponsible citizen, one of those who do not care about plastic bags, or even deny that plastic bags exist; he was as careful as any to keep his ecological footprint as small as possible, apart from the Saab, of course, that ran on fossil fuel rather than electricity; but then it was old, which redressed the balance, at least to some extent, as every new car made a further dent in what remained to us. If you took the Saab out of the equation, though, Ulf could hold his head high in the company of conservationists, including that of his colleague, Erik, who went on and on about fishing stocks while at the same time doing his best every weekend to seek out such fish as remained. Erik made much of his habit of returning to the water any fish he caught, but Ulf pointed out that these fish were traumatised and were possibly never the same again. 'It's a big thing for a fish to be caught,' he said to Erik. 'Even if you put him back, that fish is bound to feel insecure.'

Erik had simply dismissed his objection, although Ulf could tell that his remark had hit home. And that he immediately regretted, because it was only too easy to make somebody like Erik feel ill at ease. Erik belonged to that imperilled group – old-fashioned men who had yet to understand that the world was no longer sympathetic to them and their concerns. It was hard enough to be Erik, Ulf reflected, without having to fend off criticism from people like me. Ulf was a kind man, and even if Erik's talk about fish was trying, he would take care not to show it. He would listen patiently, and might even learn something, although that, he thought, was rather unlikely.

As he drove the Saab along that quiet country road, Ulf was not thinking about conservation and the long-term prospects of humanity so much as of an awkward issue that had unexpectedly arisen as a result of one of his recent cases. The Department of Sensitive Crimes usually steered clear of day-to-day offences, leaving those to the uniformed officers of the local police. From time to time, though, a particular political or social connotation to an otherwise mundane incident meant that it was diverted into the Department for more sensitive handling. This was the case with a minor assault committed by a Lutheran clergyman, who bloodied the nose of his victim one Saturday morning in full view of at least fifteen witnesses. That was unusual enough, as Lutheran ministers do not figure prominently in the criminal statistics, but what singled this out for the attentions of the Department of Sensitive Crimes was not so much the identity of the perpetrator of the assault, but that of the victim. The nose that had been the target of the assault belonged to the leader of a group of Rom travellers.

'Protected species,' observed Ulf's colleague, Carl.

'*Tatarre*,' mused Erik, only to be sharply corrected by their colleague, Anna, who rolled her eyes at the unfashionable, disparaging name. Anna, more than the others in the Department, knew the contours of the permissible. 'They are not Tartars, Erik,' she said. 'They are a travelling minority.'

Ulf had defused the situation. 'Erik is only referring to the insensitivity of others,' he said. 'He's drawing our attention to the sort of attitude that leads to incidents like this.'

'Unless he deserved it,' muttered Erik.

Ulf ignored this, looking instead in the folder at the photographs of the nose in question. This had been taken in the hospital emergency department, when the blood was still trickling out of the left nostril. In other respects, the nose appeared unexceptional, although Ulf noticed that the pores on either side of the curve of the nostril were slightly enlarged.

'There are odd little holes here,' he said, getting up from his desk to hand the file to Anna, whose desk, one of four in the room, was closest to his. 'Look at this poor man's skin.'

Anna examined the photograph. 'Enlarged pores,' she said. 'An oily complexion.'

Carl looked up from a report he was writing. 'Can anything be done about that?' asked Carl. 'Sometimes when I look in the mirror – I mean, look closely at my nose – I see little pinpricks. I've wondered about them.'

Anna nodded. 'Same thing – and perfectly normal. You find them in places where the skin is naturally greasy. They act as a sort of drain.'

Carl seemed interested. His hand went up to touch the skin around his nose. 'And can you do anything about them?'

Anna handed the file back to Ulf. 'Wash your face,' she said. 'Use a cleanser. And then, for special occasions, you can put an ice cube on them. It tightens the skin and will make your pores look smaller.'

'Oh,' said Carl. 'Ice?'

'Yes,' said Anna. 'But the most important thing is to keep the skin clean. You don't wear make-up, I take it . . .'

Carl smiled. 'Not yet.'

Anna pointed out that some men did. 'You can wear anything these days. There's that man in the café over the road – have you noticed him? He wears blusher – quite a lot of it. He'll have to be careful – he could get blocked pores if he doesn't remove the make-up carefully enough.'

'Why does he wear the stuff?' asked Carl. 'I can't imagine caking my face with chemicals.'

'Because he wants to look his best,' said Anna. 'Most people, you know, don't look the way they'd like to. It's a bit sad, I suppose, but that's the way it is.'

Ulf said, 'Very strange.' He was thinking of the case, rather than cosmetics.

The assault on the traveller might have led to a swift and uncomplicated prosecution of the assailant were it not for the fact that not one of the fifteen witnesses was prepared to give evidence. Four of them said that they had been looking the other way at the time; five said that their eyes happened to be closed when the assault took place, one actually claiming to have been asleep; and the remainder said that they could not remember anything about the incident and that they very much doubted whether it had taken place at all. This left the victim and the Lutheran minister. The victim was clear as to what had happened: he had been attending to his own business in the town's public square when a stranger in clerical garb had walked up to him and punched him in the nose. This was purely because he was a traveller, he said. 'We're used to the settled community treating us in this way. They resent our freedom.'

For the minister's part, he claimed that he had been suddenly confronted by a complete stranger who became so animated in some unfathomable diatribe that he had banged his nose on a lamp-post. He had been so concerned about this unfortunate's injury that he had offered him his own handkerchief to mop up the blood. This offer had been spurned in a most ungracious way. Any allegation that he had assaulted this man was abhorrent and patently false. 'Some people are terrible liars,' the minister concluded. 'Bless them, but they really have no shame at all. Not that I'm picking on any particular group, you'll understand.'

Ulf suggested to the victim and the assailant that it might be best to let the whole thing be resolved through the extraction of a mutual apology. 'When it's impossible for us to tell what actually happened,' he explained, 'then it is sometimes best to move on. There are different understandings of conflict – as in this case – and if both sides can see their way to patching things up . . .'

The victim's body language made it apparent that this suggestion was not going down well. He appeared to swell, his neck inflating in what looked like a dangerous build-up of pressure, and his eyes narrowing in fury. 'So, a Rom nose counts for less than anybody else's,' he hissed. 'Is that what you're telling me?'

'I am not passing judgement on your nose,' said Ulf calmly. 'And all noses are equal as far as we're concerned – let me assure you of that.'

'That's what you say,' snapped the victim. 'But when it comes to the crunch, it's a rather different story, isn't it?' His voice rose petulantly. He glared at Ulf. And then he said, 'My nose is as Swedish as yours.'

Ulf stared back. He was always irritated by aggression, and this man, he thought, was needlessly confrontational. At the same time, he was aware that he was dealing with a member of a minority disliked by so many. That must change your attitude. His reply was placatory. 'Of course it is. I didn't say otherwise.'

'But you want to let him off, don't you? Justified assault? Is that it?'

This stung Ulf. 'Mr . . .' He trailed off, realising that he did not know the complainant's name. It was recorded in the file, but he did not have that to hand. It was a particularly unfortunate *lapsus memoriae*, given that he was being accused of favouritism. He remembered the name of the minister, but not this man's. 'Mr . . .'

'See!' hissed the victim. 'You can't even be bothered to learn my name.'

Ulf swallowed hard. 'I'm sorry.' He remembered now, and wondered how he could have forgotten. Viligot Danior. 'I'm sorry, Mr Danior. I'm very busy with all sorts of problems. Things come at me from every direction, and I sometimes find it difficult to master the details. What I want to say to you is this: I am not going to let this go. I understand how you feel and I am determined that the minister should be held to account.'

Viligot visibly relaxed. 'Good. That is very good.'

'And so I am going to propose that we charge him. It will then be up to the magistrate to decide whom to believe. It will be one word against another, but we'll just have to hope that the court can work out who's telling the truth.'

'Which is me,' said Viligot hurriedly.

'If that is what you say,' said Ulf, 'then I shall believe you unless otherwise persuaded to the contrary. After all, you don't get a bloody nose from nowhere.'

'Especially when there are no lamp-posts in the square in question,' said Viligot.

Ulf thought for a moment. Then he smiled. 'I think you have just convinced me,' he said.

The court was similarly convinced, much to the annoyance of the defence when confronted with a photograph of the *locus* of the incident. Where, the minister was asked, was the lamp-post into which Viligot might have walked? After that, the minister's conviction was assured. He was fined and given a stern warning. 'A man of the cloth had a particular duty of probity,' the judge said. 'And you have singularly failed in that duty.'

Ulf felt that justice had been done. Viligot had been the victim of an unprovoked attack because he was a member of an unpopular section of the community. Ministers might be expected to be more tolerant than the average person, but presumably there were those among them who harboured vulgar prejudice and resentment. Still, it was a strange case, and Ulf was not entirely satisfied that he had got to the bottom of the matter.

That came later – barely half an hour after the end of the trial. As he left the courtroom to buy himself a cappuccino in a nearby coffee bar, Ulf was approached by one of the recalcitrant witnesses who had failed to see anything. This was the postman who had been passing, but looking the other way, at the time of the fracas.

'Mr Varg,' the postman said. 'I hope you're satisfied.'

Ulf gave the man a warning look. 'And what do you mean by that?'

The postman was uncowed. 'That man back there,' he said, tossing his head contemptuously in the direction of the court building. 'That Danior person . . .' The word 'person' was spat out. 'Do you know anything about him? Do you know what he does?'

Ulf shrugged. 'I know he's a traveller, if that's what you mean. But those people have exactly the same rights as you and I, Mr . . .'

'Johansson.'

'Well, Mr Johansson, the law doesn't discriminate.'

Johansson smiled. 'Oh, I know that, Mr Varg. You don't have to tell me that. But do you know what Viligot Danior was doing? Do you know why the minister did what he did?'

Ulf stared at the postman, thinking of the reluctance of the witnesses – fifteen people who must have seen something. Fifteen! 'I thought you didn't see anything.'

'It's nothing to do with what I saw or didn't see,' retorted the postman. 'I'm talking about what Danior was up to. He and those sons of his. There are three of them. Nasty pieces of work, every one of them. Covered in tattoos.'

Ulf waited.

'They steal tyres,' said the postman. 'We're a small town out there, Mr Varg, and we've all had tyres stolen from our cars. They arrived in our areas, and next thing – surprise, surprise, we started to lose our tyres. They just remove them – the wheels as well, some of the time.'

'Danior does this, you say?'

The postman nodded.

Ulf frowned. 'And the local police? What do they say about this?'

This brought a laugh from the postman. 'They've been told not to lean on them. It's something to do with community sensitivity. They look the other way.'

Like you, thought Ulf. And yet . . .

'So, Danior and his sons stole the minister's wheels. He has a Volvo – a nice car. But two of his wheels were removed, along with one other tyre, and the spare.'

Ulf sighed. 'And how did he know it was Mr Danior?'

'Because he saw one of the sons doing it. He chased after him, but the boy jumped into a car and made himself scarce. So next time he came across Danior in the town, he lost his self-control and took a swing at him.' The postman paused. 'It could happen to anybody. Even you, you know – if you don't mind my saying it.'

Ulf was silent. He imagined how he would feel if somebody stole the tyres of his Saab. And yet the whole point of having a system of justice was to prevent people from taking matters into their own hands and assaulting those who wronged them. That was the whole point. And yet ...

He sighed again. Suddenly he felt tired, as if burdened by the whole edifice of the state and its rationale. It was unarguable: the state had to be the sole agent of vengeance – if one could call it that – or life would degenerate into a series of vicious blood feuds. Appalachia and Sicily sprang to mind. To which one might add Afghanistan, Ulf thought. He turned to Johansson. 'I'm sorry to hear that,' he said. 'But we can't have people assaulting others because of something they've done. We just can't.'

The postman looked down at the ground. 'I sometimes wonder what's happened to this country,' he said.

Ulf looked at him. 'I understand what you're saying.'

'Do you?'

Ulf nodded. 'It's not as simple as you think, Mr Johansson. It just isn't.'

And then it had become even more complicated. Three days previously, Ulf returned home one evening to discover a note from his neighbour, Mrs Hogfors. A large package had been left for him, she said, and she had taken delivery of it. It would be waiting for him when he came to collect Martin. Martin was Ulf's dog, who was looked after during the day by Mrs Hogfors. She was particularly fond of him, as Martin was of her.

The package was crudely wrapped in plain brown paper. Ulf took it back to his flat where he discovered that it was a silver Saab grille, of the exact vintage and style for which he had been searching. His own grille had been damaged and needed replacing, and here was the exact part he needed.

There was a note. *Mr Varg*, it read. *Thank you for standing up for me. You're an honest man, Mr Varg, and I thought you might like this. I noticed your car needed it. With thanks, Viligot.*

There were procedures for such things, and Ulf knew that he should immediately return the gift. He intended to do this, and the following day he drove out to the site where he had first interviewed Viligot. This was in a caravan park outside the town. But there was no sign of Viligot, his sons, or indeed of anybody else.

'They've decamped, thank God,' said a woman in the village when Ulf made enquiries. 'Good riddance, we think.' Then she added, 'They've taken most of our tyres – and other bits and pieces from our cars.'

Ulf felt himself blushing. The Saab grille had been stolen – and now it was in his car, sitting on the back seat, in full view of anybody who might walk past and glance through the window. He thanked the woman and drove back to his flat in Malmö. Once parked, he took the grille from the back seat and carried it into his flat. There was nobody about, but he felt that he was being watched from more than one window. He glanced upwards and saw a movement at one of the neighbour's window. There was now at least one witness to his handling of stolen goods.

He knew what he had to do. The manual of proper police conduct stated quite clearly that gifts from those with whom one had professional dealings were to be returned to the donor. In certain circumstances – such as where the gift was from a grateful member of the public who would be offended by its return – it could be kept, but only with the official permission of the Commissioner's department. When a gift was thought to be stolen property, then it should be handed in to a superior officer along with a report on the grounds for concluding that it was stolen. This had to be done within twenty-four hours of receiving the gift. Ulf had intended to do this, but it had slipped his mind. Now three days had elapsed and it was too late to do anything, unless his report falsified the time of his receiving the gift. And Ulf would not tell a deliberate lie, least of all on an official form. He had been brought up to be honest, as had his brother, Bjorn. He tried to stick to that, even if Bjorn, who was the leader of a political party, the Moderate Extremists, sometimes seemed happy to take a very casual attitude to the truth.

The grille was still in his flat, tucked away in the cupboard in which he kept his overcoats and scarves. It would remain there, he thought, a constant affront, a guilty secret about which nothing could ever be done. If he tried to dispose of it, he would be seen by somebody and would struggle to find an explanation. *Why were you seen leaving your flat at two in the morning with a Saab grille under your arm, Mr Varg? Just asking.*

Don't let the story stop here

Help us make the next generation of readers

We – both author and publisher – hope you enjoyed this book.
We believe that you can become a reader at any time in your life,
but we'd love your help to give the next generation a head start.

Did you know that 9% of children don't have a book of their
own in their home, rising to 12% in disadvantaged families*?
We'd like to try to change that by asking you to consider the role
you could play in helping to build readers of the future.

We'd love you to think of sharing, borrowing, reading, buying or talking
about a book with a child in your life and spreading the love of reading.
We want to make sure the next generation continue to have access
to books, wherever they come from.

And if you would like to consider donating to charities that help
fund literacy projects, find out more at www.literacytrust.org.uk
and www.booktrust.org.uk.

Thank you.

little, brown
BOOK GROUP

*As reported by the National Literacy Trust